The Moment of Heaven
That Led to a Hell . . .

It was Emilie's wedding night. Already her
bridegroom, Guy, had done things and aroused
feelings that she had never in her innocence
dreamed possible. But the ultimate was
yet to come.

Now Emilie felt Guy's strong hands reach
under her and draw her body up closer to him.
Slowly she felt him raising her hips and legs
off the bed, opening her still wider to
accommodate the urgency of his passion.
From the very tips of her fingers and toes to the
scalp of her head she was tingling, throbbing,
yearning as she felt his manhood filling her up,
rocking her like a boat, like a cradle, like a
child, until the whole world was rising
and falling, rising and falling, faster and faster,
toward the one moment that ripped her loose
and left her shattered in a timeless ecstasy . . .

**This was the memory that would not leave
Emilie when Guy rode off to war. This was the
void that each night ached agonizingly within
her, a burning desire demanding to be filled . . .
no matter what the price in pride . . .
no matter how shocking the disgrace. . . .**

Big Bestsellers from SIGNET

Mistress
of
Desire

by
Rochelle Larkin

A SIGNET BOOK

NEW AMERICAN LIBRARY

TIMES MIRROR

NAL BOOKS ARE ALSO AVAILABLE AT DISCOUNTS IN BULK
QUANTITY FOR INDUSTRIAL OR SALES-PROMOTIONAL USE.
FOR DETAILS, WRITE TO PREMIUM MARKETING DIVISION,
NEW AMERICAN LIBRARY, INC., 1301 AVENUE OF THE
AMERICAS, NEW YORK, NEW YORK 10019.

SIGNET, SIGNET CLASSICS, MENTOR, PLUME AND MERIDIAN BOOKS
are published by The New American Library, Inc.,
1301 Avenue of the Americas, New York, New York 10019

FIRST SIGNET PRINTING, MARCH, 1978

1 2 3 4 5 6 7 8 9

PRINTED IN THE UNITED STATES OF AMERICA

To Joanie and Sandi
and all the great young editors

The overseer kept his horse at a steady pace as they approached the house. In the lengthening shadows of late afternoon, the land seemed as it always had béen. The slaves bent to their tasks in the cane, the ancient trees stood impervious to change, the horizon, now streaked with the colors of the sunset, stretched endlessly. Even the wide swath of green lawn seemed untouched. It was only when the house itself was in sight, dominating everything else around it, that the damage became sharply evident.

St. Georges reined in his mount at the foot of the veranda. The once-splendid span of columns that gave the house its regal facade was broken. The six on the right side were intact, but on the other side of the low steps, where the fire had raged most savagely, two columns had fallen, leaving the cornice they supported sagging slightly, and the other four bore evidence of the char and water damage that had ruined the first-floor interior as well.

The overseer dismounted, carelessly tossing his reins to a slave boy who stood waiting for them. He didn't even stop to see if the lad had caught them. He strode up the stairs that he could have easily bounded in a single leap. Decorum demanded that he make his entrance into the master's house in a civil way.

Master's house! St. Georges felt his throat constricting

with the phrase. There was no master to be met at
Les Chandelles any longer; no man to understand the
needs of the fields and to issue his orders in straight
strong words that another man could understand. For
the thousandth time St. Georges cursed the rotten luck
that had ended in this.

Charles Bonfils had been a hard taskmaster, but
easy in letting the overseer do as he saw fit. He had
not been a man to question the use of the lash in the
fields by day, nor of the wenches of the quarter at
night. As long as the work got done, that was all that
mattered.

Besides, there was something in it for a man to be
overseer of the largest, most important estate in the
parish. It gave him the right to swagger a bit in front of
his fellows, the ones who served lesser estates and had
fewer blacks at their heels. If a man wasn't born one
of the fortunate few, a planter himself, it was about
the next best thing. And who was to say but maybe
one day he might even get to own a couple of slaves
himself. More than one estate had gotten started just
that way.

Again, he cursed inwardly at the luck that had
plagued him and the Bonfils family. Bad enough about
the master and mistress dying in the fire, but far worse
to St. Georges' mind was the death earlier of their son
in a stupid duel. It was the prospect of young Chaz
Bonfils someday inheriting that had kept the overseer
going during the rough times. He knew the young
Bonfils for exactly what he was: a lazy, worthless
weakling good only for wasting his father's money
and breaking his mother's heart. He was exactly the
sort of man St. Georges wanted for an employer.

Chaz would have avoided the fields and given his
overseer a free hand in everything. There was no end
to the opportunities that came to a man with such a

master to serve. Chaz would have been no more anxious to burden himself with the plantation's books than he would have been to sweat in the canebrakes all day. St. Georges had heard tell of overseers who ended up with half the master's property under just such circumstances. Often he had licked his lips in anticipation of the day the son came to inherit.

But what he had gotten instead was the daughter—this stuck-up, obstinate slim young chit of a girl who ordered him around as if he were a slave, and cared more about the real slaves than she did about him, questioning him closely all the time about the whippings in the fields, making certain he knew that she held him responsible for the health of her property. Never thinking at all about what a day in the cane took out of his hide, and how he had to bear down so hard on them to keep them in line, or what might happen to him if he let go for even a minute. No, Miss Emilie didn't give a damn about him; that was clear as day to St. Georges.

But she cared enough about her property. Enough to spend hours going over the books, asking him questions that he didn't have the answers for, keeping him standing there like a damn fool, his hat in his hands, his tongue thick in his mouth without the answers she asked for. She asked about things even old Charles, her father, had never bothered about. *He* had been happy enough just to know the cane was rolling out and the money'd be rolling in, but she, she damn near expected him to know how much every grain was going to be bringing in.

He hated her, hated the way she made him feel. He always felt big and clumsy, as though the little room were just right for the size of her, but too small for him, with the walls about to close in on him. He would stand swimming in his own sweat, while she would sit, cool

and slender as an icicle, asking her endless questions,
giving him her mean looks.

Who could count how many times a day the lash
had been used? Why did she have to know? Why did
she have to make the hard, thankless job of overseeing
even more miserable and unrewarding? Everyone
knew that the planters hated the overseers, looked
down at them as a necessary evil, considered them
below their own class. Yet it was only this girl who
made it so obvious, and took no pains to hide her
loathing of him. She's not a lady, St. Georges thought;
a real lady would treat me nicer.

He took a deep breath and entered the ruined front
rooms of Les Chandelles. He stood in the hallway,
hat in hand, waiting until she was ready to receive him.

Emilie tightened her grip on the banister as she
walked down the great staircase. The house seemed
even larger and lonelier than before, and the damaged
areas looked even more menacing. This was the time
of day she dreaded most. She walked down slowly,
trying to calm the queasiness in her stomach, trying
to deny to herself that it was even there. She had taken
dinner alone in her room as usual. Now she came
down to face, as every night she must, the report on
the day's activities in the fields given to her by St.
Georges, the overseer.

Emilie did not know how to explain to herself just
what it was about the man that made her mistrust him
so. It was not merely that he was of a much commoner,
coarser breed than the planters he and his like
worked for. She felt no such animosity toward any of
the slaves, whose condition in life was so much lower
than that of St. Georges. There was just something
about the man himself that made her uncomfortable.

There was menace in the way he looked at her.

She would not admit this to herself any more than he could possibly articulate it. Such insolence would mean his immediate dismissal and the blackening of his name among any other possible employers in the area. Yet she could not deny the aura of threat she felt emanating from him. There was a shrewd cast in his eyes that seemed to say that were they to find themselves in a situation other than this, there was no question in his mind about which of them would have the upper hand.

Emilie walked slowly into the gutted library that had served as her father's office. She stared as if still disbelieving the effects of the fire. The old leather-bound plantation record books that had lined the walls on three sides of the room had gone quickly to flame. Now its shelves were barren, broken and charred by the fire, the walls staring nakedly behind them, smoke- and water-stained.

Emilie sighed. As soon as the immediately necessary structural repairs had been completed, this was the room she would want refurbished first. At least it was one which was used and had a purpose. She hated the gaunt and ugly, almost empty front salon that was the mansion's largest room, and she promised herself that when it was ready for fixing she would make it over in an entirely new way. The only time the room had ever looked pretty was the night of her cotillion debut, when it had been filled with people and flowers and music and food. Other than that, it was near as gloomy before the fire as it was now. Emilie thought wistfully of the far smaller but much more opulent house she had stayed in when she was in New York. Mrs. van Nuys, her hostess, had filled her mansion with elegant marbles and brocades and other expensive items. But with it all, that house had had a warmth and a light to it that Emilie envied. She had promised herself that she would fill Les Chandelles with the same kind of feeling.

Surely, she mused, with all the great expanse of window that the front room had, it would be easy to fix it so that it would be airy and flooded with sunshine.

She was deep in thought when she felt his shadow fall over the room. Emilie frowned slightly, then cleared her expression before she lifted her dark eyes to face those of the tall overseer.

"Evenin', Miss Emilie," he said.

"Good evening, Mr. St. Georges," she replied evenly. "How went the work today?" It was a phrase she had often heard her father use in his daily interview with the overseer.

"Well and good," he replied. "The first part of the crop has been cut down and moved to the refinery."

Emilie frowned slightly. "I have never seen our refinery," she said slowly. "I suppose I must become acquainted with it quite soon."

"As you wish, ma'am," St. Georges said. "But it's scarcely the place for a young lady like yourself, Miss Emilie. Especially when we're going full steam and the niggers are boiling down the cane."

"Nevertheless I shall be at the refinery the first thing tomorrow morning." Emilie replied crisply. "The boiling down has not begun yet, has it?"

"No, ma'am, not for a couple more weeks," St. Georges told her.

"Very well," Emilie stated. "I shall come and see it, and again when it is in full production."

"As you wish, ma'am."

"Was there any misbehavior among the slaves today?" Emilie asked suddenly.

"Why no, ma'am," St. Georges answered just as quickly. "Why would you think there'd be any? Les Chandelles' chattel generally know how to behave themselves."

"Was there punishment given out, then?" Emilie asked.

St. Georges grinned. "I always have my men kind of cracking their whips. No harm to it, and it keeps them moving along."

"I'll not have my slaves beaten unnecessarily." Emilie's eyes were blazing.

The overseer shifted his weight from one foot to the other. "Well now, with all due respect, Miss Emilie," he began, "there is a lot that you have got to learn about the management of property such as yours. If they aren't kept in their place and mindful of the lash there's no knowing what they might do."

Emilie's eyes narrowed. "We have, I believe, about one hundred and fifty field hands, don't we?" she asked.

"Yes, ma'am."

"And almost that same number of all hands are physically fit and able at any given time, aren't they, Mr. St. Georges?" she demanded.

He confirmed that fact with a brief nod of his head.

"Then why weren't a hundred and fifty people able to put out the blaze in this house?" Emilie had risen from her chair to stare demandingly into the overseer's eyes. "Why didn't the hands rise and run to help quench the flames and perhaps save the lives of my mother and father?"

"Well now, Miss Emilie, you know I wasn't here that night and can't rightly be held to answer for it," St. Georges said uneasily.

"If we had not been so quick with the lash and the manacles my parents might still be alive today and my house still proud, not the ruined hulk we're standing in right now, Mr. St. Georges!" Emilie felt as though her knees would give way under her, but she clenched her fists on her father's desk and stood as firmly as she could.

"You wouldn't be questioning the ways of the master now, would you?" St. Georges asked slyly. "The way I got it from your father, Les Chandelles chattel have been handled the same way from the time of his father, and his father before that. Are you fixing to make changes already, ma'am, before you've even warmed the saddle of a horse in the fields?"

Emilie blushed deeply. The impertinence of his remark was as ill conceived as his reading down to her of the plantation's ways.

Emilie felt the full burden of her responsibility weighing down on her at that moment. In a way she knew that the vile overseer was right; she scarcely knew enough about the workings of the plantation to be able to tell a slave when to throw feed to the chickens, and here she was presuming to change things that had prevailed since long before she was even born.

Yet in her heart Emilie knew that the slaves served them out of fear and not out of love. She knew that there was something very wrong in the way Les Chandelles' sugar was brought to its profitable harvest, and she knew that with these two conflicting feelings raging inside her she would not be able to find the steadfastness that would enable her to run the plantation as it needed to be run. Indecision could easily be fatal to her beloved home. The responsibility was hers alone.

Emilie felt something close to panic overtaking her. How can I do it all? How can I? The words stung in her mind. Yet as she stood before the grimacing overseer she knew that she must. There was no choice. She had to protect and maintain Les Chandelles.

She loved her home and her sunny Southern homeland. If there were wrongs and injustices and hardships within the system, then she must do what she could to soften them. That was all that she had within her own small power to do. She could not change the way things were, and she didn't know that she wanted to, even if she could. Surely the slaves were far better off in the hands of people like the Bonfils than they could be if left to the designs of men like St. Georges and his class.

It would be difficult, but she was determined to do the best that she could, both for the heritage that her father had left her and for the unfortunates who formed in their beings the greater part of her fortune. It would not be simple, but she was going to do her best.

The overseer was shifting restlessly again. Emilie could see that he was waiting to be dismissed. How I hate him, she thought. Nasty, odious man. Yet I need him, probably far more than he needs me at this moment. But that too will change, she promised herself.

"That will be all, St. Georges," she said airily, tossing back her thick, curly hair. "I will see you tomorrow at the refinery. Good evening."

One of St. Georges' gang of underbosses was waiting on the lawn outside the house when Emilie emerged after breakfast the next morning. He took off his hat in deference to her as one of the yardmen hitched up the small two-seater carriage for her.

The underboss rode dutifully alongside on his rather bedraggled brown mare.

The sugar refinery lay on the extreme western border of the plantation. It was solidly constructed of red brick, and from its towering chimneys would come the fumes of black smoke that indicated that the cane was being boiled down into syrup. It was located on the banks of the river, so that transport of the liquid sugar by boat could be most economically managed, and on a sloping section of land whose lowness, aided by the prodigiously tall clumps of trees which old Raymond had planted behind it, made the entire enterprise invisible from the great mansion. So secluded was it from the activities and circumambulations of the mistresses of Les Chandelles that Emilie, indeed, had never seen the place before. Sometimes, from her bedroom window, she had caught the heavily sweet drift of smoke, but in most seasons the wind from the river kept even that reminder from the delicate nostrils of the planter family.

Now as Emilie faced the buildings she was astonished that her property incorporated a veritable factory only minutes from the front drawing room.

It was as though she were entering a strange new world. Although the sun was still not much above the eastern horizon, the place was already bustling with activity. Emilie could see, as the underboss helped her alight from the carriage, that the place consisted of at least three good-sized buildings. There was no smoke from the tall chimney in the center building, as it was not yet time for the boiling. Emilie walked into the nearest structure as the door was held open for her. Before she could quite adjust her eyes to the gloominess of the place, a sudden racket started up that almost frightened her out of her skin. She jumped back slightly, glad for once to find the outstretched arm of the underboss to lean against. She collected herself and stared about to ascertain the origin of the terrible noise. She could make out the outlines of a large sloping piece of machinery that creaked and groaned as it moved. At one end now, she could see that young male slaves were loading freshly cut cane. When the machinery started up, the cane was drawn upward, almost to a precipice, and then onto a decline where it was caught between great steel rollers that crushed it flat as it spewed out of the farther side. The whole great thing propelled the cane by means of wheels and ropes and pulleys. She wanted to ask a question, but the noise was too deafening. She indicated with a nod of her head that she had seen enough, and the underboss, whose name she'd learned was Michaels, opened the door and helped her out.

"That was the mill," he told the mistress as soon as they were far enough from it to be heard. "That's where the stalks are carried to be crushed for the boiling, ma'am. The boiling is done over here in the sugar house," Michaels explained with a jerk of his thumb, "but it hasn't started yet. Do you want to see inside anyway?"

"As long as I'm here, I might as well," Emilie said. Once more they stepped into the bricked interior of a section of the refinery. The walls were smoke-darkened, and even in the absence of work and workers, the cloying smell of boiled sugar clung to the floors and the rafters. Emilie walked up to the long side, where she stepped up to a wooden platform. As she peered down she could see where the great ovens, now banked, received the crushed stalks that were ready for boiling down. Even in disuse the place seemed unbearably oppressive to her. What it must be like when the torches were lit and the smoke billowed about was something that she didn't want to think about. She could remember clearly enough how Charles Bonfils had looked during the boiling season. He would come into the mansion late at night, his face reddened, his eyes smarting, sometimes even his hair singed. His large body would be heavy with sweat, his clothes clinging wetly to him. Emilie wondered now if she too would have to spend those long hot hours overseeing this hellish stage in the refining process.

It was a blessed relief to step outside once more to the world of blue skies and green grass and the river moving swiftly but pleasantly by. She walked down the incline almost to the bank, seeing the tracks that were laid from the refinery to the very edge of the river. The track had been constructed to accommodate the small hand-pushed carts on which barrels of sugar were loaded to be put directly on board a waiting boat. There was not a step wasted in the entire process. Even her inexperienced eye could appreciate that.

When the slaves gathered the cut cane, it was carried to the crushing mill, which gave directly onto the inferno of the boiling room. From there the barrels with the sugar, now at last transformed to grains, would be placed on the carts and transported to the small dock that stood in the river. The current would take the boat swiftly downstream to the levies of New Orleans, whence it could be reshipped anywhere in the world.

Emilie marveled at the efficiency of the place. Once again she thought how extraordinary it was that all of this should be going on at such a slight remove from the gracious mansion which, while maintained from the profits of this labor, seemed in its grandeur to stand stiffly and look the other way. The amount of machinery she owned amazed her. She had thought the plantation's wealth lay solely in its slaves and acreage.

"I think I have seen enough for this morning," Emilie told Michaels. "I will, of course, be back when it is necessary."

He tipped his hat, and she was glad to return to the waiting carriage and hurry back to the house.

The sound of a horse and rider outside the mansion startled her. It was too early in the day for St. Georges to be confronting her, and the rapidity of the echoing hoofbeats told her that whoever was riding up was doing so with far more alacrity than was the overseer's custom. Emilie rose, her hand at the base of her throat, and walked slowly out onto the remnant of the veranda that still stood undamaged in front of the house.

The shattered glass of the tall front windows that had been broken during that hideous night had at last been cleared away, and the broad wood planks of the floor were smoothed clean. Still, with one row of columns nearly gone, it was a troubling place to stand. Emilie clung to one of the broad front pillars and looked curiously at the young man who was being helped to dismount by one of the small black stable boys.

He looked familiar, but she could not place him at first. She thought he was a friend of her brother's, from the plantation just north of Les Chandelles.

Emilie was suddenly conscious of the drab, rather severely cut dress she had on and of the stray curls that hung loosely about her face. The young man, by contrast, was clad in most elegantly cut riding clothes. The sun shone on his hair, making it almost silvery. Yet his face, distinguished and lean-looking as it was, seemed to her to be rather older than she would have expected for a friend of Chaz.

The lean figure mounted the steps easily. "Miss Emilie," he said, extending his hand and lifting her own most briefly to his lips before releasing it.

"I'm afraid you have me rather at an advantage, sir," Emilie said. "I am sure that we know each other but I cannot for the moment remember your name."

He smiled. "I would not expect you to know me," he said. "Although my brother was a constant companion of yours and a frequenter of your beautiful home. I myself have been away for the past seven years. I have only recently come back to the parish."

"Yet I would have sworn that I knew you," Emilie said, quite puzzled. "You remind me so much of someone else."

"That would be my brother," he explained gently, as if he had not just described the younger man.

Emilie felt stupid and mortified. What a dullard he must find me, she thought.

"I am Guillaume Charpentier of Les Saules," he said, bowing low. "And I have come to pay my respects to you and offer my condolences on your recent tragedy."

"Ah yes," Emilie murmured. "Your dear mother was among the first of the people in the parish to greet me here when I came home to—to—" With a sudden movement of her arm she tried to express the events of that terrible day. The arc she described took in the burned-out portions of the veranda as well as the windows in which the panes had yet to be replaced.

"But do come inside, Monsieur Charpentier, so that we may give you some cool refreshment. The ride from Les Saules could not have been comfortable for you."

How easily she fell into the old role; almost without realizing it she was immediately the hostess of the estate.

Emilie rang a small silver bell and one of the serving women appeared quickly and silently. The young mistress gave her instructions, and the woman hurried back to the kitchen.

As soon as Emilie had seated herself, Guillaume Charpentier lifted the skirt of his jacket and sat down in a chair opposite hers.

"You say you are only newly returned to the parish, monsieur," Emilie said, "after quite a long time. Have you been living far from here?"

"Indeed I have, mademoiselle," he answered. "I have been abroad studying and traveling on the Continent all this time."

Emilie expressed surprise. "How exciting!" she exclaimed. "And what in the world could have brought you back from all of those wonderful places?"

Guillaume's brow wrinkled. "It was a question of duty," he answered slowly, "that I be here, even though perhaps it was not my personal wish."

It was Emilie's turn to be perplexed. "But surely Les Saules is still in your father's hands? He has not brought you back here to run it?" She realized she had perhaps been speaking out of turn, asking personal questions that might make her visitor uncomfortable.

"No, it's not that at all," he said. "Les Saules is running very well indeed. It could have supported me for many more years, I'm sure. I'm afraid that the problem that has brought me home is far greater than merely my own plantation." He lifted his eyes as he spoke and seemed to take in all of the far horizon.

"But what problem is that?" Emilie asked.

The handsome face turned slowly toward her, his eyes once more settling on hers. "I believe we are going to have a war, mademoiselle," he said gravely. "And it will take every resource human and otherwise to see us through it. I have come back to accept whatever commission will be offered to me."

"A war!" Emilie was startled.

"Your Yankee hosts did not inform you of their plans, I see." Guillaume smiled gently. "I understood that you have just recently returned from a visit up North."

"There was some talk of their dissatisfaction with our system," Emilie said. "But I think that out of courtesy my friends tried to keep me from hearing much of it."

"I was really only teasing you," Guillaume said. "Although I have no doubt that war between us must come, and will come rather quickly."

Emilie gazed at the peaceful surroundings. The damage done to the house during the fire had not gone much farther than the salon they were sitting in now. The lawn stretching to the timbered area that separated the house grounds from the canefields was undisturbed. The plantation had been laid out so that the slave quarters and the refining buildings were not visible from the mansion. Nothing evil or even man-made broke the vista of sky, trees, and grass that faced them. It was impossible for Emilie to look at the blues and greens of her holdings and imagine anything so awful as war coming to change them.

She turned to her visitor. "But surely if we realize that a war is coming and the Yankees anticipate it too, it can be stopped," she reasoned. "I would think that only if one were attacked unexpectedly would it be necessary to fight back. Can't we stop this thing from happening?"

"I'm afraid not, mademoiselle," Guillaume answered gently. "There are unfortunately many men on both sides who will force us into it."

"They hate our having slaves," Emilie declared. "In New York that seemed to be all that anybody wanted to talk about. But it's hard for me to understand. It isn't as if we were asking them to live as we do. Why should they ask that of us?"

"I'm afraid it isn't quite as simple as that." Guillaume smiled. "And I fear that I have not been nearly so courteous as our Northern brothers in my bringing so unpleasant a subject to such lovely ears. You must excuse me, Miss Emilie, but I have been abroad where the young ladies in society are not as protected and sheltered as here at home. I beg your forgiveness."

"There's nothing to forgive, monsieur," Emilie said quickly. "Indeed there is very little that I can be sheltered or protected from any longer. I am mistress here now, and the responsibility for all of Les Chandelles rests with me. I have to take up my burdens much the same as you have come home to assume yours." She looked at him evenly. "Indeed, I must thank you for having opened the eyes of a silly and inexperienced girl to matters of grave importance.

"I hope, Monsieur Charpentier," Emilie went on, "that I might presume upon our neighborliness in the future. I fear my eyes and ears have much need of opening."

"I will always be at your service, mademoiselle, as a neighbor and as a friend," he replied.

"I thank you for that, monsieur," Emilie murmured. "And now perhaps we can speak of other things."

"Yes," he agreed. "It is too lovely a day to be spent on such somber matters. Let's enjoy ourselves while we can."

Emilie looked at him, suddenly liking him very much. There was so much elegance in his tall, beautifully tailored person. The cut of his soft dark-gray suit was excellent, she recognized, superior even to what the well-dressed men in New York were wearing. Yet the way his close-fitting breeches were tucked carefully into the polished knee-high boots seemed to her so very Southern in style, so very appropriate for the walking and riding that country planters had to do. His face was tanned and his hair and brows a deep sandy color that emphasized his cool blue eyes. It was impossible to imagine any woman not considering him extremely handsome.

But even more than the fine aristocratic features, what impressed Emilie was the strong set of the squarish jaw and the expression of his face. It bespoke a strength tempered with goodness, a masculinity not spoiled by pride.

She was eager to speak with him about his long sojourn in Europe. She questioned him about Paris and Rome and all of the other marvelous cities, some of which, like Prague, she had never even heard of. So engrossed was she in his conversation that she scarcely noticed Missy slipping by and curtsying slightly as she murmured something and ran quickly to the veranda and skirted the lawn. Whatever it was her maid had murmured, Emilie missed it completely.

Missy took Emilie's silence for acquiescence. Her heart was pounding as she sailed from the house, running on feet that barely touched the ground, toward the quarters. They had been back at Les Chandelles for days now and this was the first chance she had gotten to slip away from the mistress and the house and go down to the quarters to look for Young Jess.

She had used as excuse for going her desire to bring some thick porridge to the old grandfather who lay ill. She hugged the covered bowl close to her breasts as she ran. Most of the slaves would be in the fields now, but Missy prayed silently that there would be someone in the quarters who could tell her of Young Jess.

Finally she was on the dirt path that led to the squalid street of houses.

The cabin that Jess and his grandfather shared was the last one. Missy took no notice of the dust that her pounding feet raised as she once more doubled her efforts to reach the cabin.

She knocked quickly and flung open the door. Nothing inside had changed since the last time she had been there, just before leaving for New York with Miss Emilie. The only difference was that on the straw pallet where she and Young Jess first talked and then silently found and knew each other, the old man now lay.

He looked up as she opened the door. He was scarcely able to turn his head toward her. Old Jess offered no words of greeting, merely watching her as she came toward him with the food in much the same way she had first approached his grandson after the dreadful whipping that had lacerated his back and forced him to lie in this self-same place. Missy found a large metal spoon on the table. She got down on her knees and gently lifted the grizzled old head onto her lap. She spooned some of the warm gruel into the old man's mouth and watched anxiously, as, with great difficulty, he swallowed it. Missy realized that she had run through the quarter without seeing or hearing anyone else. Even the walking and crawling sugar-sucking babies whose shrills and cries could almost always be heard on the street seemed to be somewhere else. As she watched Old Jess swallow, she realized that he was unable to speak. It would be useless to try to ask him anything about his grandson, and cruel to add anything to his already enormous trials. It would have to wait.

Patiently and carefully, Missy continued to feed Old Jess. The slave averted his head, signifying that he could eat no more.

"You feel better?" Missy asked cautiously, but there was no response. She shifted his head back onto the pallet. He was asleep.

Missy rose slowly, feeling an ache in her legs from their unaccustomed position doubled up under her. She didn't want to go back to the big house, yet her inborn dread of the canefields prevented her from going past

there. Although she was a house servant and Miss
Emilie's own maid, she nevertheless lived in the constant fear that somehow she would be noticed by an
overseer and forced into the cane. Missy glanced about
the cabin. She couldn't make up her mind what to do.
Miss Emilie seemed very engrossed in entertaining
their visitor, and Missy knew she would not be likely
to be looking for her soon. Even if she were late
getting back to the mansion, her having gone to help
Old Jess would be excuse enough, and she would suffer no reprimand at Miss Emilie's hand. Still, to remain alone in the quarters was not a very appealing
alternative.

She cast about the simple square shanty, trying to
guess from its meager contents whether or not Young
Jess was still there. He had told her the last time
they spoke, before she went up north, that she must
try to escape in New York as he was once more going
to try to do from Les Chandelles. She had been unable
to talk him out of it and had spent the entire Northern
sojourn shaken by uncertainty; would he still be there
when she returned? She had not dared inquire too
closely of the other house servants. She did not know
how to approach Sully, the housekeeper, and she was
in absolute terror of Tess the cook. It was difficult to
speak to any of the other maids about matters con-
cerning the field hands, as they all disdained having
anything to do with those slaves who were not of the
house or its immediate grounds. Missy had spent the
past days as isolated from knowledge of Young Jess
as she had been all the time she and Miss Emilie
were journeying.

Now she would have to wait several hours until
the hands started returning from the cane to try to
find out anything about him. The closer she got to him
the longer it seemed to be taking to find out.

2

Emilie sat down wearily. It was not woman's work, this plantation business, of that much she was sure. Her father had never had to argue with his overseers or anyone else. His word was law, and that was that. But somehow, among all the things that he had so suddenly left in her keeping, command was not one of them. This, it seemed, was a gift she would have to develop and give to herself.

Her thoughts once more returned to her earlier visitor. She wondered how a man of such culture and courtesy as Guillaume Charpentier would deal with the problems of slaves and overseers. As the eldest son he fell heir to his father's holdings, and while Emilie could easily picture him among the splendors of the European cities that he had described, it was less easy to imagine him astride a horse giving orders, perhaps even wielding the whip, out in the cane. She shuddered at the thought.

Perhaps if he comes to see me again I can ask him about it, she thought to herself. How good it would be to have someone that close by to lean on. She sighed, thinking of how differently her life had turned out from what she had thought it would be. If only André had not died she would probably never have gone up North as she had. Perhaps there would have been no fire, no other deaths, if she had been at home.

But it was not healthy to dwell on the past and on what might have been. Emilie rubbed her eyes, as if trying to rub all those unhappy thoughts out of her head. Her thoughts had to be on what lay in front of her now, hour by hour and day by day.

"I hope he comes back soon," she murmured. "I hope he meant what he said about visiting me often."

Emilie walked slowly out of her library and drifted toward the great staircase that led upstairs. She resolved that as soon as she had the time she would pay a call at Les Saules to visit with Madame there. But then she stopped herself: that might be too forward, Emilie thought, I'll wait and see if *he* comes here again first. She almost laughed, realizing that she was thinking the thoughts of a flirtatious coquette, rather than those of a mature young woman with great responsibilities.

But Guy, as he called himself, was as good as his word. He was back the very next week.

Emilie, as she stood greeting him, was herself as different now from the young girl who had loved André Castel as indeed the two men were from each other. In the earlier situation, it had taken a long time to admit even to herself the fluttering in her bosom that told her that there was indeed one young man who was different from all of the others. She had blushed and lowered her lids at the suggestion from anyone that there was a romance between them.

But from that time to this there had been many changes: André's death had banged shut the gate on childhood dreams and fantasies. Captain Harrington, whom she had known in New York, had taken her even further from girlish thoughts. And now as she stood before Guy, extending her hand for him to kiss, Emilie was honest with herself in a way she had never been before. She saw him frankly as a man whom she might love and admitted as much to herself. His family, his background, his inheritance of a plantation bordering her own, made him eminently suitable as a husband. And she found that she was not even shocked to find herself thinking those thoughts.

"My dear neighbor," she murmured as he lifted her hand to his lips. "How good of you to come and see me. How very kind of your mother to spare you after your long absence abroad. I know that in her heart she must wish to be with you constantly, and yet she has consented for you to come here."

"Had she not, Miss Emilie," he replied, "I would have taken it upon myself to have returned to Les Chandelles. I must confess that it gives me no ease of mind to think of you here in this great place quite by yourself."

Emilie dropped her head. She herself felt no danger in her position, but she was under no compunction to deter him from playing the role of chevalier if he chose it for himself.

"I should like to visit Les Saules soon for an afternoon," Emilie said. "It is only the recentness of my mourning that has prevented me from doing so. I remember your lovely grounds so well."

"Perhaps you would like to take a turn around your lawns now," Guy suggested, offering his arm. The ruined part of the house loomed large and black behind them, and he thought to take her out of its shadow for a small diversion.

"Thank you." Emilie smiled at him. "That would be lovely. I'm afraid I have rather neglected the gardens since I returned. But we have already set about placing some new trees. Would you care to see them, and tell me something of the gardens of Europe? Perhaps I can replace our loss with a far grander embellishment than I had supposed."

They strolled around to the side of the house that was not damaged. Except for a few isolated flowering bushes, the green expanse of lawn continued right around that wing. It was here that Emilie proposed to have a new garden, one that would set off the front of the house and further obscure the outbuildings where much of their food was processed and stored.

They stood under a large sheltering live-oak tree.

"Perhaps you can plant strawberries," Guy suggested. "Although the French boast so of their *fraises de bois*, I can tell you there is no fruit in the world that can compare with our own Louisiana berries."

Emilie laughed. "And such a rich and lovely sight they are too," she agreed. "I will plan to have a good-sized patch of them, exclusively for you."

"That is as fair a promise as I have received from a woman," Guy said.

This time Emilie did very near blush. "Ah, I cannot believe that," she said. "Surely the beauties of Europe must have had far more interesting things to offer."

"I could not take more interest in anything that world might offer than I do from any promise you make me," he replied.

Emilie stared up at him. She longed to speak her mind, but the words were choked back in her throat. It was too soon after her parents' death, too much her time of mourning even to consider such things. Yet in her heart she knew that Guillaume Charpentier was everything she needed—a man she could lean on and trust and quickly learn to love. But all the pretty words he was saying to her now might be no more than that, she realized, and that knowledge, coupled with the unseemliness of such emotions so quick upon her tragedy, checked her. And so she said nothing at all to encourage him, nor to discourage any ideas, if they were real, that might be forming in his heart and mind about her.

"I think we had better go back to the house now," she murmured.

"As you wish," he agreed. "But I hope that you will organize your gardens and let me help you in the execution."

"Of that you may be sure." Emilie permitted herself a small smile.

As they walked toward the house, Emilie said, "I don't recall your saying how long you've been home."

"I arrived at Les Saules a few days after the tragedy here," Guy said. "What a shock it must have been for you."

"Yes," Emilie said quietly. "I thought I was leaving an unpleasant situation for the smiles and comforts of home. Instead I found—I found—" She faltered, unable to go on.

"Don't, Miss Emilie, please," Guy urged gently. "This is too painful for you."

"No, no," Emilie choked back a sob. "I haven't had anyone to talk to about it. I've held it all inside me for so long. It's—it's better for me perhaps to unburden myself. If you don't mind, of course. I feel as though I'm imposing on you."

"Not at all," Guy reassured her. "Permit me to be of any comfort that I can to you."

"Thank you so much." Emilie sniffed into her handkerchief.

"You have been so brave, Emilie," Guy said. "It is the least I can do."

"My mama was not well," Emilie said. "Perhaps you heard that. She had never recovered from the shock of my brother's death."

Guy frowned slightly, remembering hearing of his own brother's complicity in that sad event. But Emilie didn't notice. She went on. "Mama took a taper and lit the candles in the front windows, as if—as if they would somehow help poor Chaz find his way home again." Her voice broke again and she had to stop her narration. "Her skirt had caught fire and she went looking for my father to help her. She probably didn't realize she had spread the flames to some of the furniture. By the time she got upstairs and my father and his valet found her, the main floor was already blazing. Henrique—the valet—ran to rouse the house slaves to put it out while father took a horse to the quarters to get the other slaves to fetch water. They had left mama upstairs, but Henrique says she must have made her way down again. That's where they found her when it was finally over."

"And your father?" Guy asked, more to give her time to catch her breath than to hear the gruesome details, which he already knew.

"My father must have tried to help her," Emilie surmised. "Both of them were found just inside." She motioned with her shoulder. "If he had not gone to her rescue . . . " She left the obvious words unsaid.

Guy wondered, from the accounts he had heard, whether it had indeed happened as Emilie thought. It seemed to him there were many unanswered questions about the whole ugly affair. But no one seemed to have the answers, least of all the unfortunate young mistress of Les Chandelles. The very candles that had given the estate its name had wreaked its greatest tragedy, as well. What Mademoiselle Bonfils most needed now was respite. She was obviously griefstricken, yet he found himself admiring the composure with which she squared her slim shoulders, as if she had just relinquished a burden and was now ready to resume her place in the world and all its attendant responsibilities.

Emilie bent slightly over the silver tray that held the

cool lemonade. She wanted to avoid looking at her visitor for a moment, suddenly conscious of the great emotional outpouring she had released. He was very much a stranger, for all that he was a neighbor, and she, usually so reticent, had let her grief flow unchecked in front of him. She was a little angry at herself, a little amazed at her openness, a little in awe of this man who had caused her to speak so out of character. Yet he had encouraged her to unburden herself, and she had found it natural to do so.

There was something about him that bespoke confidence, Emilie thought, but perhaps she had been too quick to lean on that welcome quality.

The hours he spent with her were but a small reprieve from the aching loneliness that Emilie felt all around her. Later that night, she watched Missy move about their bedchamber, and wondered why the closeness that she had expected to intensify between them had not. She had always been fond of her maid, even more so now that they had both reached maturity. She looked forward to being able to exchange confidences. Although they would always remain mistress and slave, Emilie had thought that their trip to New York together would have brought about some change in their relationship.

Yet as she watched Missy now she knew that nothing of the sort had developed. If anything, the girl was more remote and quiet than ever.

How strange, Emilie mused to herself, that I hadn't noticed this change in her. I have been much too wrapped up in my own self and my problems to have seen it. What it was she did not know, but looking at the girl now she could see that a definite change had indeed taken place.

Missy went about her usual tasks, her hands moving

effortlessly as she brought Emilie's belongings back to their accustomed places. But it was as if she were moving in a trance, her hands and body performing functions from which long habit had enabled her to dismiss her mind. She moved about mechanically, the expression on her face and most especially in her dark eyes suggesting to her mistress that the servant's thoughts were far, far away.

Emilie bit her lip. Perhaps, she thought, I would have done better to let her stay up north. But she quickly dismissed the thought from her mind as though it were a sudden outbreak of a rash disease brought on by a touch too much exposure to Yankees.

Her work in straightening out the room done for the moment, Missy stood submissively in front of Emilie. Her hands were grasped in front of her, the arms and clasped fingers forming a dark V against the whiteness of the muslin apron that covered her simple dress. Her eyes were not averted but looked to her mistress for instructions, their usual brightness somewhat filmed over by the darkness that Emilie was trying to fathom.

The slave was waiting for dismissal. Emilie knew that she should talk with her and try to get to the bottom of whatever was wrong, but she felt too fatigued to deal with another single problem. What with the troublesome St. Georges and all the other details of the estate pressing down on her, it was a far easier thing to let her shoulders fall and decide to focus on this particular problem another day. "You may go, Missy," she said, and frowned with a fleeting sense of disapproval at the seeming relief with which Missy swept from the room.

Another day, thought Emilie wearily, another day and I'll sit her down and find out exactly what is wrong.

Missy flew down the broad staircase that dominated the center hall of the mansion. She went swiftly to the back of the house and into the kitchen attached to the end of the passageway. With a courage that would not have possessed her in earlier days, she completely ignored the tall figure of Tess, the cook, and went to one of the great pots sitting on the cook-oven and, seizing a bowl, quickly ladled some still-simmering broth from within it. She took from an open cupboard a flat plate to use as cover for the bowl, and just as swiftly and silently she left the kitchen through its back door and headed for the quarters.

She cut across the wide green front lawns, not caring if anyone saw her. Her recklessness was not really so grand, she reminded herself when she suddenly grew fearful of the swath that she was cutting across the forbidden manicured grass. Emilie was too occupied at the back of the house, where her chamber faced, to see her, and none of the other slaves would have lifted a voice to scold her, except perhaps Robert, the butler, but even he did not bear down heavily on the other slaves. She felt quite secure in the aura that had surrounded her from the time that it had been announced that she would accompany Miss Emilie on her long trip up North. The prestige that the journey had given her had lifted her status considerably in the eyes of her fellow slaves, and she knew that none of them, even those above her in the hierarchy of the estate, would care to cross her. Even old Tess was somewhat humble. Missy had to smile to herself at that, in spite of the heaviness of heart that colored all her thoughts and emotions. Her prestige among the other slaves would have been a crowning glory to her in the old days, but now it was merely an occasional thought that managed to press itself on her consciousness from time to time. For almost all of her waking conscious hours, her thoughts were buttressed instead by the anxiety that drove her to the quarters now.

Perhaps the old man would be sufficiently recovered

today to permit her to exchange a few words with him. She thought of nothing except his grandson and what fate might have befallen him. That Young Jess was no longer among the chattel at Les Chandelles she was certain; but nothing else did she dare even surmise.

Missy pushed open the door to the shack that stood at the beginning of the dusty street of the quarters. In the gloom she could see Old Jess on his pallet. As she entered he moved slowly to bring himself to a more vertical position. He raised his head and supported himself against his arm.

"Soup, old man," Missy said softly. "Soup to help make you better and get your strength back."

Old Jess smiled at her weakly. He opened his mouth as if to speak, but with a quick gesture Missy dropped to her knees and signaled him to be quiet.

"Hush now," she said. "Save your strength for this eating. I got to ask you something and you've only got to make a sign with your head yes or no." She crouched in front of him, drawing level spoonfuls of the liquid to his parched and slowly moving lips.

With forced patience Missy fed him three or four spoonfuls. Then she summoned all her courage. "Tell me about Young Jess," she said, scarcely daring to form the words. "Just nod your head for yes or no. Did he run away again?"

The old man nodded.

"Have they catched him?" she asked swiftly.

After what seemed to her an eternity Old Jess shook his grizzled head slowly. "Not so we know," came the reply in a voice so cracked and weak she scarcely recognized it.

Missy was shocked. Old Jess had been a man of few words, but whatever he had said had been stated clearly and firmly. Now that voice that had so often pled with the people to remember who they were and what they came from seemed as old and hurt as the very body it issued from.

"He got away then?" Missy drew in her breath sharply with the question.

Old Jess moved his thin body in a semblance of a shrug.

Missy sighed. Her shoulders dropped as if a great weight had fallen from them. "But was it a long time that he ran?" she demanded. "Soon after I went to up North with young mistress?"

The grizzled head nodded again.

Tears sprang into Missy's eyes. "He's safe then," she cried. "He's got to be! They haven't catched him all this time, he's safe in the North!"

Tears streamed from her eyes as her body wracked with sobs. She put the soup bowl down almost blindly, instinctively knowing that the contents would spill if she held it. Through her tears she looked at the old man and could see the pleading reflection of a smile on his face.

She didn't know if she cried for Young Jess's safety or for her own cowardice in not obeying his instructions to run away from Emilie while in New York and stay up North and be free. If she had, she thought wildly, perhaps she would be with him right this very minute.

But North was big, she knew, bigger than all of Les Chandelles and all the plantations around it put together. Even if she had stayed in that cold and frightening stone place, what chance was there that she would ever have seen Young Jess again? She might not be any closer to him if she had stayed in New York than she was at this very moment, kneeling in his old cabin beside his grandfather.

The only difference would be what Young Jess had told her: that she would be free, as he himself had made up his mind he was going to be. But what was that

thing called free? Missy wondered. The white, tight-
lipped servants who worked for old Mrs. van Nuys in
New York did the same things for her that Missy did
for Miss Emilie. What difference there was in their lives
she truly did not know. Besides, what good was being
free or being anything else in the world if she wasn't being it with Young Jess?

Missy started to feed the rest of the broth to Old
Jess. "You think he'll come back here?" she asked
anxiously. "You think he's ever coming back?"

The old man didn't answer. If Young Jess was still
alive and had gotten past the slave states, there was
nothing on God's earth that would bring him back to
Louisiana. Not even this girl and all of the love that
the old man knew she bore for his grandson. But this
he could not tell her, for he knew all too well that it
was not what she wanted to hear.

"Young Jess is strong," the old man summoned all
of his strength to say. "He's good. He needs to be
free." He was hurt as much by the downcast look on
Missy's face as he was by the pain suddenly surging
through his thin, hacked chest. He spurred himself to
speak again, trying to put a softness on the high, hard
edge of his quavery voice. "We all must be free. Maybe
someday Young Jess will come back and bring freedom
to all of us."

He lay down on the pallet as if these few words had
sapped him of the strength to do anything else, as
though he were capable neither of swallowing more
broth nor uttering another syllable. He closed his eyes.

Missy, watching him fearfully, was frightened. Perhaps she had taken too much from him in her wild
need to know about Young Jess. She sat on her knees,
stock still, watching wide-eyed as his labored breathing
made his chest sink and rise, sink and rise. He was

no more than a mere wisp of life, as fragile and insubstantial as the air around him.

But Old Jess, had Missy known it, had closed his eyes not from weakness or unhappiness. He wanted some moments to think himself back to the old place, the country from which he had been so ruthlessly torn. He needed, as always, to rest his mind's eye on those green abundant fields and sheltering trees, to renew himself at the wellsprings of his boyhood, to tell himself that when he closed those eyelids for the final time he would indeed be back in the good and fertile land of the fathers.

Missy sat watching for a few minutes. She thought from the regularity of his breathing that he must have fallen asleep. She got up quietly, tucking the bowl in place under her arm, and headed slowly back to the mansion on the hill beyond the quarters, beyond the trees, beyond the grassy sward she would now circumspectly avoid, as her lagging footsteps turned her once more to her place in the big house.

3

Emilie was grateful for the cooling breeze that came from the river. The horses moved at a steady clip, drawing the light carriage along the road that led from Les Chandelles to Les Saules. Several weeks had passed since Guy Charpentier had started calling on her. They had spent many hours together, hours that had come to be her only happiness. She could no longer deny to herself what his visits, and Guy himself, had come to mean to her. Her feelings toward him had been growing with the weeks, and her anticipation of seeing him now was leaping alongside the carriage wheels as they sped. She felt suddenly happy, eager to be back in the world again.

Although her period of mourning was far from over, Emilie felt it encumbent upon herself to repay his attentiveness by calling on his mother. But courtesy claimed the far smaller part of her intent this day, she smiled to admit.

It was a bright Saturday morning, a half-day of work for the slaves in the canefields, a day when she felt she was most able to absent herself from her own plantation.

Trees and brush grew thickly along the road that had been cleared years earlier through the prodigious growth which threatened at times to close over the dirt and graveled track and reclaim it once more, reverting the narrow intrusion of pathway back into wilderness. Slash pine, gum tree, and tupelo grew within leafy reach of one another, seeming to grapple for dominance. Emilie knew that somewhere beyond the surrounding thicket there lay a bayou of rather imposing size, its swampy waters the home not only of many frightening reptiles and animals, but also, so there were tales, of ghosts and haunts that supposedly drifted about the place.

Here too, she knew, were situated a few small farms, reclaimed from the nearby mire and set between the surrounding grand plantations. One such holding she knew to be that of the man Higgins, with whom her family had had some traffic, none of it boding well, in the past. She was glad for the strength and height of the trees that screened both swamp and unwanted neighbors from her sight.

She settled back into the cabriolet, closing her eyes from time to time, opening them at the flashes of unexpected color when some brilliant flower thrust itself through the pervasive greenery to demand her attention. A stand of tall cypresses, their branches held out as if in supplication, strung with Spanish moss as if in mourning, told her that they were riding past the swampy bayou. Emilie had never seen it, but she knew that its smaller shore lay parallel with the road, and she was glad that they would not have to traverse its entire length in order to reach their destination.

It would be good, Emilie thought, once more to have the company of another woman of her own class. Even though Madame Charpentier was closer to the age Emilie's mother had been rather than Emilie's, she was sure that Madame ran the household of her establishment much the same as Emilie had at Les Chandelles before the tragedy robbed her of both parents and left in their place the heavy legacy of responsibility for the entire plantation. Then too she knew that Les Saules, while much smaller than Les Chandelles, was considered to be a magnificent jewel-box of a residence, all of its treasures carefully collected and cherished and worried over by Madame Charpentier. After all of the bleak weeks isolated within the burned-out solemnity of her own home, Emilie was eager to walk once more among bright and beautiful objects. Guy, while sometimes subtly disdainful of Louisiana parish life, had, in his conversations with Emilie, displayed quite a bit of admiration for his mother's knowing eye and delicate hand.

Emilie colored slightly at the recollection of Guy. If she closed her eyes just slightly she could see him perfectly clearly just as he had been on his last visit, his long lithe form impeccably clad in soft gray doeskin, a marvelously cut jacket within which his broad shoulders found their ease down to his tapered waistline and hips. She blushed further to recollect how snugly his breeches of the same cloth had lain so smoothly against what had to be well-muscled legs indeed.

As if to condone herself for having thought rather too intimately about Guy, Emilie reminded herself primly that she had only garnered up his image to remind her of his innate superiority over one certain Captain James Harrington, in every regard. As proud a strutting peacock as that one had been in his, she had to admit, quite dashing dark-blue uniform, there was no point at which the Yankee officer could hold a candle to her elegant, newly returned neighbor.

But she had to stop thinking of him. Her purpose in visiting his home was to pay her respects to his mother. After all, Guy had told her at the outset of his first visit that he was merely being a messenger in extending sympathy and hospitality to the newly bereaved Emilie.

I'm going to see his mother and not to see him, she said to herself primly. She sat back rigidly in the seat of the carriage and for the space of the next several paces, completely believed what she was telling herself.

But as the cabriolet was drawn by the matched chestnuts and slave driver to the avenue of embowering willow trees that led to the mansion and gave the estate its name, she was once again overcome with an undeniable desire to see the handsome young returnee. The grace of the leafy branches that grew on either side of the road and met overhead in fragile lace archways bespoke his very presence. The trees were strong and tall, just as he was, yet had the same undeniable elegance of being that transformed and tempered the strength into something much more appealing than mere power ever could be.

These are his trees, Emilie thought to herself happily, indeed they might have been planted and planned by him to create the very effect that they did. But she knew that such was not the case, that the avenue had been set by his grandfather many years ago, nearly at the same time as her own forebear was setting the boundaries of Les Chandelles.

Faultless planning had indeed been the hallmark of the entire plantation, Emilie realized as they drove closer to the big house. The mansion was set on higher ground than any other habitation in the parish. There was neither sight nor sound of quarters, canefields, or refinery as they approached. One might have been driving through an English country estate or even a large private park for all the evidence of the activity that supported Les Saules. Even the small house, which was an exact duplicate of the mansion in everything but size, was nearly completely hidden by trees and foliage. If Emilie had ever known that it was precisely in that *garçonnière* that her brother had passed the last night of his life, she carried no memory of it now. Rather her mind was occupied with all the delights that greeted her eyes on every side.

The Charpentiers had forgone the use of the massive pillars that defined the front portico of Les Chandelles and had been copied by nearly every other major house in the parish. Instead the architect had used forms remarkable for their simplicity and exquisite proportions to each other. The main architectural feature of the large house was the tall jalousied galleries that enclosed all of the second floor and the sides of the first. The horizontal louvers, set between tall slim posts, gave the entire house an air of stately simplicity. The main living rooms of the interior, the salons, the dining room, and the upstairs bed chambers, were all grateful recipients of the breezes. Very few important houses in the area employed this remarkably practical feature, but the elder Charpentier knew that it was the most effective way for those inside to catch whatever coolness the nearby river might afford.

Emilie had always loved the simple white picket fencing that enclosed the house and encircled the formal gardens. She smiled when her driver brought the horses to a halt, and she was helped to alight from the cabriolet amid a profusion of ardisia whose brilliant red berries and dark-green foliage lined the walks leading directly to the house. She paused for a moment before going up the wide white staircase that led to the half-open veranda. An enormous live-oak tree, hung with Spanish moss, seemed to stretch out its benevolent arms almost in greeting to the visitor, while all around the house the grounds burst forth with rich magnolias. Their strong fragrance reached Emilie when she at last went up, a ready smile playing about her lips as she

greeted Madame Charpentier, who waited standing at
the head of the stairs.

The two women, one crowned with the silvery white
hair of majestic age, the other in shiny black contrast
to it, embraced. Madame Charpentier released Emilie,
murmured a few words in French to the waiting servants, and then motioned her young visitor into a
chair. Emilie noticed with chagrin how much better
turned out Madame Charpentier's slaves were than her
own. They wore simple enough clothes, but there was
no evidence of wear or raggedness about them; instead
a condition of cleanliness and order that was far from
the situation back home. She made a note to herself
to try to remedy it, at least as far as the house slaves
were concerned. Then she settled back in her chair, to
smile a dimpled smile at her hostess and to allow herself the feeling of almost sinking in the luxuriousness
that abounded everywhere.

It was not only in the man-made appurtenances that
Emilie reveled; it was as much in the luxuriant nature
that enfolded Les Saules. From where she sat she could
see another row of trees, almost as stately as the willows
she had driven under, lining the *allée* that led to still
another garden back of the house. Although nature's
extravagant hand was clearly at work, Emilie knew it
took a great deal of manual labor to keep the gardens
and grounds in such beautiful condition. She guessed
that Madame employed as many slaves to tend the
grounds in which the house was set as she did to take
care of the mansion and its surrounding acreage. She
remembered her talks with Guy about plans for land-
scaping the rebuilt Les Chandelles. Now as she told
his mother of her unending admiration for their gardens
she expressed her hopes for her own.

"I am sure that Guy will be of great service to you
in helping to design your grounds, my dear," Madame

Charpentier said. "And of course we shall be more than pleased to assist you with a loan of several of our own gardeners to make sure that everything is set properly."

"How kind," Emilie murmured. "I really don't know how I will be able to thank you for your graciousness."

"Nonsense, my dear," the lordly Madame Charpentier said, leaning forward in her fragile-looking chair to press Emilie's hand with her own. "Our payment will be in seeing you once more restore Les Chandelles to its deserved grandeur and yourself as happy and content there as you were when you were a child."

Just then, silently and unobtrusively, two slaves appeared behind Madame's chair. The first one carried a small silver tray on which was poised a large crystal pitcher of lemonade. Jetting out from the liquid was a jagged piece of ice that would ensure the coolness of the beverage. The other servant carried a large round silver tray on which was an assortment of delectable pastries as carefully arranged as one of the intricately worked flower beds in the formal garden. The tray was placed before Emilie, and from a pile of beignets, she chose the topmost one. She had little appetite this early in the day and thought that the doughnut would be a simple matter to nibble on and nurse and inconspicuously leave unfinished if she chose. It was expected that a young lady of her age and station display a dainty appetite, and leaving over part of the serving would in no way insult the hospitality of her hostess or the kitchen from which the delicacies came.

Emilie eyed the tray appreciatively. The table of white wrought iron before which they sat and which matched their chairs was itself too dainty to hold the large pastry tray, and so the silent slave stood within easy reach of his hostess should anything more be desired by her.

Emilie admired the impeccable training of the house

servants. As she glanced at the proffered tray she had the satisfaction of knowing that at this, at any rate, Les Chandelles need take second to no one. The gaunt giantess named Tess who tyrannized Emilie's kitchen could easily match anything that Les Saules' cuisine might conjure up. Emilie bit into her doughnut with satisfaction, knowing that in this one regard at least she could not be bested anywhere in the parish.

Then too there was the difference between the size of the respective estates. While Les Saules was sizable, it could have fit into any of Les Chandelles' corners and be accommodated nicely. Emilie almost smiled to herself at this conjecture, but then stopped. She was not being gracious-minded at all, thinking such things in front of the lady who was being so entertaining and gracious to her. She set her mind on other things.

"It must be of great comfort to you to have your elder son with you again," she commented.

"Ah yes," Madame Charpentier smiled. She did not hide the great joy that was immediately evident to her visitor. Madame fluttered a small ivory fan for a moment, then sighed, but the sound was one that bespoke great joy. It was as if her happiness with her elder offspring came from somewhere deep within her. She addressed Emilie again with a tone of great confiding, leaning forward once again from her chair as if to emphasize the intimacy of the conversation between them. "Guillaume is as fine a son as a mother was ever blessed with and as much a man as a father could ever wish for. I cannot begin to tell you the sense of loss I have suffered the last seven years while he was abroad."

"Has it been that long, indeed?" Emilie murmured. "How hard it must have been for you."

"Yes, I am glad to have him back, even at the cost

of this silly war he declares will be dropping on our heads at any moment."

It was Emilie's turn to sigh, although not with happiness. "Do you really think there's going to be a war?" she asked anxiously.

"Not at all, my dear, but then who am I to say?" Madame Charpentier replied. "My boy insists that it's all the talk in Europe and that's what has brought him scrambling back here. My husband and younger son are all for it."

"Are they really?" Emilie asked. She could not completely visualize what war meant, but she knew that men went into battle and often died or were maimed for life. Andre had described for her the terrible aftermath he had seen of a bloody war somewhere, but Emilie could not quite remember where he had told her it was. In any event it scarcely sounded like the kind of thing to bring joy to one's heart.

"My dear, if the Yankees don't actually fire on us, I think we might safely depend on Captain Charpentier's reloading his nasty old musket and charging off to get things started himself!" Madame declared of her absent husband.

It seemed to Emilie that there was something terribly wrong. It seemed somehow unfitting for men to be anxious to go out and die, no matter what their cause was, and equally unsuitable for a wife and mother such as Madame to be taking it all so lightly, as though a war would be but another diversion, like a horse race or an athletic exhibition such as gentlemen seemed to be so fond of. "What will become of us all?" Emilie sighed for the second time.

"My dear, I doubt that you have to worry your pretty head about that." Madame laughed. "It can scarcely affect us here. The men will go rushing off to shoot some Yankees and come back home when it's

over and everything will go on just as it always has."
She reached toward the tray, which the slave quickly
stepped forward to bring closer to her, and selected
a crisply thin lace cookie.

"How peaceful it is here," said Emilie, looking fondly
at the beautiful surroundings. "And how far away the
idea of war seems." She found conversation with
Madame Charpentier a bit of a chore to maintain, and
she wondered where that elder son that her hostess
spoke so highly of might be. She had quite expected
him to be in attendance on this, her first visit to the
estate since they had both returned to the neighbor-
hood. Emilie took another morsel of beignet and found
herself wishing hard that Guy would make his appearance.

"And how is your other son, Madame Charpentier?"
Emilie asked, more out of politeness than curiosity. The
younger Charpentier brother had been a close companion of her brother's, and Emilie thought that perhaps his mother had not mentioned him out of
consideration for Emilie's feelings.

"My younger son has been down in the city for
several weeks now," was the reply. "From time to
time we get a barely legible note that he has thought
to scrawl to us to let us know that he is still alive. Other
than that we hear very little." She tried to smile and
only barely managed.

"Perhaps it's just as well," Emilie replied. "The
activities of landed young men being what they are
these days, perhaps it is in defense of your sensibilities
that he does not correspond with you in more detail."

"How delicately you put that, my dear Emilie,"
Madame Charpentier exclaimed. "Indeed, I do have
a young rogue in that one, I must admit. But ah, my
dear, his older brother more than makes up for
Stephan's lacks." She beamed with pride, and Emilie

noted again the deep expression of satisfaction that
lit her aging features when she spoke of Guy.

"Guy stands to inherit, of course." Emilie posed it
somewhere between a question and a statement.

"Yes, of course," Madame was quick to answer,
looking at her young guest sharply. She was surprised
at Emilie, knowing Guy the elder son, and the law and
custom unshakable.

"Then you have the satisfaction of knowing that all
of this loveliness will pass into hands capable of main-
taining and enjoying it," Emilie continued.

"Yes, of course that affords me a great deal of
contentment," Madame acquiesced. "And all the more
reason I'm glad that he's given up his gallivanting
about Europe and finally come home where he belongs,
war or no war." She closed her eyes for a moment and
then opened them to gaze again sharply at Emilie.
"Guy will inherit here just as you have at Les
Chandelles," she stated. "Our lands have long shared
a common border. The Bonfils and Charpentier families
have been good neighbors for more years than I care to
count, at least for my generation." She laughed. But her
sharp gaze never left Emilie. "I have great hopes that
this condition will obtain, my dear, and may"—she
stopped herself suddenly, one hand gesturing in mid-
air—"may even improve. I hope that I might live to see
between you and my boy something more than neighborliness."

Emilie was taken sharply aback. She was appalled
at Madame's use of the word "boy" and wondered in
sudden terror if Madame Charpentier was proposing
an alliance between herself and the young, hot-
blooded, irresponsible Stephan. Her conversation indicated that Guy by inheriting would be well-fixed. It was
the younger son who stood in need of land of his own.

"Madame, I cannot . . ." Emilie faltered, not

wishing to give offense. "It is not permitted for me to even entertain such thoughts about myself, so early is it in my period of deepest mourning. I have come here to visit with you for reasons of that same sweet neighborliness that you yourself just spoke of, but I cannot, cannot even think of such things right now. I know you will understand."

"My dear, my dear, forgive me" Madame Charpentier pressed Emilie's hand. "Of course I meant no intrusion upon your grief, nor to suggest anything that would to both our minds be so unseemly at this time. But Emilie," she went on, "you must find it in your heart to forgive an old woman. I merely expressed what has been a fond hope of mine for many years, and now that he has returned . . ."

Emilie breathed an invisible sigh of relief. She barely heard the rest of what Madame was saying, so glad was she that she would not have to face now or in the future the fending off of such an unsuitable alliance as young Stephan Charpentier.

As far as his older brother was concerned, there her heart would be on more dangerous grounds, but still it was too soon for her to speak about such things.

Thus it was that Guy, stepping onto the veranda from the cool interior of the house, found her flustered and ill-composed.

Not so his mother. "My dear, we were just now talking about you!" Madame Charpentier chortled, and Emilie found herself plunged even deeper into embarrassment.

"Good morning, Mademoiselle Bonfils," Guy said, rising from kissing his mother's cheek to lift Emilie's hand to those same lips. "How good of you to grant us your charming presence this morning."

"Les Saules needs no gracing from anyone," Emilie declared lavishly. "What a generous Providence might have neglected to include here, you and your forebears have made certain of."

It was a pretty compliment and Guy smiled down at her with genuine pleasure. A slave brought a chair for the young master and he was quickly seated between the two women.

Once more Emilie felt herself agreeably amazed by the ease and grace with which he fit himself to his surroundings. It was not in the least bit difficult to see in him not only the lord and master of all the estate, but indeed the very embodiment of all of those virtues, accomplishments, and sensibilities that the men of the landed gentry were so often claimed to possess and were very nearly as often so deficient in. Emilie was certain, without ever seeing him mounted, that he sat as well in the saddle as he did in the settee. But when her wandering mind tried to picture him in the canefields she came to a sudden stop. It was impossible, she realized to herself, in a burst of astonishment, to picture Guy Charpentier riding herd on a gang of sweating slaves, wielding the whip, giving the orders that would bring men and yes, women to their knees. He was as alien to these practices as the sights he had dallied amid in Europe. How then was he to assume his predestined role as legatee of this holding?

In all the time they had spent together when he had ridden down to Les Chandelles, they had talked of many things, but never, Emilie now realized, had they ever discussed chattel. Perhaps, she thought, the whole subject was distasteful to him. Perhaps, and she suddenly felt as though a clarifying light had entered her mind, perhaps it was the whole business of slavery that drove him to try to find himself in foreign parts. Had not André seemed similarly driven, and had not her father admonished him for it?

So absorbed did she become in this train of thought

that she nearly lost touch with the conversation around her. Mother and son were discussing affairs of the parish, and as Emilie refocused her attention on what they were saying, she realized how much Madame Charpentier deferred to her son's opinions. She beamed at him with a smile that brooked no possibilities of shortcomings on the part of her firstborn.

Emilie was in a quandary as she watched them. It was difficult for her to concentrate on anything much at all when she was with Guy except Guy himself. Yet she felt deeply drawn to his mother and found her admiration for the older woman growing. Madame had a grasp of the problems of running a plantation and being its mistress that put Emilie in mind of how totally inadequate her own poor mother had been on this account. Madame acquiesced to the opinions that were contained in her son's answers, but the questions she so lovingly addressed to him were at the same time shrewd and piercing. Her face, while no longer young, held none of the fears and horrors that had so haunted Catherine Bonfils. Above her serene brow a crown of carefully waved white hair gave Madame the very look of the aristocratic matriarch she was. Emilie realized that she would probably never be in a close friendly relationship with her, such as she had been with Francine Desbrosses. Madame could be a formidable enemy. On the other hand, if she were approving, she could certainly make one's life a great deal easier. Emile felt a warm tinge of color touching her skin as she realized that she had been casting Madame Charpentier in the role of potential mother-in-law.

"Perhaps Emilie would enjoy seeing the rose garden," Madame was saying. "I know that we must not tempt her with anything that might be construed as entertainment in this sad, dreary time. But surely we can be forgiven if we want her to partake of such spiritual delights as the garden affords."

"By all means, Mama," Guy said. "If Miss Emilie is feeling up to walking at this time of day, I would love her to see the gardens."

"Of course," Emilie said softly. She started to rise and was grateful for the black arms that pulled the chair back from her, unseen. She smiled weakly at Madame, who remained seated, nodding with approval as Guy took Emilie's arm and led her down the white wooden stairs to the ground.

No word passed between them as they walked along the pink brick path laid flat with the earth to provide both direction to and border for the garden that stretched to one side of the house and back of it. Emilie was grateful for the shade of the towering live oaks that lined this path. It seemed to her that whoever had planned Les Saules had provided for that leafy protection along every road, drive, and path, assuring that those who moved about the elaborate grounds would do so in the shadiest possible comfort, and with great pleasure in the sight of the tall trees.

"Do you walk here often?" Emilie asked.

"Yes, as a matter of fact, I do," Guy replied. "I find that here I can be by myself and yet not feel quite alone."

"You sound almost as though you prefer the company of plants to that of people," Emilie said with a touch of irony.

"Mademoiselle, in the present case I can assure you that is not so." Guy laughed. "But there are times when I feel that there is no one with whom it is more imperative to converse than myself. I'm afraid, though, that you will find that attitude rather conceited."

"Not at all," Emilie said. "I have gotten used to being much alone, and sometimes I fear that I might not know how to converse well in company, should the occasion for it become frequent again."

"Then we are of one mind on the subject," Guy said. They had stopped walking, and he handed her onto a small white painted bench that sat surrounded by Madame's prized rose bushes. The bench was a rather small affair, probably set there, Emilie thought, for just such solitary gazing as they had been discussing. It was barely enough to accommodate the two of them with enough space between for propriety. What a romantic place, she thought giddily, and had to bite her lip to keep from expressing such a thought out loud.

"It is beautiful, isn't it?" Guy said, as if reading her thoughts. "Perhaps this is the loveliest spot in all of Les Saules."

"Do you come to it often?" Emilie asked.

"No, not really," Guy said. "It is not a vista which one should enjoy alone. That would evoke feelings of melancholy, I'm afraid. A state of mind which is most unsuitable to the running of a plantation such as this."

"Are you unhappy here?" Emilie asked outright.

He laughed slightly. "If you are asking whether I am pleased to be with you in this particular spot at this particular moment, Miss Emilie," he answered rather formally, "my response of course would be yes, but if you are questioning how I have adjusted myself to being back, I'm afraid I cannot answer you in a very positive way."

"The life of the planter does not agree with you, then." She made it more a statement than a question.

"Although we are constantly reminded of the superiority of our way of life, I must admit that I'm not quite convinced of it." His answer had an air of irony about it.

"Perhaps that is because you have lived in places of

great grandeur," Emilie said. "Compared to the European capitals our parish and even New Orleans must seem quite plain."

"Plainness is not the problem," Guy stated. "There is more than enough in our land to please the eye and enable a gentleman to live part of his life quite at leisure, but I'm afraid there is not much we have accomplished that can be said to be of much contribution to civilization."

Emilie was silent. What Guy was saying reechoed those thoughts she had heard—so long ago, it seemed—from André. But rather than being a weaker reflection of those earlier words, Guy Charpentier was, if anything, even more forthright in his views. Emilie wondered why these men who had traveled should feel so differently from the others of their class. Her own journeying about, in spite of the occasionally disturbing questions that had been raised, had done nothing to change her feelings.

"I saw life up North," she said. "And could not see how Yankee ways made life any more agreeable."

Guy laughed again. "I'm sure that aspect of New York life to which you were exposed was not meant to cast any doubt on home truths." He hesitated. "But this is not a subject we need concern ourselves with overlong. We have our duties to perform, and perform them we must as best we can."

Emilie was puzzled. "But can you do something well that you really don't believe in?" she asked.

"For the moment I'm afraid I must leave matters of philosophy to the philosophers," he said gently, "and do what I must do."

"We are in much the same boat then, you and I," Emilie said.

Guy moved closer to her on the bench. "I realized that," he said softly, "as soon as I had returned and

heard what had befallen you. We are indeed the bear-
ers of similar burdens, and yet I must tell you that I
would hope we can give each other some of the strength
we both so sorely need."

Emilie felt the color rising to her cheeks. She
looked down at the ground, not daring to answer him
or even face him. What Guy was saying was both
courteous and neighborly, and she must not be such a
fool as to assume he meant anything else, nor would
it be proper for her even to think any other interpretation could be put on his words. She stared at the lush-
ness at her feet from where the darker colors of the
roses' foliage sprang. "This green grass of home," she
murmured, "how I longed for it when I was away and
yet how different it is now that I've returned."

"It will be neither quick nor easy for you to compass the tragedy that has befallen you, Emilie," Guy
said. "Yet you must try at all costs not to dwell on the
wretchedness of the past. We must all look to the
future." He reached for her hand and covered it with
his.

Emilie dared not move. His light caress, she realized at once, was something she had coveted from
their very first meeting. It was wrong of her to want it,
wronger of him now to give it. But she had neither the
courage nor the desire to stop him.

"We should be rejoining your mother," she faltered.

"Mama wished that I show you the rest of the gardens," Guy said. "She made it my especial task for
this morning. Although I hasten to assure you, Miss
Emilie, that attending you is not to be construed as
falling within the meaning of that word. It was rather
meant that Les Saules' hospitality was of more moment than the necessities of the field."

Emilie tried to suppress a smile. She had somehow
managed to get the always impeccably poised Guil-

laume Charpentier rather flustered. "Yes, but perhaps it would be more suitable were we to return to her presence," she said.

"I'm afraid that would not be suitable at all!" Guy said insistently. "Mama always takes a nap at this hour."

Emilie burst out laughing. The idea of joining Madame Charpentier in her bedchamber was just too funny. Yet beneath the masking laughter, Emilie realized how carefully the wily old woman had planned this morning schedule. It was obvious that she wanted the two of them thrown together, and in the most romantic setting possible.

"Well, I really would love to see the gardens," Emilie said slowly, "and I daresay we will rejoin my hostess at dinner. I would certainly not wish to have my presence upset the usual pattern of life at Les Saules."

Guy rose, and rather than relinquishing her hand, grasped it more closely in order to lead her farther down the pink brick path to where the ornate side gardens lay boxed within their intricately trimmed hedges.

"How enchanting!" Emilie exclaimed, as they entered. Against the glossy dark gleam of the hedges, dwarf magnolia trees and double thick camelias bloomed, their multicolored pinks ranging from almost ruby to the palest blush of color on the outer petals of the fragile flowers. So varied and subtle were the many shadings that it seemed as if every spectrum of the prism was well represented. But Emilie quickly realized that the effect was achieved with only the one color in all its infinite possibilities.

"Pink becomes you, Miss Emilie," he said as he watched her.

"It's always been my favorite color," Emilie murmured. "And never before have I seen such a richness of it as here in the garden. The very bricks of the path seem to be blooming."

"It's beautiful indeed," he said. "But not even the choicest flower could ever hope to match the subtle shade of your cheek." And with a gently curving forefinger he stroked her face from temple to chin.

Emilie stretched her neck, inclining her head away from him. "You mustn't," she whispered fervently.

"I must," he said simply.

Emilie closed her eyes and turned slightly from him. She said nothing.

"Don't fight me, Emilie." There was almost a gentle kind of pleading in his strong-timbred voice. "Don't fight me."

Young Jess gazed down the gray length of the river till he could see no more. He shivered against the chill in the air. His worn sweater, many times mended, was scant protection from the wind that pervaded the dockside area. At least he wasn't hungry. The chores he had performed for the Canadian family who had taken him in for the past few weeks had made him enough money to pay for a good hot breakfast, with enough left over to pay his fare on the woodburner going up the St. Lawrence River. Once they passed the area just north of Lake Champlain where the river formed the border between Canada and Vermont, Jess would get off and make his way to Burlington. From there, he had been told, it would take no more than a long single hitch on the railroad to bring him to Boston. His dark eyes burned to see it.

Boston! Jess still couldn't fathom his own determination to reach that city. He had never felt quite at home in Canada, although people had been kind as he had worked his way from his landing place in Ontario to where he now waited, at a small port that stood where the huge lake narrowed at its northeastern extreme to form the river whose length he was trying now to ascertain.

He couldn't explain to himself why Boston or any other northern place would make him feel as though he were in his own country. He had never felt that, surely not in Louisiana, and although he had been helped by many abolitionists, white and black, in escaping from that hell, his journey up the Mississippi and his trek across Ohio had been conducted in stealth and secrecy. Surely not the kind of travel that would make one feel at home.

Perhaps it was because of all he had heard from the abolitionists, and from those few Canadians who had spoken with him to any extent, that he felt his direction to lie in that unknown city. He knew it was where the first concentrated efforts to see his people free had begun. The names he heard again and again, like William Lloyd Garrison and his newspaper, *The Liberator*, were Boston names. Somehow Jess knew that at the end of this new journey he would find what he had set out for in the first place: not the hand-to-mouth existence that he had known since he came North, begging for any kind of work that would put some food in his belly and a roof over his head. In Boston he would find not only work to do but the sense of what freedom was and what made it worthwhile. It would be something more than having a wife and a baby and a little bit of house that he could call his own. He had seen black men free like that in Ohio, and he knew there were some in Canada too, but even more he knew that this was not enough. Not for him.

Besides, what few black people he had met in freedom had either been so off by themselves that they didn't seem to know or care any more about what was happening in slavery, or were so caught up in helping others to escape that their lives were as precarious as those of the slaves back home.

Freedom had to mean more, and it was in Boston that Jess was determined to find out what that more was.

A loud blast from the craft at the dock told him it was time to board. Jess squared his shoulders and straightened up against the wind. Cold as it was, he didn't want to huddle into himself. He boarded the vessel tall and straight, handing over his fare like any other traveler, his lean black body taut against the chill.

Maybe he hadn't found all of the answers yet, but he knew as he found a place for himself on a bench built into the prow of the boat that at least he had learned to stand and walk as a man was supposed to do. Foreign as this place and all its usages seemed to him, he felt he was as free as his grandfather had been in the old land in the days before his capture.

Besides, he had been born into and lived through the hell that Old Jess had not known until he was thrust into it. His grandfather, at the beginning of this captivity, was armed with no such knowledge of that life as Young Jess had on the brink of freedom. Then too, there was his debt to be paid. For when he had been aided by the Underground Railroad and spirited away from Les Chandelles, he had promised that once he had reached freedom he would be willing to go back and do whatever he was told to help others get out. But when he had arrived in Canada there had been no one to receive him, to clothe and feed him and send him on his next step—back, if necessary, to help others. Jess had made his own way eastward across the vast country to the north. But he still felt he owed a debt. In Boston he would find Garrison's band of avenging angels and would turn himself over to them.

Jess shivered with the cold, but could not bring himself to go belowdeck to stay warm. There was too much activity along the shore, and it held his attention completely. This North was so different from the land he was used to. The better he got to know it and the more he could learn about it, the more help he would be to himself and to others, he felt.

All of those endlessly brutal years in the canefields had taught him only two things: to work until his body was ready to drop, and to hate slavery and all those who imposed it upon him. Cutting cane would be no useful trade up here, he thought with bitter irony; the hatred alone, if put to good use, would help sustain him in his new life.

When the vessel stopped at the great city of Montreal, the day was already getting dark. Much as he would have liked to have seen the large port, Jess was fearful of losing his way if he went ashore. He descended instead into the bowels of the boat to find himself a resting place for the night. He had been told that they would not stay over, but continue on their way to the smaller river which broke off from the St. Lawrence and flowed into Lake Champlain itself.

When he awoke the next morning and went on top for some breakfast, day had already broken. Although the air was still chill, the sun was shining brightly. It dazzled his eyes. He had to shield them with his hand even to look at the blue water through which they were skimming. Jess had never seen such a sight. Even though he had come up the mightiest river of them all and been across others and through the Great Lakes themselves, he had never seen anything as beautiful as the blueness on all sides. He could not see to a riverbank on either side, even though he knew that this lake was smaller than the ones he had traveled through previously. But never had he seen anything like the way the sunshine was caught by the waves in the wake that the vessel was making. It was as if a million stars had landed and were dancing on the water's surface. For the first time in his life, Jess realized, he was on a moving vehicle and looking backward to where the boat had come from rather than to where it was going. Taking his eyes reluctantly from the first natural vision that had ever delighted him, he turned and walked uncertainly on the somewhat rocking deck to the prow.

From that vantage point he could see land. He smiled again to realize that the expanse of lake was not some boundless ocean. The forested area turned out to be a large island. The boat made its way through the channel between the wooded mass and the shore opposite it. Jess stood watching for signs of life as they were in sight of the shoreline, but it seemed rather desolate. There were heavy woods, but he saw no signs of houses or towns or people. He stood watching for a while until his hunger prompted him to go to the vessel's galley for some hot coffee and rolls he could purchase with a few cents of the precious money he still had left.

Once he was full and warm again, he went back on deck. Now he could see the beginnings of a good-sized town rearing up in front of them. He knew that this would be Burlington.

Jess felt good as soon as his feet landed on the solid wooden wharf whose ancient green-streaked piles reached down to the muddy bottom of the lake. The vessel he had traveled on was designed to transport produce and did not accommodate itself very readily to passengers. Although there were one or two others whom Jess had noticed on board as idle as himself, none of them had spoken to him and he was just as glad to be done with it and back on solid land again.

He wandered from the dock area. The noise of a locomotive told him exactly where to find the railroad depot. Once there Jess congratulated himself on the education he had stealthily gotten back at Les Chandelles. The very locomotive that had just come into the depot, belching noise and smoke and screeching brakes and signaling as if especially for him, was emblazoned with enormous white letters reading "B&M." Jess wouldn't even have to ask which train to take. All he had to do was plunk down his fare and ask for a ticket to Boston. Then he would mount the iron monster and let the Boston & Maine Railroad do the rest.

His escape had been accomplished on a water route, and most of his transportation had been on vessels of one kind or another: a Mississippi steamer, a flatboat, and other river barges like the one he had just left. Outside of Windsor, Jess had seen a train and train station, but this was the first time he would be boarding one. It had been deemed too dangerous to use such open methods in Ohio; too much sentiment still ran in favor of returning runaways and collecting the reward money. He had been secreted in carriages and wagons, but now he was paying his fare and climbing on board like anybody else.

With his ticket Jess went inside the first in a long line of coaches that followed the locomotive and the coal car. The seats were of a dark, dusty-red color, and their green covering felt at once soft and prickly to his touch. The first car was crowded, and he walked along the aisle to the back where it coupled with the next one. He wanted to see how it felt to walk from one car to the next; also he was determined that on his very first train ride he would sit next to a window so that he could see as much as possible.

Toward the back of the second car, Jess saw an empty seat and quickened his step. He slid in next to the window, congratulating himself hugely on his good luck.

He stared out the window deliberately, as much to avoid the looks of his fellow passengers as to observe the activity that went on outside in the busy station.

Jess knew that he was being regarded with contempt
by many of the other travelers. He kept his head down
and told himself it was as much due to his admittedly
ragged appearance as to anything else. His sweater had
somehow unraveled at one elbow during the previous
night and it now hung gaping and ugly. His trousers,
though clean, were wrinkled from having been slept in,
and although he was wearing shoes his bare feet were
stuck into them without benefit of hose. He knew that
he did not present the kind of appearance he would
have wished to, but he knew as well that there were
many poor people up North no better turned out than
he was.

The train started. Once the screeches of getting un-
derway had subsided, his ears accustomed themselves
to the clacking of the wheels against the rails and the
other sounds of the moving train. Voices of children,
shrill and excited, traveling with their families, were
clear above the train's own noise. Trying not to watch
as women opened baskets and hampers and distributed
fruit and other food to their families, Jess felt an undeniable pang. He wasn't hungry; that had been taken
care of earlier on the boat, and he wasn't used to eating
overmuch anyway. It was with a start that he realized
it was loneliness. He sighed, leaning his head back
against the puzzling upholstery. He closed his eyes as
trees and telegraph wires flew past and the blue sky with
its scudding white clouds filled the rest of the space
through the window. He tried to remember the last
human voice that had spoken to him. It wasn't the man
in the train station from whom he had bought his train
ticket. The man had merely taken his money when
Jess had said, "Boston." Nor had the conductor on the
train to whom he handed the small piece of pasteboard
done anything but nod in confirmation. He had kept to
himself on the boat, speaking neither with crew mem-

bers nor the one or two other passengers. Perhaps, he tried to recollect, he had said something to the cook in the galley when he had bought his coffee and roll, but he couldn't for the life of him remember if the man had said anything to him in return. Farther back than that he couldn't remember at all.

He was staring once more at the landscape whizzing by and telling himself that he ought to be more than satisfied with where he had gotten so far. It was silly with all that was going on around him to find himself hungering for someone just to say his name. But it was a large, empty kind of feeling to know that there wasn't a soul on the train, nor in the land it was speeding through, nor even in the place that he had selected to head for, who knew that he was there and who he was.

True, he had to learn about the land, but the land was going to have to learn about him too.

In Louisiana everyone had known that he was Young Jess, grandson of the head man of the quarters. Down there that always had seemed enough for him to be. He hadn't even had to think about it. But now he was new, newly free, and he was going to be known for that. Jess looked down at his shabby given clothes and realized almost with a feeling of hopelessness what a gigantic task still lay in front of him.

Young Jess no more. But who and what would he be now?

He knew it was most important to find the Abolitionists. He had a story such as few others could tell. Not many, he knew, could have escaped from the life-sucking cane fields as he had. The abolitionists would be able to put him and his experience to good use, letting Northern people know the realities of plantation life. They would be good people and smart, and they would be able to see beyond his shabbiness. They would

know how best to put him to work. There had to be a
role that he could play in the bringing in of the Jubilee,
in the dawning of freedom for everybody. That was
what was important, not the mean looks that he was
getting from the red-faced farmwife or the snickers
from her little yellow-haired children.

Jess held himself stiff against the seat, still staring out
of the window as everything went by in a blur. Nothing
he had ever known or seen had moved as fast as this
train, yet he found himself wishing that it could go
faster still. It couldn't be quick enough to bring him to
the place that he was thinking of, that would be for
him what the preachers called the promised land.

At one stop Jess ran off the train to buy some
crackers from a vendor at the station. He was afraid
of not getting back on time before it pulled out again,
and as he hurried on board he inadvertently shoved
against a woman who was heading in the other direction.
She drew back as though she had been struck by light-
ning. Jess started quickly to apologize in his soft voice,
but one quick glance at the woman's shocked and
startled face told him that nothing that he could say in
the way of excuses would be of any use. He dropped
his head and made his way back to the empty area
where he sat alone.

Too bad she didn't curse me out, he thought wickedly,
at least that would have been somebody to talk to me.
As the day wore on the excitement of train travel began
to dull, and as the lengthening shadows of late afternoon
presented still another aspect of the fleeting countryside, Jess found himself tired and ready to sleep. The
sway of the car would be as lulling as the rocking boats
he had slept on so frequently. But there he had been
able to find warm corners belowdecks or in the hold,
places to curl himself up or stretch himself out. Here in
the confines of the narrow railroad car there was noth-

ing but the stiff lines of upright seats. He glanced around and noticed that one of the women who had boarded some time after Burlington was struggling with some mechanism at the edge of her seat. When it gave way, the back lowered and she was able to rest against its incline.

Jess tried to find the lever on his own seat, and when he did, a healthy push thrust it backward. He settled himself against the slope and closed his eyes to the mounting darkness outside.

He didn't open them again until he heard the conductor's muffled shout as he strode briskly through the car. Jess was lurched forward as the train once more ground to a halt. The noise, and the crowds lining the platform that stretched endlessly outside his window, bespoke no rural train station. There was too much activity, too much noise and bustle, too many people, both milling around the station and, as he could see now, getting off the train. They were there.

It was Boston at last.

Another city, another river. But this one would encompass all cities and all rivers for him for all time.

Jess clutched his small bag to him as he made his way from the train. He walked through the station, jostled and pushed by the crowds on all sides, but no one seemed to mind him. Indeed, no one seemed even to notice that he was there. But he was happy enough, for this meant no one to look at him in a way that said that he didn't belong. Jess made his way out of the terminal feeling almost gleeful. As he emerged into open air he looked up to see a hundred, no, a thousand tall spires reaching for the sky as if to pierce the very heavens. It was beautiful, the streets straight and orderly, the trees dark and grave, the people tall, as if they too aspired heavenward, like the church steeples leaping everywhere. It all seemed so right. He won-

dered if he would even have to ask directions of anyone, so sure was he that somehow he would find his way
without any help.

He didn't even feel cold as he walked the city's
curbs and gutters, until suddenly, as he stepped down
a high embankment to cross a street, the old stone that
his grandfather had given him moved against his chest.
It was like a reminder. He felt chilled then, realizing
that while his joy knew no bounds, neither did he know
friends or food or warm place to put his head that night.

Emilie was in the plantation office room, bowing her head over the ledger, when she first heard the noise. She tried to ignore it, certain that it was only the usual excitement of an unexpected wagon or carriage making its way up the drive. The sounds were stable sounds, she told herself, of the hands greeting some visitor. It could be business for St. Georges or for the kitchen, neither of which she had to bother herself about, and should it prove to be someone to see her she would be duly told. She bit her lip and tried again to concentrate on the long columns of numbers. It was simple enough to check and see if they were added up properly; Emilie could cipher without any difficulty. But to understand what it all meant—the amount of cane cut and boiled, the amount of syrup or powder shipped out, the amount of money coming in—that was a matter of analysis and interpretation that seemed far beyond her. It seemed on paper like a great deal of money, she realized that, but the expenses of running the great plantation was also very high, and whether the money coming in was enough was something she had to leave to Anton Bledsoe, her father's business manager down in the city.

The door to the room burst open.

"St. Georges!" Emilie exclaimed at his sudden and unwarranted intrusion.

The tall, grinning overseer pulled his hat off his head.

"Sorry, Miss Emilie, but there ain't no time for formalities," he said.

Emilie could sense the jeering in his voice and she cringed inwardly. "Surely," she began in her most practiced, level voice, "there is nothing that can excuse—"

"War!" he interrupted her. "It's war at last, Miss Emilie, and I reckon that that's important enough even to you!"

Emilie had risen in anger, but now she found herself sinking back into the large leather chair, which had accommodated her father's bulk so well but in which she seemed somewhat lost. So it's here, she thought to herself, biting lightly at her lower lip to keep from expressing any reaction in front of the overseer. She had feared it ever since Guy had first mentioned its coming as the reason for his return home. The idea of war had cast around in the back of her mind like a shadow casting gloom over everything it touches, yet still somehow ephemeral. Since that lovely languid Saturday she had spent at Les Saules, she had almost been convinced that the men were wrong. Perhaps the wisdom of the old lady would prevail, but now it seemed as though wisdom were no more than a fading memory. The hot blood had carried the day after all.

Even the usually calm Anton Bledsoe had seemed stirred by the possibility of doing battle with the North. The last time he had visited Les Chandelles, bringing the very ledger over which Emilie had been pouring so laboriously, he had seemed to her animated with the same strange excitement that she noticed unmistakably whenever she had contact with others not from Les Chandelles.

St. Georges was pacing back and forth in front of the desk, his movements filling what little available space the office afforded. He was punching his closed fist against the open palm of his other hand and muttering to himself.

"What is it, St. Georges?" Emilie asked.

"I think we're going to have some trouble with the darkies," St. Georges replied. "I know that a lot of them got the notion in their fool heads that this war is being fought by the Yankees in order to set them free."

"Where in the world would our slaves have gotten a notion like that?" Emilie was surprised.

"I don't just mean these darkies here, ma'am," St. Georges explained. "That's the feeling that's got into them all over the South. It seems to me like I'm going to have to crack a couple of heads to keep them in line."

"I think you'll do nothing of the kind, Mr. St. Georges!" Emilie said. "Our slaves are isolated from that sort of strange talk and ideas. Punishing them unnecessarily will, if anything, provoke rebellious feelings rather than stifle them."

St. Georges shook his head. "They're going to have to be dealt with, and quick. I'm not going to have as much help around here as I'm used to. Some of the other fellas, the younger men I got with me, are going to have itchy fingers to get a gun and start killing off Yankees as quick as possible."

Emily shuddered at his words. The burden of her responsibilities was suddenly unbearably heavy. She could only argue from the feelings she harbored, and she knew that the only basis for what she wanted was her own inclination of right and wrong. Against that would come the argument of her overseer, who would advance his greater experience and need for discipline as the reasons for indulging his penchant for brutality. And for all the niceness of her feelings, Emilie knew quite well that St. Georges' tactics, distasteful as they were to her, might very well be the thing needed. It was so hard to know what to do when doing the right thing might be the worst thing after all. Yet she could not let herself be dragged down into that kind of thinking, she told herself sternly. If she did, it meant she was no better than St. Georges or any of his band of young red-necked ruffians.

"For the present, Mr. St. Georges, you will increase the amount of men on guard during the workshift and at night. Closer watch is to be kept on the quarters, and the people are not to be permitted to leave the plantation unless on express orders from myself, or upon my absence, from you, in order to perform some needed task. Other than that, nothing is to change."

"Nothing?" The echo was tinged with mockery.

"At present, nothing," Emilie said. "That will be all, unless there is any incident or disturbance which you need to report to me."

"Yes ma'am." It was no more than a mumble, that reply of St. Georges'.

"And I would appreciate you bringing me up to date on all developments of this—this event as soon as you hear them. It is not advisable that we be isolated as well."

She turned her attention back to her papers. The overseer knew that this constituted his dismissal, and he grasped the doorknob and closed it firmly behind him.

Emilie raised her hand and leaned back in the chair as soon as the door was closed. If it had been hard to concentrate on the ciphers before, it would be impossible now. Why did this have to happen? she wondered. For so many years life had gone on at what seemed now to be a simple measured pace. Season in, season out, things remained the same. People grew and aged, much as the cane renewed itself from year to year. But life itself was like the great river. It flowed ceaselessly, yet remained firmly in its appointed place. Still, she remembered, from time to time the great waters flooded, seeking a place beyond their usual banks, creating havoc wherever it went. The war would be like that.

She knew she should go out and talk to the household slaves. Robert, Sully, and Tess should be reassured that everything was to go on as usual in the great house. She wondered what their feelings really were. Did they think, as St. Georges had said, that the Yankees were going to come bursting in to free them? Or would their feelings be more closely akin to her own—despondence over war and fear that actual bloodshed might reach them as well?

But much as she knew that it was her place to go out and speak with them, either to rid them of foolish notions or comfort them for fearful ones, Emilie found herself riveted to her chair. Outside her door the world was moving and churning at a far faster, more dangerous rate than she could think about or deal with; let it come in and impose itself on her if necessary. She did not want to take the fateful step of rising to meet it. Bad news surely traveled swiftly enough on its own.

Yet it was undeniable that her people would be looking to her for their answers. Not only was she mistress of Les Chandelles, but it was only recently that she had been north among the enemy; she would be expected to be more knowledgeable about things than the other parish people, who generally wandered no farther from their own domains than to New Orleans.

The responsibility overcame her uncertainty. Emilie pulled the thick silken cord that hung behind her to summon Robert.

Within moments she heard his discreet knock at the door and bade him enter.

The smooth round mask of his face revealed neither knowledge nor emotion. To look at him, Emilie thought, he might have known everything—or nothing. Yet she knew him to be a skillful and loyal servant, the one who had done most to try to save what he could that dreadful fiery night.

"You have heard the news, Robert," Emilie said.

"Yes, mistress," was his noncommittal reply.

"Robert, I depend on you a great deal, as my family always has," Emilie said, "and now more than ever, I suppose." She paused. "It is very important that I know what the people are thinking so that I may provide them with whatever knowledge and comfort I can. I know very little about what is facing us presently, but I promise that I will defend my home—our home," she corrected herself—"with my dying breath if necessary. I want my people to know that I will provide whatever I can to ensure their safety and well-being, for every life on Les Chandelles is as precious to me as anything else on earth."

He did not blink.

"I want the women and children especially to know that in the event that the worst should befall us, I—I will provide the shelter of this house if need be for their safety." She felt herself faltering before the continued impassivity of the servant who stood before her. It was as though he were listening and not hearing, or hearing and not believing. Yet perhaps he was merely awaiting instructions, as he had been so long trained to do. Emilie plunged on.

"I—I want to know your own thoughts at this moment, Robert." She had started to say "feelings" but quickly realized that that was something not likely to be revealed to her.

Robert nodded slightly. "I will tell the other servants what you have said, mistress," he replied. "And we'll have the yardmen and stable boys tell the quarters. I am sure they will be much appreciated."

Emilie realized they were at a standstill. There was nothing more that she could learn without probing deeper, questioning the other slaves herself. Yet she dreaded to. Much as she was eager to learn their feelings, she hesitated to make inquiries that were above the normal order of business, that could raise more problems than they answered. More than anything else, she knew that what she most wanted was for everything to continue as it always had, for nothing to change, for no cannon to shatter the air of Les Chandelles, no blood to stain its soil, no Yankees to come within sight of its borders.

With a brief nod she dismissed the butler. She sank once again into her reverie, remembering the Northerners she had met and known on her trip. Surely one could not picture the elegantly domineering figure of Mrs. Porter van Nuys leading an avenging army up the tree-lined avenue to destroy the cane and free the slaves.

Yet from the admittedly silly thought, it took no more than one swift turn for the mind to go back to that last dreadful evening and the searching—yes, destroying if possible—hands of Captain James Harrington tight around her waist and thrusting themselves upward on her body. Then it was all too dreadfully easy to see millions of James Harringtons, blue-clad and multiplied, swarming all over the lovely Southern landscape with nothing other than rape and conquest on their minds.

Emilie closed her eyes in horror both at the image from the past and at that of the future. She felt dreadfully disloyal to the Southern gentlemen whom she had been berating for their war calls. She, more than any-

one, should know how eagerly the Yankees looked
forward to just such an encounter.

Although the heavily draped windows kept her vision
from extending outside of the room, Emilie could tell
by the difference in the sounds of the house that evening
had fallen and it was already dark outside. She was
surprised to hear the sound of galloping hoofbeats and
then a horse being reigned in. It was an unusual time
for a visitor to be arriving. A gasp of fear stuck in her
throat. These were not usual times! Could the war
or some dreadful portent of it be at her door already?
Emilie shrank back into the black leather chair, fearing
the worst. Her mind was spinning. She had just concluded such a brave speech with her head servant,
instructing him to assure all of the other slaves that
their protectress was ever mindful of her responsibility
and devotion to them. Yet here she was cowering already, frightened to death from nothing more than the
sound of a horse.

Emilie almost laughed in spite of herself. What a
ninny I am, she thought. Surely if the Yankees are
here, they would be sending more than one solitary
horseman to conquer Les Chandelles.

She had very nearly composed herself into a normal
pattern of breathing when there was a light knock on
the door and Robert was back again, bowing low.

"Master Charpentier to see you, mistress," he said.

Emilie stood bolt upright. Guy riding here alone in
the dark of night! Whatever could that mean? There
was no time either to frame an answer or freshen
her toilette as she would have like to do before seeing
him. "I'll come out to the salon directly, Robert," she
said. "Since it is so close to dinnertime, tell Sully to
set two places."

Robert nodded and stepped aside to let her precede
him from the room. Emilie turned back to him sud-

denly. "And please see, Robert," she said, "if Tess can't fix something suited for company." Her tone made it almost more a wish than an order.

Emilie hastened down the hallway to the large front room where Guy stood waiting. She blushed with a renewed sense of embarrassment for the still-uncompleted repairs to the room. After visiting his own jewel-like residence, she felt more acutely than ever the rawness of the burned-out Les Chandelles.

One quick look at her face told him everything. "You heard?" he asked quietly.

"Yes," Emilie replied, holding her hand out to him. She didn't realize that she had curled it into a tight fist until he raised it to his lips and kissed the bottom of the clenched fingers.

"Emilie," he kept her hand tight within his, using it to draw her down to a velvet sofa. He sat simultaneously, still not relinquishing the small fist.

"It's come," he said quietly.

"Just as you knew it would," Emilie replied.

"Yes. I rather wish I had been wrong, for perhaps not the first time in my life," he said ruefully.

"Everything is going to be very different now, isn't it?" Emilie asked.

"Yes, very different," he confirmed. "There will be no time left for many of the things we loved to do, and certainly none for the pace at which we liked to do them. Everything will happen very swiftly now. It must, if the South is to rise from her knees and get on with it."

"From her knees?" Emilie was puzzled. "Surely we aren't in that woeful a position? The talk of war has gone on for so long, it seems to me an army must be ready to spring into the fields at a moment's notice."

"Would that it were so, sweet Emilie," Guy said. "Unfortunately the talk has been that and no more.

We must rouse ourselves quickly indeed, and prepare to engage the enemy."

There was a somberness in his voice that startled her. She scanned his face and found it changed. The handsome features had been set into a different cast, another expression informing them now. He was harder somehow, and the elegance seemed to her to have turned to iron. Yet it was mere days ago that he had been so carefree when she had visited him. If pronouncement of war could provoke such a singular change so quickly in so strong a man, Emilie thought fearfully, what would it do to the rest of us when we felt it in its full force?

"Are you—" She hesitated to form the words, yet knew that she must. "Will you be going soon?" she asked, fearing to hear his answer, her heart racing wildly, her mind thinking only, What will become of me if he goes?

Guy pressed her hand tight once again. "I must leave immediately for the city," he replied tersely. "I am to command a regiment of men drawn from this area. I must see to their provisioning and supplies and a great many other details that I do not wish to bore you with."

"Or frighten me with," Emilie amended quietly, her eyes downcast, not daring to look up and seek his.

He squeezed her hand. "I will be in New Orleans for about a week," he went on. "Then I will be coming back here to await my orders."

"How long will that be?" Emilie asked.

"Perhaps a few days, a week at the most," he replied. "But it will be enough time . . . " His voice trailed off.

She looked up at him. "For what?" she asked.

"For you to marry me, and for us to be able to spend at least a little time together before I go."

Emilie's head was spinning. She knew then how much she loved him and wanted this very thing he was asking. Yet the suddenness of it was as confusing as her own emotions. "But what can I say?" she turned her face toward his at last. "I am still in mourning for my parents, and there are so many other things that would have to be decided. I don't know what to say to you. Although you must by now know what is in my heart." She paused for a moment, looking at him again. "And that that heart is yours completely."

"This is a time of madness, Emilie," Guy said. "War always is. We have no time, my dearest, for the niceties and formalities on which we always based our lives. Now everything that is to be done must be done and done quickly. I know that your wedding should be the most beautiful in the world. One that would have taken many months to prepare for. But time is the one thing we do not have, and lovely as it would have been, it still is not as important as making you my wife as quickly as we possibly can manage it."

"But why?" she cried. "Why all this sudden haste? We should have the marriage announced and guests invited and the house prepared. I cannot imagine how your mama will accept what you are proposing."

"I love you, Emilie," he said. "And there may not be time enough left in the world for me to tell you that as often and for as long as I would like. I can do little more than tell it to you now and hope that your feelings toward me are the same, and that our love is strong enough to carry us over the sacrifices that we must make."

"The sacrifices . . ." Emilie nearly choked on the words. She knew that he was leaving, perhaps

never to come back, and the thought of that was unbearable.

He had his arms around her now, and his words
were murmured with his lips pressed close to her
hair. "I can carry nothing into battle with me more
precious than the memories I will own of making love
to you, and the knowledge that I have brought you to
womanhood. I love you enough to believe that these
can sustain me in battle and I will be strong enough to
come home to you to live our lives the way we wish
to."

"What's going to happen to us, Guy?" Emilie cried.
"I'm so frightened, so very frightened. When I heard
you gallop up before I thought it was the Yankees
come to kill us all." She began to sob.

"Hush, hush, my sweet," he whispered, stroking
her hair and holding her close as she hid her face
against his shoulder. "Everything is going to be all
right. I can at least leave you the protection of my
name if not my person."

"I'm so afraid, Guy, I'm so afraid!" Emilie cried.

"It's not as bad as all that," he assured her. "The
Yankees are far from Les Chandelles and will probably always be. We are the last line of the South,
Emilie. They would have to penetrate through the
Virginias, the Carolinas, all of the states that lie north
of us. From what I understand, Lee is already mass-
ing the Army of Virginia. He plans to make his battle
on the enemies' soil and not ours. We are fighting for
our women and our homes."

"But I don't want you to go!" Emilie couldn't help
saying it even though she knew it was pointless.

"First I must go down to the city," he said, releasing her slightly, "and get everything in order. It
shouldn't take more than a few days. On my way back
up here I will stop and arrange for the priest to come

and perform the ceremony on the Saturday following. Thus I hope to give us as much time together as man and wife as possible."

"I can't leave Les Chandelles," Emilie said suddenly.

"I realize that, dear, and I will make arrangements for the nuptials to be celebrated here and to stay here with you until I must leave."

"I can't imagine what your mother will say to all of this unseemly haste," Emilie said. "It will seem so strange to her, I'm sure."

He laughed slightly. "Not at all," he said. "You must not underestimate Mama. She has seen a great deal in her lifetime and garnered sufficient strength from it to be able to compass anything that might happen."

"Have you told her about—about us?" Emilie asked.

Guy suppressed a smile. "I'm afraid I must admit that I have, my darling," he answered. "I am sorry that you weren't the first to know of this plan that concerns you more intimately than anyone else, but I knew we would need Mama and her help."

"What did she say?" Emilie asked fearfully.

"She was all for it!" Guy was able to laugh quite heartily now. "She's been after me about you ever since I got back from Europe. In fact"—and he took Emilie's chin with his finger, lifting her face toward his—"I almost thought it was the major reason for my return from exile."

Emilie was staring up straight into his eyes now. The confusion lifted suddenly, and she felt her mind as clear and as unshakable as her heart. She loved him truly, and if all of this war nonsense was responsible for bringing them so close together so quickly, well, then some good had come out of it after all. Guy started to get up from the sofa. "Be ready for me, my darling," he said.

"Surely you're not going so quickly," Emilie pleaded. "You aren't going to ride all the way to New Orleans in the dead of night?"

"No, only as far as the landing," Guy said. "I'll stop overnight and catch the boat in the morning."

"Why can't you stay here?" Emilie pleaded, clinging to him.

"Emilie!" Guy was astounded at the ferocity of her grasp. "Haven't I already thrown enough impropriety your way? Are you of a mind to totally scandalize the entire parish?"

"Hang the parish!" Emilie exclaimed passionately. "I am not a child, Guy," she said evenly. "I too have seen something of the world. It is far from the storybook place my father wished me to believe it. I know that a young woman is not taken for a bride by some handsome young gallant on a white charger. I have seen women in New York and how they behaved when they wanted a man. Yes, I've seen it," she repeated, when she saw the shock in his gray eyes. "And I have seen too that those who get what they want are not made unhappy, do not suffer for what they have done. I have seen and heard the laughter on the dance floors and in the darkened galleries and yes, from behind the closed boudoir doors."

"Emilie!" Guy exclaimed. "What little you have seen of life has nothing to do with us here. I admire your father for the upbringing that he gave you and the virtues that he instilled in you. My darling girl, let me tell you, I have seen far more of life than you have. And yes, I must admit it to you in all honesty, my fair Emilie, I have drunk deep from its cups. And more than once tasted its dregs."

Emilie said nothing.

"These are not confidences which I wish to share with you, nor shall I disturb your sensibilities with details I prefer remained buried. They have nothing to do with you and with the life I want for you. Please believe that, Emilie."

"I do believe it, Guy, I do," she said, close to tears. "But I know that there is sweetness, not bitterness, when two who love as you and I do drink, as you say, from the same cup."

She blushed again for the very boldness of her words, surprised as much by them as her listener.

"Emilie, much pleasure as I know we are going to find in each other, I shall not risk destroying it this way." Guy was adamant. "We have all of our lives together to look forward to. The affection and respect that a good marriage requires of both husband and wife shall not be flung away by us in one heedless, passionate moment such as this."

"I want you, Guy," Emilie was emboldened enough again to say.

"As I want you, my dearest," he replied. "But not this way, Emilie. Believe me, I must in this instance as in all others be the stronger, and I know only too well the truth of what I am saying."

"But do we have all of our lives?" Emilie cried. "You're leaving for the war. How can you be so sure that anything will be left for us?"

"All the more reason," Guy said, his lips set in a thin fine line whose grimness frightened her. "There is so little of beauty and honor and goodness left in the world, Emilie," he said. "This war that we are going to fight may be the very last stand that will ever be taken to honor and preserve those virtues. For that reason alone, if for no other, I must hold you to this difficult course which I know to be the best for us. Please believe me."

Emilie felt almost chastised, as though she had been a naughty child, and, but for Guy's sensibility, she knew full well she might have been. One day soon now he would be loving her as a husband. But for the moment he was protecting her more as a father would have.

That thought quickly gave rise in her mind to another, more seemly, problem. She brushed the wanton thoughts of keeping him with her that night from her mind and turned immediately to the more practical question of all that needed to be done for their nuptial preparations.

She rose quickly and laid her hand on his arm. "Who's going to give me away? There is no one here, of course, and it cannot be done by your father or brother."

Guy frowned in concentration. "Perhaps one of the planters in the parish," he said. "I can make several stops on my way back. The time taken will serve to extend invitations to them as well."

"Oh no, I would rather not," Emilie said. "I don't want all the fuss of a large wedding under these circumstances. I think it should be very private, with only the immediate family in attendance. Unfortunately"—and her voice took on a bitter tone—"that will be your responsibility, my dear, as I don't have anyone to call my own."

"My poor Emilie, what I'm putting you through!" Guy said. "All I can do is promise you that it will be worth it. And so long as the father says the appropriate words, I'm sure that it will be all right to forgo the other formalities."

"I suppose so," said Emilie slowly.

"And then I promise you," Guy grinned, "that on our tenth anniversary we will throw a ball so lavish, so elegant, so spectacular, that it will be ten times greater than anything this state has ever seen."

"Oh Guy! How can that be?" Emilie laughed, caught up in his gaiety.

"It can be because in ten years I will surely love you even ten times more than I do now."

"I'd settle for five times as much," Emilie answered quickly, "and the celebration in five years. I daresay that ten is too long a wait!"

"Five it shall be, then. Whatever you want."

She held to his arms, unwilling to relinquish him so soon. Yet she knew that she must and that she was doing him no good in staying his journey. The time he would spend in New Orleans would be immeasurably difficult, and he deserved as good a start as he could muster. At the thought of the city, another idea flew into her mind. "Guy," she exclaimed. "I just thought of the very thing! You must make inquiry of my factor, Monsieur Anton Bledsoe, and instruct him to follow you on your return to the parish. He is a great old friend and associate of my poor father's and would be the fitting one to give me away at the ceremony."

"Splendid idea!" Guy said. "I'll attend to your Monsieur Bledsoe before taking care of any other business."

"Wait just one minute more and I'll write out his address for you," Emilie said, casting about for paper and pen. "I suppose while you're about it you can extend an invitation to his wife as well. There should be at least one lady to attend me, I suppose."

"Done," Guy promised.

She folded the slip of paper in half and handed it to him. "Until we're together again, my darling," she said softly and stood up on her toes to plant a kiss fully and lovingly on his mouth.

"My dear!" Guy looked at her with an expression

that combined surprise and delight. "You may be sure there'll be nothing able to stop me from claiming the promise of that sweet, sweet kiss."

The way he looked at her set Emilie back for a moment. She flushed, wondering if perhaps she had been too forward. But little more than a week separated them from becoming man and wife, and she was as truly his in heart and mind already as she was soon to be in body. For all the sacrifices that Guy was going to make and all the danger he would soon find himself in, a real kiss from his intended was little enough prize to be freely given and eagerly snatched. He was promising to bring her from girlhood to womanhood in the space of their wedding night, but Emilie determined that she would surprise and please him by being more of a woman than he was expecting. Every fiber in her being told her that this was what they both wanted.

She stood on the veranda clinging to one of the remaining pillars until long after she could actually see the swiftly fading horse and rider, and the final echoing of the hoofbeats no longer resounded in her ears. It seemed as though all creation were standing alert and prepared; even the trees and the stars above them seemed outlined with a hardness she had never noticed before. It filled her with a great longing she could not quite identify, to realize that scenes such as she had just experienced were happening in houses all through the land. She could feel the agony of parting that would soon be the common lot of all womankind. She gazed about at the half-ruined front of the house. In all likelihood the war would prevent its repair, and progress on that had been slow enough without complications. It was a sorry-looking place from which to celebrate her wedding, and Emilie tried to fight back the tears and the melancholy that suddenly seemed to descend on her. Somehow, she told herself determinedly, everything was going to be all right. Les Chandelles had always been the life force that had nourished her, and so it would continue to be. She had made that determination the very day she had returned home to find it still smoldering with tragedy. Now, she thought, with a determined lift of her chin, she would continue to replenish her spirit from its blackened walls. Her mother's old chapel, three walls intact but one open to the elements, would be the place where she and Guy exchanged their sacred vows. Some of the niceties might be absent, but Emilie, daughter of Catherine, would accept her new responsibilities and her new life under the eyes of God.

She thought proudly of Guy. He had taken total command of their situation, determining its difficulties, deciding on what steps to take to ensure what little joy they might derive from the awful events around them. For the first time since she had come back home, she felt that there was someone to take care of her. Even the wrenching loneliness Emilie knew she would suffer when he left for the war would be easier to bear for having had him.

Whatever had sent him away for so long and so far had not been enough to keep him from his duty. In the way he had just spoken to her, Emilie could see nothing of the melancholy she had noticed at other times, times when they had spoken of the past. It was as if the urgency of the situation had chased all the doubts from his mind, leaving him free to do what he felt he must. And now she was herself being brought under his protection, his strong will and great honor to serve her as proof against the vagaries of a cruel world moving swiftly beyond control. She would wrap herself within his love when his absence afforded nothing more solid. She shivered suddenly, and cursed inwardly, as if at an unseen spirit of the night who stood silently mocking.

The strength she took from Guy would be enough, she told herself as she climbed wearily up the broad stairs to her lonely room.

6

Young Jess flexed his toes in the highly polished brogans, trying to feel the outer edges. He was pleased to have his feet encased in hose as well and to be sitting in the beautifully furnished room wearing a full suit of clothes which, if not quite as fine as those of his host, were at least of the same style. The room itself was beautiful, much like the study at Les Chandelles which held all of the master's books, but Jess knew how seldom those books were touched, except for dusting by the slaves, while Mr. Higginson referred to the volumes on his shelves constantly.

But now Higginson sat at his desk reading the papers that Jess and the other visitor, Reverend Martin, had brought him. Thomas Wentworth Higginson was a well-known abolitionist, an editor who loved poetry and fine writing with the same sort of passion with which he hated slavery. The notes he was perusing were for a speech that Reverend Martin was going to make at a mass meeting of the free black citizens of Boston the next night. Jess and the minister sat patiently waiting for Higginson to finish and make his comments.

Much as Jess was impressed with the aristocratic Bostonian, his deeper feelings rested with the black man who sat patiently waiting with him. He thought once again of the great good luck that had directed his feet to the Joy Street Baptist Church when he had arrived in Boston months earlier.

Of course he had to admit that he hadn't found Joy Street all by himself and that he hadn't known of this man. But when he found himself outside the railroad terminal in the huge and bustling city, he turned to go in a direction he had chosen arbitrarily. One street, one section, meant no more to him at that point than any other, so strange was he to the metropolis.

It was only when he caught the notice of an elderly black man who was loading vegetables onto a flatbed wagon that Jess heard the name of the church and its leader for the first time. Still, he felt that it was his own instinct that had led him to that particular street and that particular old man. Then he had followed the narrow curving streets, some of whose names he could read, until he saw with exactly that very emotion, the legend JOY STREET. From there it was easy to find the rest of the way. The church choir was holding practice at that very moment, and the sound of voices, joined in a melody much like those he remembered from the day of Ephraim's preaching, told him that he had found his destination.

When he had come into the church and told the first person he saw where he had come from, he was hugged briefly but enthusiastically and led into the cramped room that served as Reverend Martin's study.

The Reverend J. Sela Martin was a renowned speaker not only from his own pulpit but also throughout the North wherever Abolitionists gathered and held public meetings to plead their cause. As Jess unfolded to him the story of his own running away and search for freedom, Reverend Martin's eyes widened with approval.

Then he told Jess of the role that he and other black

men, free and far from the slave states, were playing in the Abolitionist movement. He told about the bonfire rallies and prayer meetings that were constantly being organized, sometimes working with the white movement and sometimes on their own. The two branches had frequently split in the past because their policies and wants often differed, but just as frequently they rejoined ranks in the search for an end to the evil that disquieted all their hearts and minds. Generally, Martin explained, the blacks who were free tended toward more radical means of solving the slavery issue, and it had been when the white brothers weakened and opted for such unacceptable schemes as a return to Africa that the movement would split. When blacks again decided to join forces with whites it was to the more radical and demanding leaders, such as Garrison and the group that had formed around him, that they turned.

Jess was home.

After talking slavery and abolition non stop for almost three hours, Reverend Martin had finally halted the conversation to address himself to his young visitor's more immediate physical needs. Almost before he knew what was happening, Young Jess had been promised a place to stay with Reverend Martin and his family, was being measured by one of the church members for a new suit of clothes, and was stoking down his first home-cooked meal in a long time. It was only when he saw that these things had been attended to that Martin turned once more to discussion of their mutual cause. He told Jess about the mass meeting that the free black men of Boston had organized for some nights hence. They were going to declare themselves publicly on the side of the Union and their willingness to fight in the war that had just been declared.

Now they were sitting in Higginson's comfortable

study as he perused the speech that Reverend Martin was to deliver at the rally.

"This is excellent, my friend," Higginson declared. "Especially here where you say, 'Our feelings urge us to say to our countrymen that we are willing to stand by and defend the government with our lives, our fortunes and our sacred honor.' I wouldn't change a word of that. This is a rallying cry that all black men can stand behind and no truly free white man can ignore."

"Thank you, my brother," Reverend Martin said, smiling. "If all white men thought and acted as you do there would be no problem that could not be quickly solved between us, but I do not stand so convinced as you are that this will indeed be the case."

"Now that the country is finally at war, Lincoln can have no excuse not to push forward for the enactment of everything that we have been asking for all these many long years. The South no longer merely constitutes a section whose economy is different than ours and loathsome to us. The slaveholding states are now the declared enemy of the Union, and as the ideals of the Union must be preserved, so must those hideous conditions which are so in conflict with them be abolished once and for all."

Jess was thrilled with Higginson's words.

"Amen to that," Reverend Martin sighed, "but there is much more to be done now than speechmaking."

"The declaration of all free black men of their willingness to risk their lives for the Union cause will not go ignored," Higginson insisted. "We have made the abolishment of slavery and the acceptance of black men into the Union forces our dual demand precisely because the acceptance of the latter will ensure the former. Tomorrow night should be a turning point in the history of both our races and our single nation."

Jess was fired by the words. He had listened to Reverend Martin as he had written the speech and rehearsed parts of it. Jess found himself wishing that his black mentor could speak with the great force and power which their host displayed. Still, the words of the speech, if one listened carefully enough and they were properly reported, should be enough to ensure their success.

The two men rose to leave, Reverend Martin gathering his papers and thanking Higginson once more for his time and comments.

"I'm sorry that I won't be there to hear it delivered tomorrow night," Higginson said with a smile. "I do so enjoy your oratory, you know."

Jess shook hands with Higginson and followed Martin out of the study and then to the Boston street. The row of stone houses gleamed in the sunshine of the early spring.

"Such glorious weather," Reverend Martin sighed. "God alone knows how many men will live to see the next one."

Jess fell in step alongside the deeply worried leader as they made their way back to the Joy Street church. He wondered if the distinguished Mr. Higginson was being sincere with them. He had felt confident that Higginson was acting in all sincerity until he had made his remark about Reverend Martin's oratory. From what Jess himself had heard so far, the Reverend was not going to be any great shakes as a speaker.

It wasn't until late the next evening that he found out how wrong he was.

The rally had been set for eight o'clock in a large open square of the city. Torches had been set up on tall stakes in front of the speakers' platform, which held a number of chairs for the community's dignitaries. When all of the chairs had been filled, Jess understood why

Higginson was not present: All of the men on the platform were blacks.

In front on the sidewalks crowds of men and women had been gathering for the past few hours. Some of them led small children or held babies on their shoulders. It was clear to see that the rally was considered an important event.

The darkness made it impossible to estimate the number of people who had gathered, but Jess could tell that the crowd was considerable. He hadn't ever seen that many people gathered in one place. Moreover, almost everyone was standing still in anticipation of the evening's events. There was very little of the milling around and general movement that such gatherings usually induced in restless people.

Having arrived with Reverend Martin, Jess was assured of a place close to the speakers' platform, although he had to stand up for the entire rally and crane his neck constantly in order to see the speakers. He didn't mind at all. He could not remember when he had ever felt so elated in his life.

He was sure, just as Mr. Higginson was, that their plea to join white men in donning the uniform of the country would be heeded by the new President in Washington and that this singular occurrence would be the great instrument by which the forging of freedom for all black people North and South would be assured. Speech after speech told him that he was not the only one to hold this grand conviction.

Jess admired all of the men who spoke and wondered how his friend would be able to match their brilliant and fiery declamations.

But when at last the name of the Reverend J. Sela Martin was announced, the crowd broke into a roaring approval that seemed to Jess to top that they had given to any of the previous speakers. Or maybe, he told himself, it was just the sound of his own fervent hands clapping that was sounding in his ears and making him think so.

But when Reverend Martin launched into the opening lines of the speech they had reviewed with Thomas Wentworth Higginson the previous day, Jess realized that all of the men who had gone before had done no more than set the stage for his mentor. He heard the words come alive in a way he had not thought possible. As good as the speech had seemed on paper, it was but a pale hint of the grandeur of his eloquence. The words that had seemed to Jess to burn on the paper, only to receive scant life in the monotone in which they had been recited as the Reverend rehearsed them, were now the foreshadowings of a clarion call that Jess knew for once and for all would not be ignored. They were the words of men, spoken to men: the declaration of willingness to sacrifice everything, even sacred life, in the service of the homeland which would now grant freedom to its darker inhabitants.

The sentiment was the same one that all the speakers had been proclaiming, but in the thundering accents of J. Sela Martin, they reverberated from the brick and stone of building and street and seemed to the enraptured young listener as though they too were made of the same New England granite.

Now Jess knew himself at last to be on the brink of his quest. He was ready to go out and fight for freedom. Now he knew that this was how it had to be earned. Not in the crevices and hidden byways through which he had been taken, nor in the handout of food or feeble wages he had been paid as a free laborer, but in the willingness to risk everything for the prize that such a risk alone would earn.

The next day's newspapers carried full accounts of the rally. Jess read some of them out loud to Reverend

Martin, who was resting after his herculean exertions of the night before. Reading the Boston papers had been Jess' means of rapidly improving the skill he had previously practiced by himself. Now as he read the commentaries he found that he was stumbling on fewer and fewer words and needed less spelling out and prompting from Reverend Martin. He was pleased with his growing facility and the compliments of his friend.

All of the dailies carried accounts of the rally, and most of them seemed quite favorable. They were even commended by an editorial in one of the gazettes. For the black abolitionists of Boston it was a moment of triumph, but it was followed by tedious, anxious weeks of silence from the leadership in the nation's capital. Day after day, abolitionists, black and white, told themselves and each other that surely on the morrow word of the acceptance of black soldiers would be forthcoming.

When at last the man in the White House spoke on the issue, the answer was no.

By the eleventh day after Guy's hasty proposal and
equally hasty departure, Emilie was hopeful, fretful,
anguished, and finally exhausted. It did not seem to her
that time could ever drag on so. She thought of calling
on Guy's mother the day after that fateful evening but
decided against it. She hadn't wanted to leave Les
Chandelles even if she had dared. By the time she re-
versed her decision and felt that it would be quite the
right thing to do, it was too late. The day of his possible
return had come, and now she was as riveted to her
own plantation as if she had been stitched in place there.

Each ensuing day brought with it only the frustration of proving no more fruitful than its predecessor.
When at last the silence was broken by the sound of
horses arriving, it was not a gallant single rider who
greeted her happy sight but an elegant coach, drawn
by two carefully groomed white horses whose reins
rested in the hands of a black driver in silk knee-
breeches, powdered wig, and all the other accouter-
ments of a hundred years earlier. Behind him, well
into the shade afforded by the overhanging hood, sat
Anton Bledsoe and his wife.

Emilie sprang forward to meet them, carefully hiding
her disappointment.

Madame Bledsoe was helped down. She was a pretty
woman in a rather fussy way, Emilie thought, her lace-

trimmed bonnet with its many ribbons framing a face already haloed with clusters of bright golden curls. Emilie made a simple curtsy, as she had been taught to do as a child when greeting adult guests.

Madame Bledsoe laughed and grasped Emilie to her, kissing her on both cheeks rather noisily.

"You don't have to indulge yourself in such pretty formalities, my dear!" Madame Bledsoe exclaimed. "You're very nearly a married woman yourself now, and I can't tell you how happy my husband and I both are to be with you on this most joyous occasion!"

Emilie blinked at the brilliant lights that bounced from Madame Bledsoe's diamonded neck and fingers. She moved a step forward to greet the more austerely dressed husband. Forthright as he had always been on previous visits to Les Chandelles, especially since he had taken her under his wing, somehow the rather frightening Mr. Bledsoe seemed little more than an afterthought in the company of his resplendent wife, and Emilie was somewhat amused. It was the female of the family who held center stage.

Glad to see them, knowing that their arrival at the very least heralded that of her fiancé, Emilie welcomed them to her home and led them to the veranda, where a slave stood waiting silently with a tray of cold drinks and light refreshment.

"I declare there isn't a cook in all of New Orleans who can make pralines as light and delicate as these," Madame Bledsoe said. "It is a fortunate set of circumstances indeed, my dear Emilie, that permits you to remain mistress of your own estate rather than having to relocate yourself to some smaller holding which may have at best an uncertain staff. My husband always exclaimed over the hospitality and cuisine of Les Chandelles whenever he came to visit your poor dear papa in the past, and now I can see he did not exaggerate."

"Lucky indeed," Bledsoe echoed his wife's sentiments. "My dear young Emilie, you are going to have the best of both worlds. Your own place right here in your home and the love and strength of a perfect young consort to share it with you and relieve you of its onerous burdens."

"I thank you very kindly for your sweet sentiments," Emilie said, "and I wish I could share your confidence in my good fortune. I dearly love Monseiur Charpentier and do wish to make him a good and loyal wife, but what chance will I have to do so, with this terrible war that is going to take him from me nearly as soon as the vows have been said over us?" Her lip trembled and she bit it, trying to force back the tears that were suddenly forming in her eyes.

"There, there, my dear." Madame Bledsoe leaned forward to place a comforting hand on Emilie. "You mustn't think about that nasty business at all. It isn't proper matter for a young bride to dwell on. Think instead of all the happiness that will at last so deservedly come into your young life."

"But where is Guy?" Emilie asked, looking from one face to the other. "He told me that he would stop here on his way back to Les Saules to let me know definitely what our plans will be."

"He left that to us, my dear," Bledsoe replied. "It was advisable that he hurry back home as swiftly as possible to settle whatever business he could there. He adjured us to confirm that the ceremony will be held as he had told you, two days hence. We can expect the arrival of old Père Lachaise sometime tomorrow. Young Charpentier and his family will be here early on Saturday morning."

"That will give the cook plenty of time to prepare as

festive a board as she can for us," Emilie said. "I will give her my instructions this afternoon."

"I wish that we were more of a wedding party," Madame Bledsoe said. "I'm afraid that two elderly people such as ourselves are scarcely sufficient to constitute the gay, extravagant company that should be celebrating your wedding party."

Emilie smiled at her gratefully. "Madame," she said, "my fiancé offered to stop at all of the neighboring plantations, indeed, at most of the houses in the parish, in order to invite everyone to our celebration. It was I who demurred, feeling that in times like these it was not proper nor necessary. I asked him only to favor me with making inquiry in New Orleans at the Bledsoe establishment and to prevail on you to come and attend me, if you would. I asked for and need no others."

"Thank you, my dear." Madame Bledsoe's voice was husky with emotion. "That is quite the loveliest tribute that has ever been offered us, and I thank you for it."

"I can only echo my wife's sentiments, dear Emilie," Monsieur Bledsoe added.

That was about as much as anyone could do, Emilie quickly realized as she spent the next few days primarily in their company. Madame Bledsoe was one of those women who could attach herself to any purpose, take it over, and make it completely her own.

Emilie was pleased enough to find her time so totally occupied. Madame Bledsoe, when she was not exclaiming over the size and treasures of Les Chandelles, entertained Emilie with news and gossip from New Orleans. Much of it touched on people she had heard of but did not know. Nevertheless, she was glad for the diversion. When she told the couple of her desire to have the ceremony held in her mother's old chapel, Eurydice Bledsoe immediately seized on the idea and insisted on being shown to it forthwith.

She exclaimed over the beauty of the dark-blue-silk-covered walls, smoke-stained now, but otherwise intact. Even the wall that had been sundered was proclaimed by her a blessing, for the warm spring air would help to dissipate the closeness that was sure to fill the chapel when it held such an unaccustomed number of people and a multitude of burning wax candles.

The two women returned to the main part of the house, and Eurydice set about at once to commandeer a small army of house slaves under the direction of Sully and set them to work scrubbing, polishing, and refurbishing the chapel as best they could. The hard narrow wood benches would accommodate a half-dozen people, and the nuptial couple would be able to kneel at Catherine's prie-dieu to hear the blessings pronounced over them. All in all, it would be quite satisfactory and exactly the proper size for such an abbreviated wedding party.

"I wonder if the good little father would object to vases on the altar," she murmured. "I do so want to fill two quite large vases with enormous bouquets of blooms. Flowers are so appropriate to the spirit and meaning of a wedding. Don't you agree, Emilie?"

"Yes, of course, whatever you think is right." Emilie replied as she did to most of Madame Bledsoe's suggestions. She was pleased to have the older woman take such forthright charge of all the necessary arrangements.

But it needed all the sophisticated townswoman's ingenuity to arrange a proper wedding dress for her young bride. There was nothing in Emilie's wardrobe that suggested anything nearly as ornate as Madame would have liked. The only dress that quite caught her fancy was the daring black-and-white-striped ball gown that Emilie had worn on her last night in New York. She colored deeply at seeing it again, but Madame Bledsoe

exclaimed over and over about the smartness of the
style and its exquisite construction. But for all the
quality of the gown, it was scarcely serviceable for a
blushing young bride. Something was going to have to
be done with another of Emilie's garments.

"What a pity that you don't own a single white dress,"
Euridice said for at least the seventh time. "It would
be a simple matter for any competent seamstress to
embellish it with enough laces and ribbons to make it
perfectly suitable." But in the end she was obliged to
settle for a demure dress of palest pink. This garment's
most evident lack was that of long sleeves to cover
Emilie's arms to the wrist. But happily a lacy crocheted
shawl was found in very nearly the same ethereal
shade, which Euridice cleverly folded and tucked until
it made quite a perfect covering for what the dress
itself left bare. Then, dress and shawl over one arm,
she proceeded to rummage through the cabinet of sew-
ing materials, searching out trimmings with which one
of the slave sewers could embellish the dress, making it
at once more elaborate and more in the style of what
passed for fashion currently in the city.

When with a flourish Eurydice presented the results
to Emilie on the very day before the ceremony, the
new bride was completely taken aback. She proclaimed
Eurydice her great benefactress and said a miracle of
couture had been performed. They quickly but fervently embraced as Emilie prepared to retire for the
last night that she would ever spend as a single girl.

Bathed and in bed, she lay awake. There was not a
great deal to think about in regard to the phase of her
life she was about to leave. When the fussy little priest
had arrived with his sullen new slave that morning he
had insisted on hearing her confession, and Emilie
found herself wondering if he had been as bored by the
procedure as she was. There was so little to tell him,

and what little there was was of no importance. Finally
he was put to asking her questions regarding her observances, and she had to admit that she had not regularly prayed for her mother and father since learning
of their death. He at once and with great satisfaction
set her a penance of doing both those observances and
some other prayers for the good of her soul.

When he tried to instruct her on the ways of a proper
and dutiful wife, Emilie cut him short, claiming the
press of domestic responsibility kept her from enjoying
his comforts for any longer a time than she had already
given over to it. She went away wondering if, other than
herself, anyone in the world could possibly be more
ignorant on the subject than the dry little priest.

As she lay in bed now she tried to conjure up a
vision of what this marriage would be like. The picture that she held in her mind's eye of being held in a
crushing embrace by the dashing young man she was
marrying seemed to her to afford as much excitement
as anything in the world possibly could. Alone on this
night, she allowed herself to seek dreams and visions
she would have blushed to admit before. She knew what
it had felt like to be held in his arms, pressed against
his body, and kissed full on the mouth. She shivered
with the memory of it and again in anticipation of
more. And yet, she knew that the marriage bed held
far deeper mysteries, and couplings of a nature much
more intimate than that of a kiss and hug, no matter
how fiercely given. It was difficult to imagine what
those deeper embraces might be, and shyness joined
with ignorance in preventing her from trying to picture too much. There was such a great deal that she
did not know, but she closed her eyes to all of it with
implicit faith in the ability of her new husband to both
teach and pleasure her in all things that passed between
man and woman.

When the morning sun rose at last on her wedding day, it shone on an Emilie more curious than frightened, eager for the embraces of her husband rather more than a bit anxious for the formalities of the day to be over and done with, and for the door to close on everything but themselves.

She had chosen her own bedroom for their nuptial chambers. It was large enough to accommodate a couple easily, and she had felt uncomfortable at the prospect of spending her first night with her new husband in a room as coldly forbidding as Catherine's or as somber and intimidating as that of her father's. Afterward, she felt sure, when the war was over and she and Guy could assume their lives in the natural order of things at Les Chandelles, there would be plenty of time to make over the master bedchamber in a way that would be suitable for them. By that time the ghosts of the unhappy past could be properly exorcized and she would be able to feel completely at home. Until then she was rather pleased with the idea that when the ceremony and dinner concluded, she would be bringing Guy back to her own bed, the very one where she had spent so many nights alone thinking about him in a way she had scarcely dared to, a way that would now be justified.

A loud clamor outside the house interrupted her thoughts. The Charpentier family was arriving en masse and in style. Guy and his brother both rode big bays, while a cabriolet contained Monsieur and Madame and an open-top flatbed wagon carried a number of Charpentier chattel.

Emilie greeted Madame warmly and was given a rather dry kiss by Guy's father. She presented her hand to his younger brother, Stephan, and then to Guy himself, with no great show of emotion. Her fiancé lifted her rather trembling fingers to his lips, but barely did skin touch skin. Emilie was pleased to see that he was conducting himself with all the reticence proper to a young bridegroom. Had this wedding been held in earlier days without the cloud of her recent tragedy over them and the gathering storm of the war on everybody's mind, he would not even have been there. From the time of his arrival at the home of his bride, he would have been hidden from her and they would not have caught so much as a glimpse of each other until he drew up her veil at the conclusion of the wedding ceremony. But all was different now. Practical informality was the fashion of the day, and within its simpler confines Guy was still conducting himself seriously as a man of honor. Emilie was deeply touched.

Eurydice acted as hostess, drawing all of the company inside to an elaborate wedding breakfast spread in the dining room. It had been a very long time since there had been so many at table at Les Chandelles. Emilie's heart was lifted at the sight of it, and in the knowledge that her home was once again the setting for the grandeur and hospitality it had long been noted for.

With a cosmopolitan grace, Madame Bledsoe took her place at the end of the table and seated Emilie at her right hand. Monseiur Bledsoe sat at its head, the couple playing their roles perfectly as surrogate parents. Bledsoe drew Guy to his right and the elderly Monsieur Charpentier to his left, and Madame Charpentier and her younger son took their places in between.

Emilie had not overseen the kitchen activity. All of its details had been directed by Madame Bledsoe, at her own insistence. She had found Tess, the cook, a rather formidable personage to deal with, for a slave; but after lavishly praising several repasts that Tess had prepared during the previous days, she had completely won the cook over as few people ever had before. Now in payment Tess was determined to surpass all of her prior endeavors and reached not only for the best in the Les Chandelles larder, but into the recesses of her own memory for the grand feasts she had prepared in the past. Thus the breakfast was beautifully and bountifully served.

Silent slaves pattered around the table, bearing huge platters of cold meats. Elaborately decorated hard-boiled eggs had been sliced thin as wafers and color-fully garnished. Fresh raw vegetables had been similarly treated, and hot and cold beverages were held by small black boys who darted forward at the mention of a desire for the contents of their silver pots and pitchers. Small plain cookies dusted with the planta-tion's own sugar was served after all the previous courses had been completed and the table cleared away to the accompaniment of the piping-hot chickory-fla-vored coffee favored by New Orleans' society.

Emilie nibbled lightly at her food, taking no more than a few bites from some of the proffered platters. She tried to concentrate on the chatter of conversation that passed between the two older women. She was amused to see how quiet Guy was, his usual gallant social manner for once subdued. His demeanor seemed to be affected by the same reserve that held her in check as well.

But young Stephan Charpentier felt bound by no such constriction. To Eurydice's pleasure he seemed to know all the New Orleans people whose carryings-on she delighted in retailing. The young scion was a familiar visitor at most of the best salons in the city, and could match her point for point with racy bits of gossip about much of New Orleans society.

Emilie was grateful that she was not expected to participate very fully in their chatter. It was pleasant to let the words stream about her without having to pay close attention to what was being said.

Madame Charpentier was in radiant bloom. Not only was she seeing her elder son, the delight of her heart, take a step that would ensure his continuing to remain in the area rather than go gallivanting all over the civilized world, but her younger son, generally the cause of much anguish, was being delightfully gallant and sophisticatedly amusing. His mother nearly gloated at the fine compliments and great attention being paid to him by the worldly Madame Bledsoe. Although the entire proceeding was going to be a far cry from the enormous and elaborate wedding she had always pictured for her son, the prime purpose was being well achieved: his marriage to the most eligible young lady in the parish and the ultimate annexing of their neighboring plantations. There was little more she could hope for beyond the continued well-being of her offspring, only that God grant her the boon of living to see the fruit of this union, a grandson who would someday be lord over the bordering dominions of Les Chandelles and Les Saules. No grander achievement could she foresee or even wish for.

The nonsense of war seemed very far away to her then, and she wished that it would be done with quickly as well.

There was a lull in the conversation when Father Lachaise made his belated appearance and was given his place at table. The ensuing conversation, Emilie noted with wry amusement, then turned from the gamier aspects of New Orleans' society to a discussion of the more important wakes and memorials that had taken place during the last several years. No wonder the young black who attended him looked so grim, Emilie thought. She wondered what had become of the tall, coffee-colored man who had been with the priest for so many years. She did not remember when she had last seen him.

Breakfast was at last over. Madame Charpentier was given a bedchamber in which to retire, and Eurydice Bledsoe hurried Emilie off to her own room. There the separation for the nuptials and what would follow it would begin in earnest.

"First I want you to take a long nap, my darling," Eurydice instructed. She turned to the silent servant hovering in the room's shadows. "You, Missy, draw the draperies so that the room is cool and quiet for your mistress." She eyed the girl critically for a moment and then turned her attention to Emilie, who was seated at the edge of the bed. "Has young Charpentier got a suitable male for this girl? I didn't particularly pay attention to that wagonload of chattel that came with them, but I suppose he would have thought to bring someone, especially as he himself is going to make his home here."

"I really don't know," Emilie admitted. "We haven't discussed it." Now it was her turn to gaze at the slave who had been at her side for so many years. The girl had slipped to her knees and was removing Emilie's shoes so that she could lie comfortably on the bed.

"Loosen your stays, Emilie," Eurydice went on. "Turn your back so that she can help you."

"I'm not wearing anything but my camisole under this dress," Emilie admitted.

"I declare, it's a long time since I've seen anyone look so firm without a corset. You're a lucky one," Eurydice said.

"I'll just loosen my dress a little and be perfectly comfortable here until time to get ready," Emilie said. "Missy, have one of the servants knock when it's two o'clock."

Missy hurried off to obey. Neither of the women had

noticed the conflict that had crossed her face when they discussed the possibility of a mate for her. Missy ran down the broad stairs, her heart knocking in her chest as she tried to remember the passel of slaves sitting in the open wagon. Had they indeed already selected someone for her? And might he already be at Les Chandelles? For the thousandth time she wished that Young Jess hadn't gone off. If only they had been able to marry. Then there would be no chance of their throwing her in with someone unwanted as they were now talking about doing. Missy knew that she would rather die than be put with any other man but Young Jess. Even if she had to be alone and barren all her life she'd rather wait for him than go with anyone else. She went through the main-floor rooms looking for Sully to give Emilie's instruction to. At last she found the short round housekeeper standing on a stepstool checking the shelves in a vast linen closet.

"Miss Emilie says . . ." Missy lowered her eyes and faltered. She didn't like being forced into the position of conveying instructions to those slaves who were her seniors.

"Miss Emilie says what?" Sully asked. "Speak up, girl, you've been sent to tell me something. It might be important."

"Sully, did you see—did you see any of the people who come with the wedding party from the new master's plantation?" Missy asked quickly.

Sully turned from the shelves to stare down at her. "Is that what Miss Emilie sent you to ask me?" she wanted to know.

"No," Missy admitted. "But I got to know. It's important, real important."

"Well, suppose first you tell me what the mistress did say," Sully said patiently.

"She say to send someone to knock on our door at

two o'clock," Missy said. "But tell me, Sully, tell me, did you *see* any of those people?"

"Why is that so important to you, gal?" Sully asked.

"I got to know, Sully. I got to know." Missy was pleading now. "That lady from down the river, she's talking to Miss Emilie about marrying me off to one of them Les Saules men."

"That so?" Sully raised an eyebrow. "I wonder why they never think to bring someone for me?"

"Did you see them, Sully?" Missy persisted. "Was there anyone you think they might see likely for me?"

Sully stepped down from her stool. She felt an almost maternal concern for Missy, whom she had helped raise as a child and had supervised when she was first brought into the house as a companion and then nursemaid for the baby Emilie. "What are you so scared of?" she asked, not unkindly. "You should be glad if they've got a man picked out for you."

"Oh no, Sully, oh no." Missy was scarcely breathing. "I can't do that with no one else, I can't."

"No one else but who you talking about?" Sully looked at her closely.

Missy hung her head. "I can't tell you that."

"Then why you be asking me so many questions if you can't be tellin' me nothin'?" Sully asked. "You best get along with you and let your mistress do your worrying for you. If she has someone in mind you'll do it whether you think you will or not. Now get on back upstairs with you in case she's needing you. It is her wedding day, strange as it seems."

Missy trudged up the staircase with none of the fervor that had sent her flying down it only moments earlier. She opened the door to the room she shared with her mistress quietly, so as not to disturb her, and found her own place on a blanket roll near the bed. She crawled up on it, hugging herself with her arms, rocking slightly back and forth, saying over and over in her mind, Let it not be, oh let it not be. She lay rigid then, with no idea of how the time was passing. She was almost dozing off when one of the housemaids knocked on the door and opened it slowly.

It was two o'clock then, time for her to wake the sleeping Mistress Emilie.

"It's time, Miss Emilie," she whispered softly. "Time to get up." She walked around to the other side of the bed and pulled back the concealing draperies. The full flood of sunshine filled the room.

Emilie woke with a start, blinking her eyes to the unaccustomed brightness. She stretched exultantly. "This is going to be the happiest day of my life!"

She slid her legs over the edge of the bed and sat there smiling. Then she turned to her servant. "Please don't stand there looking so glum, Missy! This is my wedding day. Now go and draw up the water for my bath."

"Yes, ma'am."

Emilie looked more closely at her slave as Missy turned to leave the room. "Wait a minute," she called out to her. "Come back here, Missy."

Dutifully, the girl turned around and walked slowly back to her mistress.

"What's the matter with you, Missy?" Emilie asked. "Aren't you happy for me?"

"Yes, ma'am." Again the same listless monotone.

"Missy, what's wrong?" Emilie's voice softened. She could tell that something was gnawing at the slave.

"Nothing wrong, Miss Emilie," Missy said.

"There must be something wrong for you to be looking in such a state, today of all days," said Emilie insistently. "Tell me what it is, and at once. I haven't got all the time in the world, you know."

"Do I have to get married now too?" Missy asked finally, her eyes downcast, her head bent over.

"Is that what's bothering you?" Emilie asked. "To tell you the truth, I haven't given it a single thought." Then with a sudden start she realized how thoughtlessly cruel she was being—so wrapped up in her own happiness, she had completely forgotten that her servant must have had some feelings about her own fate. Feelings, it seemed, that were frightening her half to death.

"Missy, I'm your friend!" Emilie told her, laying a hand on the girl's shoulder. "I want to keep you with me forever. Surely you don't think that I would just let you be married off to any man you didn't care for."

"No, ma'am." But the dark lips trembled.

"Missy, I'm really surprised at you," Emilie said. "After all we've been through together. Now put all of this foolishness out of your mind and go and get my water. I don't want anything in the world to spoil this day. Lord knows, I'll have little enough happiness before Master Charpentier must go off to that dreadful war."

Missy went out of the room and Emilie flung herself back on the bed. She had promised herself that she would not mention or even think about that war all this glorious day, and she was angry with Missy for having made her spoil that promise.

"But it really doesn't matter," Emilie murmured to herself, as if forgiving the absent slave. "Everything is going to be wonderful."

By the time the tin tub had been filled with water and lavender and Emilie was submerged in it up to her chin, her thoughts had been completely turned around. There was a loud knock on the door. She looked up rather startled but motioned for Missy to open it, just a crack.

There was Madame Bledsoe loudly sparkling and

thrusting the door wide open. "Close it quickly, girl, so your mistress doesn't get a draft," she said as she rustled into the room and stood looking down at the embarrassed Emilie.

"I've come to attend you, my dear," she said gaily, "with all of the attention that a young bride should be getting." She opened a small cloth bag she had been carrying and from it withdrew a quantity of pale-pink rose petals, which she held high in the air and then released to flutter slowly into Emilie's bath.

"Roses and lavender!" Emilie laughed. "What a lovely combination."

"And what a fertile one," Eurydice Bledsoe added.

Emilie blushed. She busied herself with her cloth, working furiously under the water at every part of her body.

"There, there, I think that's quite enough," Eurydice said. "If you spend any more time in that tub, your skin is going to be as wrinkled as a prune. Missy, get your mistress' towel ready, and help her out of the tub."

Missy moved to obey. Eurydice went to the window and studied the scene below, discreetly turning her back on Emilie's nakedness as Missy helped dry her.

"Plenty of powders and scents, mind you," she called from her position at the window. "Today is the most important day of your life."

Emilie lost track of the number of times she had been told that, but again she reminded herself that she wasn't going to let anything spoil her mood.

"You will wear stays today, won't you Emilie, dear?" Eurydice asked. "Although you don't really need them, you do want to look perfect, and besides, I'm afraid your young man might find you rather immodest if you eliminated any of the expected undergarments."

"Well," said Emilie dubiously, "I'll wear them if

you think I should, but I don't want to draw them so tight that I can't breathe."

"I know exactly how to do them, my dear," Eurydice replied. "And as soon as you've got your drawers and shift on I'll do the stays for you."

"I'm ready now," Emilie said. She did not especially like the idea of anyone fussing at her like that; sometimes it was all she could do to let Missy perform the usual assistance. But Eurydice was treating the whole business of Emilie's dressing as if it too were a kind of ceremony. The center of attention stood still and decided she might as well let them do what they would. It would be the last time, most likely.

White hands and black thrust and tugged at her for what seemed to Emilie an eternity. After the stays had been properly adjusted, Eurydice circled her, staring from every angle until she finally announced that what was needed was more petticoats. So Emilie had to submit to having the stays undone once more so that Eurydice could add several stiffened muslin petticoats to those already encircling her waist and belling to the floor.

"We needed the petticoats for fullness below," Eurydice said. "But all of that extra business around your waist has thickened it considerably. We'll have to pull the stays a bit tighter this time, Emilie."

Emilie gritted her teeth. She was beginning to feel that that was the real reason for the additional bulk she had to carry. Eurydice seemed to be inhaling delight with every tortured exhalation Emilie made. But at last everything was in place and she held her arms up over her head so that she could be helped into the newly festive pink wedding dress.

Eurydice was down on her knees patting and smoothing, pulling and stretching until every fold and pleat of the gown was hanging perfectly to her satisfaction. "The shawl," she told Missy. And when that garment was handed to her she spent a good quarter of an hour draping it around Emilie's shoulders, arms and body, until she announced herself at last satisfied with the results.

"Now the veil," Eurydice breathed and turned herself to get it from the stand on which it had been placed. The crown was a circlet that fit on Emilie's head. Pink satin was twisted all around to give it color. Sewn into the satin were various lengths of stiff white veiling to cover her face and upper arms completely, barely affording her enough light to see where she was going.

Eurydice arranged the folds of the veiling till she thought she had achieved the greatest affect. Then from a basket she drew several tiny pink rosebuds still enclosed within themselves, the petals folded together like fingers in prayer, and wound them intertwined with the pink circlet on Emilie's head.

Even Eurydice was content with the results. Missy stared up at her mistress and knew that she was quite beautiful. Emilie stood stock still, the tightness of her stays and the stiffness of the veiling making her feel entombed within herself. She had no clear idea of how she looked until Eurydice took her hand and led her carefully to face the long pier mirror that stood against the wall.

"I can't see," Emilie said. And Eurydice came and carefully lifted the hem of the veiling up above Emilie's face so that she could see herself more easily.

Emilie stared at her reflection, but before she could quite make up her mind, Eurydice, standing behind her, had let the veiling drop again and everything was once more obscured.

There was a light tapping at the door. Eurydice called out, "We are ready." Then she turned to Emilie.

"There, my dear, it is time for us to leave for the chapel. Missy, you follow behind and hold your mistress's dress up from the floor. Then when we get to the chapel I will continue to lead her inside to the altar and you may stand just outside. You'll be able to see and hear everything."

Emilie made the familiar passage down the broad staircase and through the house and then from the veranda and around the side of the mansion as though she were in a trance. It was as if this most familiar of all places had been transformed into an obscure maze through which she was being led for the first time in her life. Had not Eurydice been holding her firmly by the elbow, she was sure she would have stumbled and fallen and never found the place. She was vaguely aware of the house servants standing about and watching as she passed by them. She wondered suddenly if anyone had thought to give the slaves a half-holiday in honor of the occasion. She started to ask Eurydice but could not quite form the words. There will be time afterward, she told herself, for Guy to make such an announcement. After all, he will be master here now. She continued to be led, past the lawns and into the chapel.

Eurydice stopped her suddenly and said, "Here, put these on, my darling." She helped Emilie to draw on a long pair of satin gloves, and once these rather stiff items were in place she thrust a tiny white-covered Bible and an even smaller nosegay into Emilie's hands.

"Hold on to these firmly, my dear," she cautioned. "If you ever feel yourself going faint during the ceremony, just clasp the book tightly. It will steady you and you will be all right."

Emilie nodded and they proceeded to walk to the chapel.

The wall that had been destroyed had contained the chapel door, and now the emptiness served as entrance.

Eurydice nodded to Missy, who now hung back at the opening while the bride and attendant walked slowly inside.

Through the haze of her veiling Emilie could see the little black-garbed priest standing facing her. The tall man standing with his back to her must be Guy, she realized. In a light-gray suit she had never seen before, he loomed in front of her almost terrifyingly tall, larger than she remembered him being. She was suddenly taken with great fear. Was she indeed given into the keeping of this large unknown creature? For a moment she faltered, but Eurydice's firm grip at her elbow urged her silently onward. When she at last reached Guy, Eurydice slipped into a seat in the front pew and Père Lachaise motioned for the couple to kneel.

As she sank to her knees, Emilie, eyes downcast, caught a glimpse not of Guy's face but of the gray cloth-covered body. She realized why he had looked so different from the back. Instead of the impeccably cut, close-fitting jackets she was accustomed to seeing him in, he now wore the full dress uniform, with the boxy jacket, of an officer of the Army of the Confederate States of America.

The priest was droning the dead foreign words that would bind the two of them together forever. Emilie had no idea of what he was saying, but even had he been speaking in English or the somewhat familiar patois of the New Orleans Creole, she was sure she would not have heard a word of it. The entire ritual went by in a blur, as if it were a dream too hastily dreamed to be recalled.

At a signal from the priest, she rose and knelt again mechanically, feeling like a puppet on a string. When at last Guy half turned to her and took her hand in order to place the ring on her finger, she was startled until a slight smile from him reminded her what he was doing. Then he helped her from her knees for the last time and it was over.

Still holding her hand, he led her outside the chapel, past Missy, who was watching the whole proceedings wide-eyed, and in front of the other slaves, who had gathered in small groups to hear and watch the ceremony. He lifted her veil and in the full sunlight of the day kissed her very tenderly on the lips.

"Guy . . . " Emilie started. But before she could get any further they were completely swamped by the other members of the small party coming out of the chapel. Emilie felt herself kissed again and again by Eurydice and Madame Charpentier. Her face was suddenly wet and, startled, Emilie realized that her new mother-in-law was crying. But before she could think why, she was being claimed for embraces by the men.

After much kissing and laughter they trooped back to the main entrance of the mansion, Emilie and Guy leading the others.

But once inside, seated at the laden dinner table, Eurydice once more, "and for the last time," she insisted, again acted as hostess. "When next you sit at this board, as master and mistress of this beautiful house, may God bless you and keep you so for ever and ever." As she finished speaking she raised her glass in salute to the young couple, and amid cry of "Hear, hear," all of the others did the same.

Round after round of champagne toasts was drunk—for the bride, for the couple, for their home, for the family they were certain to be blessed with, each round accompanied by much cheering, hand-clapping, and stamping of feet. Then in the midst of the gaiety, old Monsieur Charpentier rose lightly and steadily to his feet.

"Gentlemen," he said, looking around the table

slowly, "and ladies, I give you the Confederate States of America and our glorious cause." Everyone fell silent for a moment. No one moved until the old man picked up his own glass and downed it in a single draught. Then all of the others followed suit, even the ladies. Emilie made a brave attempt, but was sure she would choke if she tried. She managed to şwallow most of the champagne in one swig and then tentatively finished the rest of it.

The servants darted back and forth from their stations to the table, refilling glasses as fast as they were emptied.

Tess, standing unseen in the passageway that stretched from the dining room to her domain, was angry. All of the drinking would spoil not only their appetites but their appreciation of the magnificent feast she had prepared. She stood impatiently tapping her foot, glaring at the butler as though she could contain herself no more. She longed to give the signal for the food to be brought in, but that of course was the province of the served and not the servants. There was nothing she could do but watch and wait.

After what seemed an eternity Madame Bledsoe signaled to Robert that the food could be brought in.

Great platters, piled high with oysters, were set at either end of the table, and serving slaves quickly filled the guests' plates.

"Oh la la!" Madame Charpentier exclaimed gaily. "Champagne and oysters!" She winked broadly at Emilie. "Enjoy them, my dear, they are meant especially for you!"

Emilie blushed and bent her head over her plate, forking the seafood into small pieces. She felt suddenly weary of it all and wished that the festivities were over and the visitors gone back to their own homes. Then she admonished herself, remembering that Guy too would soon be gone and Les Chandelles would all too quickly revert to its usual lonely solitude. Then she would be quick enough to appreciate diversion such as she had now.

The oysters were quickly demolished and new platters of food were brought out to the table and duly attacked. It hadn't been since her cotillion years before that such a variety of food had been served up at Les Chandelles. Emilie had good reason to be proud of her table, she thought happily. The plantation's kitchen had brought forth an abundance of food that would be hard for any establishment to match. There were cold and hot meats, all carefully carved, each accompanied by three or four different vegetables. Tess had prepared great pilafs of rice, each flavored and seasoned differently so a guest might partake of the grain in a half-dozen different ways. The fields, forests, inlets, and bayous of the region had all been carefully culled to provide a freshness and variety of supreme excellence.

Emilie chose very little for her own plate and found she could do no more than nibble at the choicest viands, but she was gratified to see the relish with which most of her guests attended to their plates.

She tried to see if Guy's plate was full and whether he had a healthy appetite or was feeling as constrained as she was. She watched unobtrusively throughout the long meal and satisfied herself that he was partaking well of the meats, fish, and fowl, and rather neglecting the sweet and fancy side dishes that accompanied them. She felt silent approval, happy that he was being well fed at her table.

At long last, amid accompanying groans, the guests began one after another to push their chairs slightly from the table, declaring it was impossible to consume another bite. The table was swiftly cleared by the dining-room slaves, and coffee, brandy, and cigars were brought to the men in Charles' large study while the ladies retired to the front salon.

Emilie wondered if this phase of the celebration would be endless. But as if reading her mind, Eurydice whispered in her ear as they settled themselves on a small sofa, "Don't worry, my dear, I'll see that your new mama is off to sleep in short order and then I'll attend you to your bed."

Emilie could only smile weakly in thanks, wondering what further business would have to be fussed through before she would at last be allowed to be alone with her groom.

She was rather passive in the conversation that went on between the two older women, contributing only now and then when a direct question was put to her and she had to answer.

It seemed as though the elder Madame Charpentier's memory for weddings and balls was inexhaustible, and she delighted in recalling the dates and details of all of them until Emilie thought that she was going to die of fatigue and boredom before ever getting to explore the mysteries of the wedding bed.

At last Eurydice took pity on her and made a rather obvious remark about Emilie's apparent state of fatigue. With that Madame Charpentier sat up abruptly and announced herself more than ready for bed.

Eurydice rang a small bell on the table that brought a slave from Les Saules to accompany Madame upstairs. Then in a few moments, after extinguishing the salon's candles, another slave preceded Emilie and the lady from New Orleans up the stairs. The door was open to Emilie's bedchamber, where Missy already waited. Then the slave darted ahead, stationing herself at Eurydice's door until such time as she would be needed.

Missy closed the door behind them, and with a great sigh of relief Emilie threw herself down on her bed. But then she had to get up again as Missy helped her undress and Eurydice thrust about the room, smoothing down the blankets and puffing up the bed pillows.

"Emilie," she declared, "I am going to talk to you as your own dear mother would have, had God granted her the boon to live to see this happy day. Missy, help Madame into her nightdress and brush out her hair. Then you may go and sit at the other end of the room while we talk."

Emilie was quickly out of her elaborate gown and into the nightdress she and Eurydice had previously chosen. It was white, of the lightest lawn, with lace insertia running from the gathered neck all the way down to the wide hem. The wide sleeves were made with the same lavish use of lace. The neck was gathered on a drawstring, which tied loosely and could easily be undone. As Missy tied it under Emilie's chin the young bride was trembling. She knew that she would not be the one whose hands would next undo that string. It seemed so fragile a thing to constitute her sole defense against the male onslaught for which she was now preparing herself. She pulled the satin bedcover up almost to her chin, but Eurydice pulled it down a little and pulled out her arm and clasped her hand in her own.

"The duties of a wife are simple, Emilie," she began. "They are foremost to do the bidding and the wishes of one's husband. He is your lord and master in all things and is to be obeyed."

Emilie nodded silently.

"You have the great good fortune to be married to one of the finest young gentlemen ever to come out of this parish, and I know that he will be as good a husband to you as you could wish. Therefore, my dear, set your mind to complete obedience to him, even in those matters which we of the feminine gender have no great desire to. Still, it is the will of God as well as that of our husbands, and the nature of things, to submit in that as in all things."

"I understand," Emilie said in a small voice, although she knew that she understood nothing but that she must do all of these strange unspoken things that Guy would ask of her. She hoped fervently that he would explain to her so that indeed she would understand and would be the best wife possible for him.

"All things must be, in order for us to fulfill our tasks and purposes here on earth and to continue the family which your great-grandfather established to live on and rule over this domain. I know that you will not fail him, nor what you know in your heart to have been the fondest wishes of your poor dear papa, who wanted nothing more in the world than to see his precious Emilie safely ensconced in the bosom of a gentleman who would love and protect her for all of her life."

Tears started coming into Emilie's eyes at the mention of her father, but Eurydice admonished her.

"Here, here, we'll have none of that," she said somewhat brusquely. "Tears on the wedding night are a sign of nothing but bad luck. You mustn't cry tonight, Emilie, no matter what." She kissed her lightly on the cheek and got up from the bed, sweeping quickly across the room, stopping only to order Missy to extinguish the lamps and to remind her that she was to take her blanket roll and sleep outside the chamber in the hallway that night.

Emilie was alone in the dark.

8

There was no knock at the door this time. Emilie heard only the muffled noise of its opening and, as swiftly, its closing. She was half sitting up against the pillows and she felt her body suddenly tense. Her hands were clenched into fists, a habit she had first noticed she was developing the night that Guy had told her of the war. She forced her fingers open and lay with her hands in a more natural, graceful state. She could not see in the unlit room, but felt his presence as he drew near the bed. She felt the impact of him on the mattress and knew he had sat down.

"Emilie, I can't see you," he said, but his voice was soft and without annoyance.

"Do you want me to draw the draperies?" she asked timidly, suddenly as mindful of her new obligations toward him as she was of his very presence.

"No, my darling, you stay as you are and I'll do it," he replied, and she felt the bed move once more as he got up and somehow found the window of a room he had never been in before.

The moon was up and gave them some light. Guy sat down at the edge of the bed again, took both her hands in his, and asked, "How do you feel?"

Emilie did not know quite how to answer. She didn't want to burden him with her fears or her ignorance, yet she did not want to be dishonest with him either. "I—I don't know how I feel," she admitted finally.

Guy pressed her hand tightly and laughed. "You're going to feel beautiful, just as you look beautiful, I promise you." He drew close to her and kissed her.

"Oh Guy!" And before she knew what she was doing, Emilie had thrust herself forward. Her body aching and straining against him, she threw her arms around his neck and clung to him, his mouth still firmly on hers, their kiss unbroken as his hands found her and held her tightly to him.

At last she broke away for breath. "I love you, Guy," she said.

"And I love you," he replied. "And I want you more than anything else in the world. I love you, Emilie."

Then through the fine soft fabric of her nightdress she felt his large hands cupping her breasts, holding them and squeezing them gently. Emilie gasped with the air that she felt being pushed up through her throat. She sucked in greedily, and gave herself over to the sensations that were now surging through her. Guy was kissing her again, not fastening on her mouth as in their initial embrace but showering kisses on her forehead, eyelids, cheeks, and throat. He kissed her everywhere he could reach her bare skin. When he had no more such places for his lips to touch he hurriedly undid the poor weak tie at the base of her throat and kissed her all along her shoulders. He drew the gown gently aside and down her arms and then pushed her breasts upward till his now greedy mouth was kissing first between and then on the rounded flesh.

"Oh!" Emilie could not believe what was happening inside her. It was as though her flesh now moved with a will of its own, fueled by swiftly running bloodstreams which she had always known were there but had never felt before. Now it seemed as though her whole body throbbed with a coursing of hot unstoppable power. She felt herself growing alternately strong and weak, at first eager to meet his embraces and then thrown back, weakened by the fervor of them. She realized for the first time in her life what wanting someone really meant, this wanting with the body that took physical mastery over the brain. Her mind could no longer decide what it wanted; her body was the complete tyrant now, and her thoughts could only do the biddings of the throbbing flesh that surged and surged again under the demanding lips and fingers of her husband.

When she thought that she had known all possible delight and nothing lovelier could ever happen to her, she felt Guy's body move away from hers and realized that he was lifting the hem of her nightgown, drawing it above her waist and leaving her totally exposed not only to the hands she loved to feel on her but to his eyes as well. She suddenly blushed furiously, realizing now that he could see as well as feel her. What had seemed so wonderful in the dark with her eyes shut tight now embarrassed her as she knew that he was looking at what no man had ever seen before.

It had been so easy to give in to his unspoken demands—such a delight to acquiesce to every motion and hunger that he expressed on her, that all the loaded warnings of Eurydice had flown from her mind. But now as she shrank before his gaze, she realized that it would not all be so simple and pleasurable as she had just thought.

She knew her legs were trembling, but she could no more stop that than she had been able to control the hot racing of her blood, only moments before.

"Don't be afraid, my darling," she heard Guy's whispered words. "You are so very lovely, my Emilie, and you must know there is nothing that I would ever do to hurt or damage all this beauty."

She felt his hands gently stroking her legs. The sweet feeling this roused in her made her stop trembling, and suddenly she found herself longing for even stronger, quicker movement from him. *More,* she thought, *more.*

But instead of stroking and rubbing her as he had been, he suddenly moved his hands to the insides of her thighs and gently drew her legs apart.

"Guy," she faltered, when she felt his fingers touching her there.

"Don't be afraid, Emilie." His words were whispered hoarsely. "I'm not going to hurt you, my love. I want you to know as much pleasure as I do."

She let her body relax, giving in to the soft rhythm he was producing between her legs. She felt almost drowsy, lulled by the simple soothing motion of his fingers.

But then she was suddenly alerted in all her senses as the pace of his touches increased and she felt more of a probing nearly inside her. This sudden shock drew forth wetness, and Emilie thought she would collapse with shame, not knowing what she had done or why he had touched her in there. She longed to call out to him, to beg him to stop, but she knew that she mustn't. She was relieved when she felt his body shift and he was lying once more alongside her. She cuddled against his chest, resting her head on one shoulder, her hand lightly on the other one. But then the movement between her legs started again, more swift, more insistent now. Before she could open her mouth to protest, the same surging feeling was running through her, but even stronger, as all her senses reveled in the glory and mastery of his touch.

She let out a small cry in spite of herself and then pressed her mouth against his chest, trying to muffle the sounds which came from her of their own volition.

"Don't bury yourself, Emilie," he urged her. "Give

vent to your pleasure. It makes me happy to know that
I'm pleasing you."

She lifted her head up to look at him and was struck
by the awesome beauty that was his face. It was as if a
veil of softness had been drawn over him, putting an
expression there that was almost ethereal. She could not
believe the peace on his face and the almost sleeping
softness in his eyes. It was only the increased vigor of
his hands on her that made her realize that he was far
from sleeping.

She groaned out loud again when he lifted his head
from the pillow and bent over her, kissing her breast
and taking the nipple deep into his mouth as he continued his probing. Everything in Emilie moved until
she felt she could stand no more. Everything racing
through her was released in a long throbbing shudder of
pure delight.

Then she felt everything returning to normal, all of
the coursing and quavering finally subsiding, leaving
her filled with a sweet peace completely unlike any
she had known before. It filled every crevice of her
being until she could not tell which she loved more,
the exciting arousal which drew her unchecked cries
or the sweet leveling off and peace that was its aftermath.

"Oh Guy," she murmured. She did not know what
else to say.

He patted her arm. "I know, I know, my darling."
She could tell he was smiling through the words. "Don't
try to describe it, sweetest, it's impossible."

She opened her mouth to try to explain, but he
stopped her with a kiss.

"You can't describe it, Emilie," he told her again.
"No one in the world has ever been able to. It isn't
necessary. It's more than enough for me to know that
I have made you happy."

"So very, very happy." She was nearly sobbing in his arms.

"This is only the very beginning, Emilie," Guy said. "There is a lifetime of delight stretching out in front of us, and I mean to take you through every aspect of it."

"Oh do, Guy, do!" Emilie exclaimed, and he laughed at the unchecked enthusiasm she was at last permitting herself.

"I want to know you, Emilie," he said suddenly, his voice strong again. "Know you in all of the most intimate ways in which a man can know a woman." He paused for a moment. "Are you ready, my darling?"

Emilie was not quite sure what he meant, but she told him yes, and once again she found him in that place and once again he moved her to that wetness. But this time when he drew her legs apart, he had her spread more open on the bed. And he released her hand and moved until he was on his knees in front of her. It was then that Emilie realized that although he had long since cast her nightdress aside, he was still in his shirt and breeches. Now as she watched he slowly undid his shirt and drew it over his head. She stared at him, delightedly watching the ripple of muscle across his chest and in his strong arms. But she immediately averted her eyes when his hands, now free of the shirt, went to his breeches and began to unlace them. She kept her eyes shut tight as she felt the movements on the bed that meant he had freed himself of all his lower garments. Then her eyes flew open as she realized he was on his knees again, hovering over her and watching her face for only a brief moment before he turned his attention to the rest of her body.

Her legs had come closer together of their own volition, and now he set about spreading them again.

She did not fight him as she felt him reach under her hips and grasp them, drawing her body up closer to his. She felt the pressure of something from him against where she had gone all wet, and slowly, slowly she felt him raising her hips and legs off the bed, opening her still wider to accommodate his hardness, at first against her and then slowly entering inside her.

Her feelings surprised her. There was no pain, there was no sense of shame at finding herself in this totally unexpected position, no thought but wonder filling her mind as she felt Guy filling her body from below.

Then she felt as though she had clasped it all inside her and stayed very still until she felt him begin again those same motions that had brought her to such giddiness only moments before. But this time it was not with his fingers, but with a full long rounded hardness that he had put in her and that was directing this new movement, rhythmic as the other but longer, stronger, and ultimately making her feel as though he had filled not only that nether opening but the farthest reaches of her body. To the very tips of her fingers and toes, to the scalp of her head, now tingling with it, she felt his manhood filling her up and then rocking her like a boat, like a cradle, like a child, until the whole world was rising and falling, rising and falling with the motion of him and the completeness of it until at last he released her and she could sense his body subsiding as hers was.

Then he lay down beside her and silently held her close to him for a long time.

"Will it be like this forever?" Emilie asked dreamily.

"Forever is such a long time, darling," he answered. "And we have so little of it."

"Why, Guy?" Emilie asked, rising up on one elbow to look down at him as she spoke.

"Because, my sweet . . . " He hesitated. "I hadn't wanted to tell you this so soon, but I must leave very quickly."

Emilie felt her heart stop. "How quickly?" she demanded.

"In two days."

She sank back on the bed. Two days! It didn't seem possible.

"Emilie, you remember I explained all of this to you at the very beginning," Guy reminded her.

"Yes, I know, but . . . " She felt so helpless. She had very nearly convinced herself that the war and the emergency and Guy's departure had all gone away. But they hadn't, and now at the happiest moment of her life here she was confronted with it again. Now it seemed harsher and crueler than ever, and it would be even more difficult for her to accept it. She had loved him with her heart and mind before this. She had known she had loved him even before she was able to bring herself to admit it. But nothing she had felt about him before this night could compare with the strength of her emotions now, now that she knew him in the same sense in which he had said he had wanted to know her.

She knew too what he had meant when he had promised her that when he did leave her, she would be a woman. She was that now, she was sure of it, and she did not need any further suffering in her life to prove it.

"I can't let you go, Guy," she protested.

"Emilie, you must," Guy said. "We both know what I must do, and you will only make it that much more difficult for us."

"Yes, I know that," she admitted, "but it's so unfair, my love, it's so wrong to be torn from you like this when we have only just found each other."

"We have two days, Emilie," he reminded her, "two days in which we will create enough happy memories to last a lifetime."

"It will seem like a lifetime to me all the time that you're away," she told him.

"All the more reason to find our happiness now," he said.

He took her in his arms again, pulling them both on their sides facing each other. Emilie clasped his back, burying her head on his shoulder, not wanting to move away from him, even when he drew her back for a moment so that he could enter her again. When she realized what he was doing, she relented, and let him put her leg over his hip so that he could bury his hardness and his anguish in her once again, and over and over again until at last with the awakening day they both fell soundly asleep.

"Nobody wants to hear talk about freeing the slaves now. Nobody's interested."

Thomas Wentworth Higginson stared at his visitor. "I can't believe that," he said slowly. "This whole war is being fought for expressly that purpose."

"No, it is not," the Union general insisted. "The war is being fought to preserve the Union, and anything else that might happen is just a side issue."

"Slavery aside for the moment, although I must say that I do not accept your premise," Higginson went on, "why in damnation is the President still refusing to let our free black men serve the Union cause?"

The general spread his hands as if to say he did not have the answer. "Lord knows we can use any kind of help we can get to carry supplies, build fortifications, do any number of things that will free regular soldiers for combat. I've expressed myself on the matter many times, even to the Secretary of War, but Lincoln's afraid of it."

Higginson pounded on his desk. "But you're not even talking about arming them," he exclaimed. "What harm could it do to enlist them just for the purpose you've now explained and let them wear the uniform of the country?"

"They seem to be afraid in Washington that it would get out of control. Once you've put them in uniform, even if it's behind the fighting lines," the general replied. "Nobody wants to take the chance that in the confusion of battle or the aftermath things won't change around." He cocked an eyebrow speculatively. "Suppose you were leading your company, Higginson, and you were outnumbered and outfought, your troops being decimated. Hell, you'd shove a rifle into the hands of anyone who you thought could shoot. That's what they're afraid will happen."

"And what if it did?" Higginson contested hotly. "They're citizens, and they constantly have declared themselves as willing to sacrifice their lives for the Union as you and I are."

"But you and I are white," the general reminded his host. "That's where the difference lies, right there."

Higginson wiped his hand across his mouth as if to indicate he had said all that he could on the subject, at least for the moment. Then he asked, "What is the latest news from the front, General? Is the war going as badly as we're told?"

The general frowned. "It isn't good," he said. "The war's been going on for a year now and they're still coming at us pretty badly."

"That's why we need all the men we can get," Higginson declared hotly. It was as if he could not stay off the subject, even if he wished to. "Dammit, some of the generals in the field have been using contraband slaves in their commands to do all the kinds of work we're talking about. Why in the name of heaven can't free men have the same rights?"

The general did not reply, but turned around to face Jess, who had sat silently listening. "Tell me, young man," he said, "are you willing to volunteer to risk your life for your country?"

"Yes sir," said Young Jess without hesitation.

"I shall certainly report to the Secretary on the

enthusiasm of both you gentlemen," the general said with a twinkle in his eye. "As soon as I return to Washington. Seriously," and he addressed himself in a more earnest tone and principally to Higginson, "our best chance lies in persuading them to reactivate Hunter's First South Carolina Volunteers. If we can get the President to agree to that, it may be the key that turns the whole issue."

Jess spoke up. He had heard of the regiment that the general spoke of, and wondered what had happened to it. "Why did they disband the First South Carolina, sir?" he asked.

"Lincoln felt that General Hunter was overstepping his authority when he took slaves out of the Sea Island cottonfields and impressed them into military service," the general answered. "The fact that he had not used them as mere contraband, the way other commanders had, but had armed them and sent them into combat raised too many problems for the Administration. They were afraid that arming darkies would do them more harm than good. They did manage to see some action, though, and acquitted themselves pretty well." He turned to Higginson again. "Now if I can get them to authorize the reconstitution of that regiment, would you be willing to serve at its head?"

"I certainly would," Higginson replied. "On the condition that I would be allowed to take my young friend here with me as an aide-de-camp."

"I'm sure that such decisions would be left to your own discretion," the general said. "The important thing is to get them to agree to it, first."

He stood up. Higginson, who was now Captain Higginson of the 51st Massachusetts, saluted smartly. The general returned the salute and the two men shook hands. Then the general left.

"Brigadier General Saxton is a fine man," Higginson

said to Jess. "And it was a very fine thing for him to have made me this offer and for a superior officer like the general to convey it."

"Does this mean you'll leave the 51st?" Jess asked.

"Yes," Higginson replied. "Much as I am loath to do so. It has long been my ambition, as you know, to raise a company of free black men here in Massachusetts. The First South Carolina Volunteers are slaves who were taken right from the fields. But if that is the instrument which we are given in order to prove that black men can and will fight for this country, then, by God, that's the instrument we will use."

"Do you really want me to come with you?" Jess asked.

"Yes, I do." Higginson's voice was studied. "I know it's asking you to assume a lot of hardship and much danger. You will have no official status. I don't even know if I can promise you a uniform, but it could be worth it, Jess, it could be worth it." He paused for a moment. "If you can see firsthand what black men are capable of in combat, especially ex-slaves, and you can come back here and influence others by your accounts, then maybe we can accomplish all that we set out to do in the first place."

"I'm coming with you no matter what the risks are," Jess stated.

"I thought you would." Higginson grinned. "Mind, you'll have to stick close by me so that no one, Yankee or Reb, decides that you're contraband and makes off with you."

Both men grinned.

"Actually it's quite a promotion I'm being offered," Higginson went on. "From captain of a company to colonel of a regiment. Either somebody has apprised Saxton of my enormous capabilities or, more likely, someone in the administration has finally cast about and found a way to do away with me altogether."

Within weeks the two set out for Port Royal, South Carolina. The journey, made mostly by sea, was extremely long and tedious, with interminable stops along the coast and long waits at each one. Jess had expected to experience some great emotion when he knew that he was once more in slave territory, even though it was held by the Union forces, but when the time came he was so thoroughly exhausted that he had little reaction to the fact. Port Royal was situated on the second-largest of the South Carolina Sea Islands. In order to reach it they had to shift to military barges. But at long last the journey was over.

After the incredible lurching, crowding, and discomfort of the boats, the army camp seemed to be almost a model of order and regularity. The most difficult part of it for Jess to comprehend was the fact, relayed to him by Higginson as being absolutely indisputable, that there were influential proslavery forces both in the federal government and in the military commands such as the one to which they were now attached.

Captain, now Colonel, Higginson had his work cut out for him. He would have to train a newly freed body of field hands into an effective disciplined fighting force. Only then, with combat experience and victories to cite, could the cause for which they had been working so hard be achieved. Some of those he hoped to convince were the very ones who created the obstacles.

Jess had not been permitted a uniform of the Union Army, but between them they had managed to procure simple dark-blue shirt and pants which kept him from looking as conspicuous as a civilian in regular clothes would have. Despite his lack of status, he quickly found himself plunged into the thickest of military life.

The command had only allotted the space of a few months for Colonel Higginson to get his men battle-ready. From the start, Jess insisted on taking the same training as the other men. Colonel Higginson tried to talk him out of it, wanting him more as a reporter than merely as another recruit among the five hundred he already had, but Jess was insistent. Day by day for two long unbroken months, he took military drill with the others. After the first several weeks, his commander no longer berated him for it. There was now an unspoken agreement between the two men that when the regiment was ready for combat, Jess would fight alongside his brothers.

The discipline of army life and all its regimentation lay rather lightly on his shoulders. It was no more of a burden than had been the routine of the canefields, with its early-morning rising and endlessly long day. Nor, for the same reason, did Jess find military training a great strain on his body. Even though the Sea Islands were notorious for their miasmic climate, the sun somehow did not pierce through as brutally as it had in the cane. Moreover, much of the muscle he had developed working in the brakes had not been exercised fully since the time of his escape, and now he found a certain physical joy in being able to perform quite easily all of the tasks to which he was assigned.

It was with quiet satisfaction that Colonel Higginson received him one night in the house that served as his regimental headquarters.

"Here are your papers, Jess," the Colonel announced with a great deal of pride in his voice. "You've been mustered into the First South Carolina Volunteers. From now on you're a regular soldier, receiving soldier's pay." He passed the papers to Jess, who scanned them quickly.

He was relieved that he was able to read them quite clearly except for a few long and unfamiliar words.

"There's only one difficulty," Colonel Higginson was saying, as Jess read on. "Merely a technicality, but I will not be able to sign these and have them filed at headquarters until we can fill them out with a proper last name for you. Unless, of course," he added, "you want to continue to be called Young Jess officially."

Jess shook his head vehemently. "That was my name in slavery," he said. "Not in freedom."

"Many of the ex-slaves have taken their masters' names, since those were the names that they were known by," the Colonel said. "But I doubt that that would be acceptable to you."

"Since I've been free I've only really known two people," Jess said. "The war came so quick I never got settled. There's only yourself and Reverend Martin. The Reverend took me in as soon as I appeared at Joy Street and always treated me like a son. I have the strongest admiration and affection for you, sir, but I would not take it on myself to assume your name. I'm afraid it might prove an embarrassment to you, especially in our present circumstances. But if you think it's all right I would take the name of Martin."

"Very well taken, Jess," the colonel said, "and I feel myself highly flattered even to be considered in providing you with a surname, but I think you are right in that we must consider what the reaction might be had you chosen to do so. But Martin is a good strong Yankee name, and I'm sure you will bear it with pride and distinction."

"Thank you, sir," Jess said, saluting. "Am I dismissed, sir?"

"As you wish, private." Higginson grinned. "Private Martin, that is to say."

Jess returned to his company with spirits high. At

last he was officially one of their number and not merely someone hanging on like so many of those who flocked to the military settlements. He was a soldier now, in the army of his country, in rank and in name confirmed. Private Jess Martin.

Christmas and New Year's passed with observances suitable for a military camp. Training resumed after the brief respite. Toward the end of January, rumors started drifting through the camp that an expedition by the regiment was imminent.

The chief purpose of most of the expeditions being mounted was as much the confiscation of good timber, of which the army stood in dire need, as engaging the enemy. And to this purpose an expedition was planned for the First Volunteers. The men were to be transported by boat south to Georgia, to the mouth of the St. Mary's River, along whose upper banks it was reported there were stores of timber in Confederate hands but in vulnerable positions.

Jess was delighted when the report was indeed confirmed. He felt himself to be as tense as a cocked trigger after the seemingly endless months of training, and he was sure that most of his comrades felt the same way. The weeks of drill and target practice had taught them as much as such rehearsal could, and it was now in actual fray that their mettle and their training had to be proved.

He felt no fear. He assured himself constantly that the military maneuver was a far less dangerous one than the journey he had undertaken as a runaway slave. There, except briefly as he was passed from hand to hand, he had been utterly alone; here he would be a man among many comrades in arms. Yet Jess had to acknowledge a secret longing in his heart to prove himself to be more than that: he ached for the opportunity to prove himself in battle, to his fellow soldiers, to his colonel, and to his country above all. He wanted to show the world what black manhood, free as it was meant to be, was capable of.

With as much secrecy as could be mustered, over four hundred men and officers left on a variety of commandeered vessels to move down the coast to the St. Mary's. Jess was beside himself with excitement. He no longer had to stay close to Colonel Higginson, as had been their plan when they had first sailed from Boston. Now he was free to go to the very forefront of battle if the opportunity arose. He checked his rifle time and again, cleaning it and polishing it with special care, all during the day before they were to leave.

Finally the great hour came. After arriving at the island of Hilton Head, Jess was chosen along with about a hundred others to accompany Colonel Higginson on a further foray up the river. Under cover of darkness they made their advance.

The first rifle shots were startling. Jess was with the advance group. He thought he felt a man fall by his side, but could not tell for sure in the darkness. He crept forward, stealthily crouching alongside the shrubbery that massed along the river bank. With several of his comrades, whom he knew to be among the most daring of the young men in the company, he moved forward quickly. They grinned at each other in the dark as if some secret signal were being passed between them. It was as though they had decided that this was to be something more than the usual foraging expedition. They were, in the words of the military, going forward to meet and engage the enemy.

Jess tightened his grip on his gun. In the black night he could almost see the sweat trickling down his body. He knew that the next time he saw daylight he would be a different man. For between this time and that, he was going to kill. He was going to shed the blood of those who had trampled and whipped him all of his life. He was going to kill those who had taken his mother away from him and sold her off to some unknown hell. He was going to kill some of those who had robbed Old Jess of his birthright as the chief of his village back home. He was going to kill those who had put a thousand miles between him and Missy. He was going to kill some of those who had stood over him and cracked the whip deep into his back as Charles Bonfils had stood back and counted off the numbers of the lashes to be dealt him.

He was going to kill Charles Bonfils himself, if that were possible. But should the master not be among those in the rebel camp, he would kill whoever stood there in his place, whoever stood for protecting the master's lands and the master's properties. He was going to kill some of those who would not let him learn to read, who would not let him learn to think, who would not let him learn to live to be a man. All of these things he had managed to do in spite of them, yet he would kill them all if he could.

Jess knew he stood high in the regard of his soldier comrades; partly that was due to his closeness to the colonel, but even more it was because these men from the cottonfields of Florida and South Carolina knew of the canefields only through terrible tales and rumors. The fact that he had survived the cane and run away to freedom before the war made him a kind of hero to them. He knew that if he chose to burst into the very center of the rebel camp, the four or five men running beside him, although they were under no explicit orders to do so, would follow him and take from him the same steel courage that urged him forward now.

He would kill some of those who had stolen their wives and their mothers as well.

The moonlight shining down reflected off a bit of

metal that Jess recognized as part of the strappings of a horse. He knew that meant that they were on the outskirts of the camp where the animals would be quartered. With a sweep of his arm he signaled the other men to follow him.

He cut a wide swath away from the animals, thinking that there would be at least one sentry guarding them. Since the only prior rifle shots he had heard had come from another direction, before they reached the camp, Jess figured they had encountered a single sniper. There was a good possibility that the camp itself had not been aroused.

But a sudden burst of rifle fire coming from the direction they were headed in quickly informed him that this was not so. Now he could hear the shouting of voices as well as the intermittent crack of bullets. He and his men had immediately dropped to their stomachs and flattened themselves as best they could against the earth. Jess lay still for a moment, determining where most of the noise was coming from. Then he signaled the others again and they crawled quickly forward until they found themselves face to face with the enemy rifles.

"Now!" Jess shouted, and the four men with him began returning the rifle fire.

The months of intensified target practice were paying off. Against the guns of the Rebels in the sleepy isolated outpost, the rigid training standards that Higginson had insisted on quickly proved their value. Now it was the scattered outbursts of widely separated enemy guns that were coming at them, rather than the concentration of front-line defense that they had first encountered and that they seemed to have silenced.

Jess had no time to count the number of men still with him. He whispered, "Come on!" and lurched forward on his belly again.

If the bullets aimed at them were now less concentrated, they were even more dangerous, as there was no knowing where the next attack would come from. The crack and whine of bullets everywhere assured him that he had not done much more than penetrate that first fallen defense line. If he was to secure the entire camp he would have to wipe out whoever was doing the sporadic shooting.

For one weary moment it seemed as though bullets were flying at him from everywhere. Jess felt as if he were now at the center of the target. He did not want to waste too many shots because he knew they had not carried a very heavy supply of powder and shot with them. This raid had been set up initially for the main purpose of foraging. Now that he had taken it into his head to make it a punitive raid against enemy personnel, he would have to fit this new operation to the small amount of men and material he had with him.

A bullet came whizzing so close to his ear he thought he had seen it. Instinctively he pointed his shoulder in the direction it had come from, and his own shot rang out within seconds of the other. Suddenly, in what little light there was, he saw the figure of a man pushed upward into the air, arms and legs bent and dangling, rising almost upward for a moment and then falling back to earth. Jess knew he had killed him, but there was no time to think about that. Instead he crawled in the same direction he had sent his bullet so purposefully. Since there had been no returning fire he surmised that his victim had manned a solitary post, and Jess determined to take that ground and direct his attack from there. Then one by one he and his men would pick off any of the rebs that remained to oppose them.

He cautioned the others to be as careful as he was with their bullets, but the grin of the man at his side told him that no such instructions were necessary. Each of the other former field hands was as trained and disciplined as he was. Jess grinned back.

There was more noise of men shouting, and another exchange of gunfire. The men who had stayed near the opening to the camp were fighting the remaining Rebels, while from their vantage Jess and his comrades waited until they could see enough movement to assure them of their targets. Jess tried to determine from the firing coming from his men how many of them were still there. It seemed to him as though there were two Union guns answering the Rebels. That meant that one of the First South Carolina Volunteers had fallen. He tried not to think about it. He wondered for a moment how long they had been fighting. It could have been ten minutes or several hours. Time itself seemed to have been a victim of the battle. There was no way of knowing how much of it had passed.

The noise of men was growing less loud and less frequent. Jess realized that no blood-curdling Reb yell had sounded for a long while now. Over the sporadic crack of the bullets he could hear the neighing of horses. He realized that it had never ceased from the time of the first outburst, but the sounds of the fighting and the dying men had made the animal noises a mere backdrop. It was only when human voices had stopped and the last bullets had been shot by his own men that Jess realized it was over. They had won.

Just then the neighing of the horses grew louder and Jess realized that the animals were coming closer. He crouched on his knees and swung around quickly, rifle at the ready, but just as he thought they were about to be stampeded, he heard a voice crying, "Whoa! Whoa there!" in accents that no Johnny Reb could have made.

It was quite another Johnny, a young Florida field hand by that name, who had made his way to the South Carolina camp of General Saxton at a time when the ex-slaves, labeled contraband, had been freed from land taken from the Confederacy. When the First Volunteers had been set up, Johnny had been one of the first to sign up. His signature had been a penciled X made with someone holding his hand to help form the letter, but he had proved himself to be one of the most adept soldiers in almost every phase of the training.

Now he walked toward Jess, his rifle slung over his shoulder, hands gripping the reins of the horses he was leading. It seemed to Jess that his grin was nearly as wide as the span of animals.

"How about *this* foraging?" Johnny asked eagerly.

"That really is something!" Jess admitted. "How many reb horses you got there?"

"Six," came the delighted answer.

Jess called out to the men who were still stationed at the camp entrance. In a few moments they ambled over. No one said anything for a moment, then Jess slapped the man closest to him on the shoulder and with that they all broke out in whoops and hollers, hugging each other and congratulating themselves on the outcome of their first battle.

They quickly lit a bonfire so they could see exactly what they had done and what booty other than the horses they would be bringing back to the Union side.

With himself, Johnny, Sam, who had taken over the stand within the camp with him, and the two other men, Ben and Mose, all five of them had made it.

Unconsciously Jess touched the stone that hung inside his army blouse. They had taken over a Reb camp, killed all its inhabitants, captured a fine span of horses and still more as yet unaccounted-for loot. The First South Carolina Volunteers had more than proved itself in battle, and it would be a fine gift to hand to the colonel from Boston.

Jess turned to Sam, who was the fastest runner in the

group, and dispatched him back downriver where the colonel was with the bulk of the forces. They would hold the camp until the colonel arrived or sent back orders for them to return.

Jess felt like a general. The four men with him were as good at their soldiering as he was. Each of them had performed everything that had been required. Any one of them might have been able to assume the leadership position, but he had been the one to actually do it. More than that, more important even than the fact that each move he had made had turned out to be the right one, more important than anything else, was the natural and willing way in which all of the others had followed him, obeying his every order, going with him unquestioningly to the very heart of danger.

And perhaps sweetest of all, they were all free men acting freely and had fought for and won that right.

10

Emilie didn't quite know how she had gotten into the habit, but now her brief morning visit to Catherine's ruined chapel had become a fixed part of her life. Even before she sat down to breakfast she would cross the veranda and circle around to the side of the house. She never lingered there, staying only long enough to drop to her knees and pray for Guy's safety. She didn't even know how or why she had gone there alone in the first place. Perhaps it had been to recapture her wedding day, when for once the little chapel was filled with people and flowers and candles and was being used as it should have been, as the setting for a significant rite of life.

Even though her mind and her prayers were only on Guy, she could not be in the chapel without seeing it as it was then, with people filling the small and narrow pews. She could not recall anything much about the actual ceremony. It was only the sense of being surrounded by warm and loving people that seemed to comfort her somehow.

Emilie got up quickly and went up the aisle and out into the open air, regretting as she did every time the press of war that made it impossible to rebuild the missing wall or make any of the other repairs at Les Chandelles. Someday, she promised herself, someday.

It was more than a year now since Guy, resplendent

in his uniform, had ridden off. Now it had been almost a month since she had heard from him, and she did not want to admit to the worry that was pressing down relentlessly upon her.

She heard the distant roar of thunder, and the sound surprised her. It was rather early in the season for storms. Emilie stood for a moment on the steps of the veranda as another volley came roaring up from the south. She stared in the direction of the river over which the storms usually traveled. She could not see it from where she stood. The lay of the land and the tall trees that grew almost unchecked on the other side of the road made that impossible. But as she stood poised, waiting, the air about her seemed almost crushing with the heaviness of expectancy.

By the time it roared again, mere moments later, Emilie was distracted by other, more earthy sounds that seemed to be coming closer.

There were horses and carriages speeding up the embowering drive of Les Chandelles, and Emilie stood stock still as the unexpected morning visitors drew close. They were nearly upon her before Emilie recognized the frightened occupants of the carriage and the outriders on horseback who were restraining themselves to keep pace with it.

Emilie called inside for slaves to come out and help the sudden visitors.

Coming down from the carriage were Madame de Pommeri and her daughter Amie, a girl a year or so younger than Emilie. They lived on a plantation that spread near the southern borderline of the parish.

One of the riders slipped quickly off his horse to assist the old lady as she tottered toward Emilie. Emilie stretched out her hands to the old woman, both to welcome her and to keep her from falling.

"Oh, my dear, my dear," the old lady quavered. "It's

the end, it's the end. They've come to kill us all!" She fell into Emilie's arms, and Emilie almost staggered with her weight.

Before Emilie could ask the question or an explanation be given, an enormous roar, much louder than the others, made all hearing impossible.

When it stopped, Philippe de Pommeri, who had hastened to his mother's side, stared down at Emilie and said grimly, "The Yankees."

"Oh no!" Emilie stared at him, horrified.

"Their ships are on the river," Philippe continued. "They are fighting down in New Orleans. So far the forts below the city have held out, or so we've been told."

"Then how have they gotten so far north to us?" Emilie asked in terror.

"The damn—begging your pardon, Miss Emilie— the naval commander, that man Farragut, has slipped some ships past them and come upriver."

Emilie looked at them, unable to speak. The fright of the two women was so apparent she did not want to disturb them any further by pressing with more questions.

She motioned to Robert, who in turn gestured for two housemaids to help the ladies inside.

The other man, who had dismounted and hitched the horses to a small post at the side of the house, now came toward them and bowed low to Emilie.

"I'm afraid the news is very bad, ma'am," he said. "The city will be cut off by this maneuver. The Yankees will have it in no time. I only just managed to get out in time to come upriver and help warn as many families as I could."

"You must forgive me, Miss Emilie," Philippe de Pommeri said. "In our great haste and anxiety, I neglected to introduce you. This is Captain August Hammond, of General Breckinridge's command."

The captain bowed again to Emilie. She nodded her head.

"I am hoping to join up with the rest of General Breckinridge's forces farther upriver at Baton Rouge," the captain explained to Emilie. "I am stopping only to warn as many of the planters as I can. As it is, I'm only one step ahead of the Yankees."

"Then all of that noise, that thunder . . ." Emilie left the obvious unsaid.

"Yes, ma'am, I'm afraid it's Yankee guns you've been hearing this morning."

"Then they must be very close," Emilie said quietly.

"What we're hoping is that in their haste to get upriver, they will move past the plantations and leave you undisturbed," the captain went on. "They are interested in controlling the Mississippi, and in so doing will be able to divide the state in half."

Emilie blanched.

"But don't worry, ma'am," he hurried to assure her. "We'll keep on fighting from the other side and drive them from every inch of our land." He continued to stand restlessly as he spoke. His foot tapped the earth much as an impatient stallion would paw the ground, and his last words seemed more directed to Philippe de Pommeri than to the young mistress of Les Chandelles.

Philippe seemed to sense this, and he cleared his throat nervously. "As soon as I have seen to my mother and sister, sir, I shall feel free to join you and General Breckinridge," he said.

"Splendid," said the captain. "We have need of every man we can get." So saying, he turned his gaze to Emilie again. "I understand your magnificent estate to be the largest holding in this area," he said. "I'm sure that you have already given much in defense of our

Confederacy, but I must urge you, ma'am, that if there is any white man still employed by you who can be spared, let him come with us at once or make his way as quickly as possible to Baton Rouge."

Emilie considered. All of St. Georges' underbosses had long since left, either of their own volition or having been recruited. This had left the cruel overseer in complete charge and in direct contact with all of the field hands. The situation had enabled him to give vent to all the fury of which he was possible, now that his work load had been so intensified. He had no hesitation in venting his brutal anger on the slaves who bent before him in the canebrakes. Emilie knew how frequently and harshly the whip lashed out every day at Les Chandelles. In order to get the work done, St. Georges had appointed two of the strongest male slaves as drivers over the others. In their sudden and unexpected rise to authority these men had quickly begun to ape the tactics of their work master, if anything surpassing him in swiftness with the lash and immediacy of punishment for any imagined infraction or slowdown. Emilie was proudly told this by St. Georges himself when he reported to her, gloating over the fact as if to show her how senseless her own soft ways with the slaves were, as if the even greater cruelty which they exercised on each other proved his point.

But far different was the version she would hear unintentionally when she passed by slaves talking in the kitchen or front rooms. She was not meant to hear these whispered exchanges among the house slaves, and so therefore she chose to close her ears to them. But she knew that someday she would have to face the growing and excessive brutality to which her chattel were being subjected.

Emilie knew that not all slaves would treat each other the way St. Georges insisted. All her life she had seen

Robert supervise the smooth running of the entire household with scarcely the hint of a raised voice, let alone a raised hand. And while Tess had the reputation of being a veritable tyrant in her kitchen, she acted very nearly alike to white and black. Nor had Sully as housekeeper ever reprimanded one of her helpers with more than a light slap when necessary.

Emilie knew too of the respect and esteem in which all of the slaves held Old Jess, to whom they still looked as their head man, even though his body had grown so feeble. Emilie turned from these inner thoughts back to the waiting face of the captain. Then she turned aside briefly, saying to Robert, "Send one of the stable boys for Mr. St. Georges immediately."

"We will settle soon, captain, I promise you, and you can be on your way to rejoin the general," Emilie said. "But please first avail yourself of what scant time you have to rest and refresh yourself at Les Chandelles. Everything we have here is yours, and if you are in need of supplies let us provision you with everything you can possibly carry when you leave."

"Our glorious cause lives in the hearts and spirits of ladies like yourself, ma'am," the captain said. "It is with such memory so strong in them that our men are able to go and do battle against the stronger forces of the enemy."

They were standing on the veranda now, and Emilie put her hand on the captain's arm as if to forestall him from going inside where she knew the de Pommeri ladies were still in a state of distraction.

"Tell me, Captain, you must," she whispered fiercely, "are our forces always outnumbered? And what news have you of the fighting elsewhere?"

He looked at her frightened face and could see the trembling which had overtaken her entire body. "Your husband, ma'am," he said gently. "Where is he?"

"In Virginia, sir," Emilie said, her voice almost breaking but with a forced tone almost military in its tenor. "As near North, I suppose, as the South can get."

"General Lee's armies have won victories whose names will be recounted till the end of time," the captain answered. "My only wish, ma'am, would be that I were numbered among those gallant men myself. They have been advancing steadily, determined that the blood be spilled on Yankee soil, not on ours."

"But that spilled blood, wherever it may stain the earth, is it not as much ours as it is theirs?" Emilie asked.

The captain lowered his eyes; he did not answer her.

"Come, gentlemen," Emilie said loudly with a strength she scarcely felt. "Let us go inside. There is nothing to be gained from your standing here before you continue your journey. You must partake of whatever refreshment I can provide you."

They had been seated inside for a few moments when the overseer appeared, hat in hand. Emilie rose instantly, and as she did Philippe and Captain Hammond joined her. St. Georges understood he was to follow the three of them as they headed for the study.

Emilie seated herself behind the huge desk which had served her father more for drinking than working. She did not bother to introduce the commoner St. Georges to the two gentlemen who had taken seats on either side of the room, nor did she gesture for the overseer to find a chair.

"What is the condition in the fields at this very moment?" she asked him.

"The harvesting is nearly finished and the refinery is being loaded with cut cane," St. Georges answered. "The boiling is going on as usual, but there's no telling whether we are going to be able to ship the barrels." There was immediate understanding among his listeners that he for one had not mistaken the morning's noises for thunder.

"I see," Emilie said, folding her hands on the desk.

"If there's no further need you have of me, Miss Emilie, I ought to be getting back down there. Them niggers need minding every minute, and it ain't easy, me being the only white man on this plantation."

"Indeed I agree." Emilie sighed. "That has not been easy on any of us." She started to say something about the condition of her property, but stayed silent. It was not necessary to discuss Les Chandelles business with outsiders.

The silence was heavy in the room. Finally St. Georges broke it. "If you've no further orders for me, ma'am," he said uncertainly.

"But I do, Mr. St. Georges," Emilie answered evenly. "My orders are for you to accompany Captain Hammond and Monsieur de Pommeri to Baton Rouge or wherever else necessity may force them to take you. You are under the command of Captain Hammond and are as of this moment a soldier in the Confederate Army." She stared at him, her dark eyes bold.

St. Georges turned red. "But ma'am," he shouted. "We've been told that we've got to continue to get the sugar out. The Confederacy is depending on us to help raise the money we need. We've been ordered—"

Captain Hammond broke in. "You have been ordered, man," he said. "And it is for you to do as your mistress says and for your betters to decide where it is you are most needed. We leave at once."

Emilie stood up. The three men followed her out of the office. She paused in the corridor to turn briefly to Philippe de Pommeri and assure him that his kin would find whatever comfort and refuge were possible. "As long as my lands are safe and my house stands, your mother and sister can stay with me. All I can promise is they will share a fate no better or worse than my own."

"I thank you for that, Miss Emilie," Philippe replied. "May God watch over Les Chandelles and protect you all."

In the front salon the young planter, the last of his male line, bid farewell to his family. Emilie was proud, seeing that even the tears and ministrations of his mother and sister did not break him down. He wore his new burdens and responsibilities manfully, with a strength that would never have been guessed of the young dandy she remembered slightly from only a few years earlier. But when she looked straight in his face to say goodbye and wish him well, Emilie was shocked by the doomed expression of his features. It was not strength nor belief in the cause that was propelling him, she realized with a start, it was more the acceptance of an implacable doom. She wanted to cry out for him, but she knew she must not. The existence to which he had willed himself had to discipline her as well to a strength to perform whatever had to be done.

"If they want to leave here and join Mama's cousins up in Arkansas, I guess it'll be all right," Philippe said. "But try to convince them to stay here with you if you can, Miss Emilie. I'd feel better about that somehow."

Impulsively Emilie reached up and kissed his cheek tenderly, patting his shoulder in farewell. Then, feeling more like an already grieving mother seeing her sons off to battle than a brazenly coquettish young woman, she turned and kissed Captain Hammond as well.

"Thank you, ma'am," the officer said. "I will carry that with me into battle as my talisman."

She walked with them outside and stood on the veranda watching as they remounted and rode off.

No one had noticed that the roaring of the gunboats had suddenly stopped. A horse from the stable was saddled and another one quickly outfitted with as many provisions as it could carry without causing it to slow the others down. Emilie went back inside to arrange for bedchambers for her two new guests and to try to raise their spirits as much as she could, but the pressing needs of the plantation prevented her from giving herself over much to this unexpected task.

She summoned Robert, not to the large study that had been the scene of her encounter with the overseer, but to the small office where the real business of the plantation was conducted.

Much to the elder servant's surprise, she gestured for him to sit down. Slowly he took a seat facing her from the opposite side of the small battered desk.

"As you've no doubt seen, I've sent Mr. St. Georges to join his comrades in the army, where he is much needed. It will be more than ever in our hands to see that all continues as it must on this plantation."

"Yes, ma'am," was the only reply.

"I know that St. Georges has set up two of the field hands as drivers over the rest of the people," Emilie went on, "and I know that they are mean and hated by the other slaves. Therefore our first task will be to find someone who can oversee the fields properly."

Robert remained silent. He would do as he was bid, but as expert as he was in the ordering and running of a large household, he would be nearly useless in the fields.

"I have in mind the person I think could replace St. Georges, at least for the time being," she went on, "and I think he would be able to provide himself with more suitable drivers from among the field hands. But before I take such a step, I wanted to talk with you about it. I well know, Robert, the high esteem my poor father always held you in and how much your good judgment has helped me through these terrible times."

Robert regarded his young mistress. In all his years of unending service to the house of Bonfils, never had any sentiments regarding his worth been expressed. From Emilie's poor father, as she termed him, Robert had heard almost nothing other than orders and abuse. The only time any mention was made of his value as a servant was when Charles would roar about how much money he would bring on the auction block should the master choose to send him there.

"I will always do my best for the mistress, as I always have tried to do in the past," he said quietly.

"Good," said Emilie fiercely. "I am thinking of Henrique, Papa's former valet. I know that he is a house servant, but I remember hearing too that he has served in many varied capacities in his life. I see little of him about the house these days, but I know he busies himself about the horses and in keeping the grounds in order. Do you think that he could serve as overseer? Would the people listen to him and obey him?"

"I believe our people will do whatever our mistress tells us," Robert answered. "And if Henrique is put in charge of the fields I believe they will obey him."

Emilie plunged in. It was not often that she wanted to find herself in the position of asking advice from a slave, but she knew it was necessary. "Can he do it, Robert?" she demanded.

"I believe so, miss," Robert replied. "All of us who are loyal to you will do everything we can to help."

"Thank you," Emilie said. "We have always tried to give the people a good home here," she paused. "I know that there have been bad times for many of you, but I do believe they have been less frequent here than on other places. At least"—and there was a measure of appeal to him in her voice now—"that was the case before St. Georges ran unchecked. But now that I have dismissed him, surely the people will see that I have their good at heart and that they must continue to serve me because it is in the best interest of all of us to preserve and protect our home."

"Yes, mistress."

"Then send someone now to the stables and have Henrique come to me at once," she ordered. With these swiftly uttered words, all of the warmth and pleading quality had gone out of her voice. Once more she was unquestioned mistress of the plantation and Robert no more than another slave to do her imperious bidding.

And so she remained when Henrique stood in the doorway. She felt the pang at her heart as she always did at the sight of him, so closely was he associated in her mind with her father. Indeed it seemed that with Charles dead Henrique was not the totality he had been before. It seemed to Emilie as though something were missing from him. But this was not the time to plague her mind with such thoughts; there was much more immediate business to be done. She did not invite the slave to sit down.

"I have sent Mr. St. Georges, the overseer, into the service of his country," she said. "I am setting you in his place to supervise all of the work in the fields. I have been given to understand that you have much experience of many kinds, gathered in the years before you came to serve my father. I shall depend on your loyalty to his memory and to this house to serve as well in this position as I thought you to do in your former one."

"Yes, mistress." The softly uttered words were those of any subservient slave, but the intelligence that was

etched on his smooth light-brown face was obvious.
Emilie realized how much of a mask he had worn as
her father's valet, and while the thought irked her she
was happy in this instance to see that she had not, at
least at first reckoning, made a wrong choice. Her
shoulders dropped for a moment and she felt herself
relaxing. But when she spoke it was again in the tones
of the mistress. "Tell me something about yourself
Henrique. What did you do before you came to Les
Chandelles?"

The simple recounting of his past would have filled
volumes, Emilie realized. She wished there was time
to press him for the details of his life. It seemed as if
from childhood years until his arrival at Les Chandelles
his life had been a string of adventures, one closely
following another. He had served French, Spanish, and
English masters before arriving in New Orleans, and
had served them very nearly everywhere in the known
world. He had been to places she had dreamed of and
others she had never heard of. But there was no time
to be entertained now with a slave's memoirs. Instead
she dwelled on the time when, in one of his less fortunate escapades, Henrique had found himself bound
and chained and sentenced to the canefields on the
far-off island of Barbados. It was several years in the
unimaginable heat of the tropics before his English
master realized the value of the slave whose life was
being burned away, as was that of countless lesser
beings.

It was that time in the fields that Emilie needed to
draw on now.

"I want you to assume the overseer's job at once,"
she said. "I do not like what I have heard about those
slaves that St. Georges set up as drivers, but I will not
impose my feelings in this matter on you as I did not on
him. Whether they are retained in their posts or re-

placed with others is a matter for you to decide. Should it prove unsatisfactory in the outcome I will make a decision then. Meanwhile let us get to the business of what must be done and what I shall expect from you when you report to me at the end of each day."

Whether Henrique was pleased or not with this sudden change in his fortunes, he did not reveal. Instead he listened closely as Emilie spoke. It was only when she had come to the instructions about the accounting of each day's production that she stopped herself.

"Can you read?" she asked him.

"Yes." That answer to that question given several years earlier might have merited him anything from the loss of a part of his anatomy to immediate sale on the auction block. But now it was different.

"Good," said Emilie. "Can you figure?"

"Yes, ma'am."

Emilie felt her shoulders relax again and gave a sigh of relief. She looked up at the still-standing slave. "Henrique, I think this is going to work out for the best," she said.

"Yes, ma'am," he answered, still impassive, displaying nothing.

"Do you have any questions?" she asked.

"No, ma'am."

"Then I want you to set out for the fields at once," she instructed. "I want Robert to go with you to make the announcement of your position to the hands, and I want Jones and Hubert to go along as well to ensure that there is no trouble." She knew that the last two named were yardmen whose position close to the house and long years of service gave them status and respect in the eyes of the fieldhands. "Then report back to me at six in the evening. That is to be our regular routine unless something unforeseen happens that requires my knowledge."

The slave bowed low, murmuring a "thank you, ma'am" that was almost inaudible as Emilie turned her attention to her ledger. But she could not stand to look at it for more than a few seconds. She hastened out of the office and through the front rooms to the veranda.

Other stragglers and refugees from downriver made their way to the mansion during the next few days. Emilie knew that they would put a strain on Les Chandelles's resources, but she gave instructions that some bit of food was to be given to anyone who requested it, that shelter was to be made available in the barns and stables for overnight travelers. All of the gentry who might arrive, of course, fleeing their own plantations, were to be immediately shown into the house and accorded every courtesy that hospitality demanded in bad times no less than in good. Further, anyone who had traveled from New Orleans or close to it and had news of what was happening in the city was to be brought to Miss Emilie at once.

When Henrique came to the little office that evening he was able to report to his mistress that all had gone without incident in the fields. For the time being he would retain the drivers that St. Georges had installed, to afford some continuity of command in the fields and also to prevent the two from possible retaliatory troublemaking. Still, he had already warned them that he would not tolerate unwarranted heavy-handedness with the people and he would watch closely to see that Miss Emilie's property was not abused.

Emilie dismissed him with a feeling of thankfulness in her heart that she did not directly express to the slave. He had been taken from innocuous duties in the stable and given his own big roan to ride and the command of all the field hands. This was recognition enough and needed no embellishing words from her.

Over the next several days the stream of refugees coming to the door increased steadily, and with these newcomers came the news that the city had fallen into the hands of Federal forces. Having been cut off by Farragut's gunboats from any communication with the territories lying above it, New Orleans was in an isolated and hopeless position. The Union Army, with fifteen thousand troops under General Benjamin Butler, marched into the city on the first of May and put it under military government.

Emilie was relieved. At least it meant that the fighting had stopped in their part of the world. If the Yankees were satisfied with their capture of the Queen City, perhaps the plantations upriver would be left in peace.

11

Les Chandelles hung suspended like an island in space. Travelers had ceased coming as traffic on the river road all but ceased. The unearthly quiet after the tempest seemed almost as unbearable to Emilie. It was as if they were cut off from the rest of the world, not knowing what was happening elsewhere and how quickly their seemingly peaceful existence might be turned completely inside out.

It was fortunate, Emilie realized, that the plantation was self-sustaining. They needed no import of goods from the outside world in order to keep going. More than once did Emilie stop in her daily routine, to thank the insight of her long-gone ancestors who had planned their estate so efficiently. But with less war news and fewer war victims to worry about, her mind was left almost totally free for concern about her husband. There had been only two letters which had come to her in all the time that he had been gone, but occasionally news of his company had been received in New Orleans and relayed to her by some traveler or other. That seemed to mean that all was well. But it had been a long time now since she had heard anything at all, even at second or third hand. Emilie was tortured day and night by thoughts of what might have happened to Guy. The unnatural stillness all about her seemed to increase her anxieties. The de Pommeri ladies had elected to return to their own holdings as soon as all the signs of fighting had ceased and the road was declared once more usable. Madame de Pommeri had thanked Emilie effusively for having sheltered them, but declared herself to be quite capable of returning to her own home. No soldiers of the occupying army had set foot in the upriver parishes, and the land lay peaceful and calm.

Emilie was determined that the sugar crop would be harvested as usual, later in the year. At the time of the battle for New Orleans she had thought that all their activity would be for naught. If the city was unreachable and the countryside at war, there would be no way of shipping the syrup and therefore no point to boiling the cane. But now it seemed that the Federal Army had chosen, or had had chosen for it, a policy of occupation rather than conquest. What little news she heard from the city seemed to point this out. There was a feeling that the planters would be permitted, even encouraged, to keep up the work of their great estates.

It was growing too hot out on the veranda, and Emilie went back indoors to seek some respite in the quiet gloom of the salon. She sat musing for a few moments, her head back, her eyes closed. She was almost dozing when she sensed the presence of someone close by. Her eyes flew open.

It was one of the housemaids, Selena. The girl almost never spoke even when spoken to, and Emilie did not know whether her demeanor was from an excess of modesty or from unusually slow wits. But she did her work carefully and well and was permitted to remain in the house. This morning, however, wild fear ignited her usually docile features as she waited for her mistress to address her.

"Well, Selena, what is it?" Emilie asked. "You look frightened half out of your mind."

"Yes, ma'am, I come to tell you there's a gentleman here asking for you."

"A gentleman?" Emilie echoed. "Who is he and where is he from?"

"We don't know, ma'am, and Tess said for me to come and tell you quick. He's in the kitchen."

"The kitchen?" Emilie was sure she had misunderstood. What could anyone who wanted to see her be doing in the kitchen?

"Tess say to make sure you be by yourself and no one around to hear," Selena went on.

Emilie went white with fear. "Let me hurry then and see who it is." She jumped up and raced for the kitchen, Selena following in her wake.

At the table which Tess usually used for kneading dough sat a man. A chair had been pulled up for him and he sat there, leaning his elbows and chest on the table in a way that Emilie knew Tess could not possibly approve of. But this was no time for such niceties. He looked tattered and bedraggled, but torn and spotted as it was, there was no mistaking his light-gray shirt for that of a soldier in the Confederate Army.

"I am Madame Charpentier," Emilie announced. "Did you wish to see me?"

"Yes, ma'am." The words came more from a croak than a voice, and Emilie grew frightened. She leaned her hands on the table to steady herself.

"Where are you from?" she asked in a softer voice, recognizing from the way he looked and spoke that he was certainly not of the planter class.

"I was with your husband, ma'am, at the Battle of Chancellorsville. I was at his side when—" His voice broke and he could not go on.

Emilie was beside herself. She wanted to scream

out, but knew she could not put on such a display in front of the slaves.

"Go on, go on, I beg you," she urged.

The man was beaten and exhausted, and she dared not ask him to get up and walk another step. She did not know how far he had come, nor how long it had taken him to find her.

"I promised—I promised the colonel," he started to say, as though reading her thoughts.

"Perhaps there is some mistake," Emilie said. "My husband had only the rank of major."

"No, ma'am," the man mumbled. "He was made colonel after Fredericksburg. We really showed them at Fredericksburg." There was an almost insolent smile on his face.

"Are you sure you are speaking of a gentleman named Guillaume Charpentier?" Emilie asked again, meanwhile directing Tess to put some hot broth in front of the man.

"Yes, ma'am, and I promised him I would find you for him. He told me the name Les Chandelles and told me I would find you here. It was what he wanted, and now I've done it."

He had not pronounced the words that Emilie so dreaded to hear, but she did not need them. One of the slave women had started wailing, a keening sound that Emilie recognized from earliest childhood as accompanying death. She wanted to sit down next to the weary soldier, plead with him somehow to take back the words he had said, to tell her that it was not true, but Emilie could do nothing but stare down at him as she clenched the edge of the table and begged, begged inwardly that it not be true.

"We be sent back," he muttered again. "The colonel knew we had done it and he told me to get this back to you."

Emilie stood stock still as he reached inside his coat pocket, but before he could withdraw his hand one of the stable boys had burst inside excitedly yelling, "Mistress Emilie, Mistress Emilie!" He ducked to avoid the arm that Tess swung out at him at this invasion of her domain. He stood in front of the young mistress, so excited that he could not read the expression on her face but immediately began to speak. "There's a whole troop of Yankees coming up the drive, Miss Emilie!" he shouted. "There's blueshirts riding up to Les Chandelles!"

Emilie's head sprang up as if something in her neck had snapped. "What did you say?" she breathed.

"Yankee soldiers, ma'am. A whole bunch of them," the terrified boy repeated. "They almost at the house now!"

Emilie couldn't believe it. The Union forces at Les Chandelles now, of all times, when she had a Confederate soldier right here in the house! For a moment the dread message he had brought her was pushed back in her mind as she realized the terrible danger that they were in.

She turned to Tess. "Get him outside and hidden in one of the storehouses quickly," she told the cook, and turning to the boy she added, "You help her. Hurry, hurry!"

Between them the two slaves managed to lift the soldier, and supporting him under his arms, started out of the kitchen.

"Don't worry, you're in safe hands," Emilie called after him. "We will take care of you and make sure that you get back safely." She urged them quickly out of the house.

He started to say something, but Emilie didn't dare wait to catch the words. Not until the Yankees were gone could she dare seek him out. She bit her lip and glanced hurriedly at the clumsy trio trying to make their way from the kitchen. "Move quickly, move quickly," she shouted after them. "We are all in the gravest danger!" She looked at the frightened faces of the kitchen maids. "Not one word of this to anyone, do you hear me? One word and I'll take the whip to you myself!"

She walked swiftly from the kitchen, thinking luck was with her when she met Robert in the passageway. She ordered him to station himself at the door and be ready to open it for the invaders, while she sat on a sofa and tried to appear as calm as she possibly could.

Guy, Guy, she thought, the name like a knife in her heart.

There were three of them, each in the detested dark-blue blouses and trousers, yellow kerchiefs knotted around their necks and insignia which she could not read of the same color on their sleeves. The first man touched his hat with his fingers in a sort of salute, while the two others, whom she thought to be his subordinates, removed theirs.

"Is this the Bonfils place?" the first soldier asked.

"This is Les Chandelles," Emilie replied. "I am Madame Charpentier; I am mistress here."

"I can see that," he replied, not unpleasantly. "But I was informed that this place belonged to the Bonfils family."

"It does," Emilie answered smoothly. "I am Emilie Bonfils Charpentier."

"Is there a Mr. Bonfils?" he asked.

"My father is dead, sir," Emilie replied sharply.

"I'm sorry to hear that, ma'am," and he touched his hand to his hat again. "May I ask then where is Mr. Charpentier?"

"My husband is fighting with General Lee's army." This time her words were cold. Her heart beat furiously. She realized, had to realize, that the statement was no longer true. Oh Guy, oh Guy, why did it have to happen to you? Her mind raged with the unspoken question. She could barely hear the man in front of her talking, her mind was so full of her anguish. Yet she knew she must keep a firm grip on herself. The presence of the Confederate soldier had to remain hidden from these dangerous intruders.

"We understand this to be the largest plantation in the parish," the Yankee officer was saying, "strategically placed for observation of the river."

"I know nothing about that." Emilie smiled sadly. "My great-grandfather cleared this land solely for the purpose of raising cane sugar."

"The United States Government has no wish to interfere with the peaceful running of your plantation and the continued export of your crop," he went on. "We have made contact with the owners of most of the estates between here and New Orleans. Those who are willing to sign an oath of loyalty to the United States Government will be permitted to continue on as they always have."

"I see," said Emilie slowly. "And just what does this oath declare?"

"That you are loyal to the Constitution of the United States and that you are in no way engaged with her enemies in her destruction, that you neither aid, abet, nor harbor any Reb soldiers nor engage in any other activities harmful to the war effort of the United States of America."

"And if I do not agree?" Emilie asked, her heart pounding.

"Then under the regulations of the military government which is administering this area, we are obliged to confiscate your property, either to be given over to the United States Government or attached under a lien to one of your neighbors who has declared himself in support of the Federal Government."

"I see," said Emilie drily. "And which of my neighbors have already agreed to your oath?"

"That is military information which is not to be shared with suspect citizens," the soldier replied.

"Indeed!" Emilie said. "And am I suspect?"

"Everyone who has not declared himself loyal to the government is suspect, ma'am."

Emilie sat still for a moment. She was no more prepared to deal with this totally unexpected development from the Yankees than she had been with the Confederate soldier who had appeared only moments before at her back door. She was more than aware of the terrible danger which his presence thrust on her and the entire future well-being of Les Chandelles, but he was a special emissary from Guy.

And, from all she could gather of his message, perhaps he was the last person who had spoken with Guy while he was still alive. Her mind spun with the danger and confusion she now found swirling all around her.

She looked up at the Yankee captain. "You must give me a moment or two in which to consider, sir," she said. In her heart she was prepared to do anything that would save the plantation. But someday the war would be over and there would be all of the rest of parish to still have to live with. Until she knew what others had done, she felt afraid to make a decision on her own.

"My husband's parents are the owners of the plantation that lies just north of here," she said at last. "I must ask your permission to confer with them on this matter. It is of too grave a consequence to me to decide by myself."

"The roads have been closed to all but military travel, ma'am," was the immediate answer.

"Then I suppose I shall have to rely on your gallantry, Captain," Emilie countered. "Since you are visiting all the plantations in this area you may surely escort me the several miles to my in-laws."

For the first time since entering the mansion, the young officer looked unsure of himself. Emilie noted this with a grim satisfaction. She tried to keep her mind clear, for she knew only too well how a single wrong word or step could seal her fate as well as that of the plantation. Yet the name of Guy kept tugging at her heart. She felt as though she were going to choke, unless she could learn at once what fate had befallen her beloved and either know that he was still somehow alive or be allowed to fling herself into grief were that not the case. She could scarcely breathe. Yet here she was, with three Yankees staring at her, looking only too ready to pounce at the slightest provocation.

"Surely there is no danger to your conduct of the war nor your governance of this parish to permit one helpless female such as myself to travel to her nearest relations," she challenged.

"Are you the only white lady on this whole plantation?" the Yankee captain asked, changing the subject completely.

"Yes, I am," Emilie said haughtily.

"Aren't you a little afraid, ma'am?" It was almost the same kind of challenge she had thrown him, with an even more cutting undertone than Emilie had dared assume.

"Only of you, Captain," she answered sweetly.

That didn't deter him. "And if I agree to take you along with us to this other plantation," he said, "who would be left in charge here?"

"My butler Robert is completely capable of watching over the household while I'm gone," Emilie said, "and I do not contemplate being away for more than part of a day. It is not a long trip by any means."

"That would be the place called Les Saules, I believe," the captain said.

"Quite right," Emilie said, making her voice sound a little warmer. It suddenly seemed to her that the very best thing would be to talk with Guy's parents. Even if they could not confer privately she would at least be able to follow the old man's lead in dealing with this newest problem.

"I can be ready in a moment," Emilie declared. "And my carriage will have very little difficulty in keeping up with your horses."

"You'll drive yourself, ma'am?" There was a hint of mockery in the captain's voice now.

"No indeed, captain," Emilie replied almost gaily. "How could I hope to make such fast time with only myself at the reins? I'll have my best driver."

"The lady seems quite determined," the captain remarked to the other soldiers. Both men grinned back. "Colonel Phillips is going to have his hands full."

Emilie didn't know what he meant and didn't care. The words were spoken when she had already turned her back. She started quickly up the stairs for a wide-brimmed bonnet and shawl. She told the startled Missy to run to the stables and have the small two-seater readied for her, with Hubert at the reins.

"I don't want to go down there, Miss Emilie," Missy said.

Emilie stared at her as if dumbstruck for a moment, then she raised her hand as if to slap the disobedient slave into moving. "What's come over you, girl?" she snapped. "How dare you!"

"That's Yankee soldiers down there, Miss Emilie," Missy was sobbing. "I'm afraid to go down!"

Emilie almost laughed despite the grimness of the

situation. So this was her slave's reaction to the great liberating army of the North! "Go on along with you, Missy," she said in a kindly voice. "Those soldiers won't do anything to hurt you. Besides, they're coming with me to Les Saules."

Missy's eyes widened. "You're going traveling with Yankees?"

"Yes, I am," Emilie replied firmly. "And if you don't go and do what you're told this minute I'll take you along and leave you with them."

Missy moved swiftly down the stairs. Emilie stood at the balcony watching, amused to see that the girl scampered to the back of the house. She would exit through the kitchen rather than go near the three blue-clad men who stood in the front salon.

Emilie drew on her gloves and then walked slowly down the stairs. "I will be ready to leave as soon as I have informed my butler," she said. And before any of the men could stop her, she too went off to the kitchen. She continued the same measured pace, walking for all the world as though she were truly mistress not only of the plantation but of the entire situation in which she found herself intricately bound.

"Robert is to be in full charge of the house until my return," Emilie declared loudly to the few servants who were in the kitchen. The butler nodded briefly, then Emilie turned to the cook and whispered, "Is he well hidden?"

"Yes'm," gaunt Tess answered. "He be safe for sure."

"Robert, I shall hold you completely responsible for the next several hours until I return. These are sorry times for all of us. But I want the servants not to be afraid. The Yankees are coming with me, and if all goes well I shall return without them. In any event everything is to go on as usual."

"Yes, ma'am."

Emilie walked back to the front salon, indicating with a nod of her head that she was ready to leave.

The small carriage had been brought out front, and Hubert helped her to mount. Seeing Missy sidling back to the house, Emilie called out to her.

"There's room in here for you too, Missy," she said. "Come along with me to Les Saules. I may have need of you."

The terror in Missy's eyes softened somewhat when she realized that she was to accompany her mistress on the inside seat, something that had never occurred before. Usually a slave would have sat up on the front bench with the driver, totally exposed to the heat of the sun and dust of the road. Missy forgot her fear of the officers and clambered up alongside Emilie.

The Union officer wheeled his horse in front of them, and the small convoy set out at a regular clip, the officer remaining in front of the carriage and the two soldiers on either side of it.

As they rode along Emilie tried to clear her mind. She wanted only the sweet peace in which to cry out the grief that clutched at her heart. Guy was dead, she knew it, even though the soldier had not been able to tell it to her in just those words. Yet in order to save everything that Guy held dear, she had to clamp an iron bond around her emotions and conduct herself as though she knew nothing at all about him. The terror which had first struck her at the sight of the dark-blue uniforms had been changed to pure hatred. How she wished she had a gun with which to put a single small bullet in each of the backs that stood out so clearly in front of her. The two men kept their horses alongside those of the carriage. Emilie was sure that with the proper weapon she could have dispatched all three quickly to a much further destination than even that cold hard North from which they had come.

Emilie had not been able to visit her in-laws since the morning of the great thundering battle on the river. Now as she hurried toward their presence she wondered who would be the comforter. Would she, from the strength of youth, be able to instill some hope in Guy's parents, or would she be the one to lean on their strength and maturity? She realized with a start that even if she knew for sure that the beloved elder son had indeed fallen for his country, almost as hard as being able to bear that loss herself would be having to convey it to his parents.

Against the greenness of the foliage they were passing, Emilie's mind kept superimposing images of Madame Charpentier, the wise and willful face with its white tresses. She remembered easily how the old woman had looked at and spoken to Guy. Emilie shivered, praying inwardly that the day would never come that she must bear the news of that loss to his mother.

She sat stock still in the carriage now. Hubert reined in the horses to set them on the drive leading to Les Saules, and for a moment the Yankee soldiers wheeled about in confusion at the unexpected turnoff.

Emilie smiled to herself, but only for a moment. At least there was this one small satisfaction to be gained.

Now they were riding along under the graceful trees that arched and met overhead for the length of the avenue. The drive was much narrower than the road they had come off, and the Yankees were obliged to ride in single file, the captain in front of the cabriolet and the two other men behind it.

Emilie leaned forward to urge Hubert to drive faster. She wanted the sound of galloping hoofbeats to reach the main house as quickly as possible, as a way of warning her inlaws.

When at last they were in sight of that graceful white house she could hear the stir of many voices and much movement from within. As they drew up front, Emilie was startled to see the aging figure of Guy's father standing on top of the stairs that led to the veranda, his hand on the hilt of a sword that was buckled onto his waist.

"This is Charpentier property," he shouted at the bluecoats. "What business have you here?"

The young captain touched his fingers to his cap. "The business of the Army of the United States of America," he said, "and the accompanying of your daughter-in-law from the next plantation."

The old man peered into the carriage. "Emilie, here!" he exclaimed starting down the steps. "If you've done anything to harm her—" He didn't finish the sentence.

Emilie jumped quickly from the carriage without waiting for anyone to help her and ran up the stairs. She threw her arms around him, kissing his cheek and hastening to assure him that she had not been touched.

"I've asked them to bring me here, *cher Papa*," she said, "because I must speak with you."

She took his arm gently and they turned, mounting the stairs to the veranda. Just then Madame Charpentier came out.

"Emilie! What are you doing here?" she exclaimed. "We have been told that the roads are closed and completely unsafe for travelers."

"I'm quite all right, my dear Mama, I assure you," Emilie said, kissing her. "I have my military escort, as you can see, so I am quite safe from all dangers." She regarded the three soldiers lightly, but Madame

Charpentier glared down at them as though they represented the very shades of hell.

"What are they doing on this property?" she demanded, but the question was directed to her husband and not to the soldiers.

"We must go inside and talk," Emilie urged, hoping to draw them inside before the soldiers could follow. "They have asked me to sign an oath to the Union," she continued quickly, once they were inside the front salon. "Otherwise Les Chandelles will be confiscated and turned over to the Yankees or to someone else in the parish who has sworn loyalty. They claim they are demanding this of all the planters."

"Whatever are we to do?" Madame Charpentier asked.

"I don't know," Emilie admitted. "That's why I came here. It seems to me that we must do whatever is right in order to retain our property, but I did not want to make such a move without consulting with you first." She turned to her father-in-law. "I cannot conceive of swearing loyalty to them, nor can I willingly let them take Les Chandelles from me," she said. "But I come here, dear Father, to take counsel with you. I will act as you do and however you may suggest. Perhaps it is best for us to go along with them, at least until the time when our country is ours again."

"But what of the other planters?" Madame Charpentier asked before her husband could answer Emilie. "What have the others done?"

"Alas, they will not tell me," Emilie said. "At first I had thought that I must do the same as the others, but since they will not say what that is I begged them to permit me to come here to see you."

At that moment the captain and his men entered.

Armand Charpentier put his hand once more on his sword, but the gesture was meaningless; neither weapon nor bearer had seen service since the Mexican troubles in 1846. Even the young soldiers who stood watching recognized that the gesture was no more than the last effort of an old man to declare himself.

Madame Charpentier felt no such need. She made no offer to her unwelcomed visitors to sit or to partake of refreshment. The three Charpentiers stood facing their adversaries, equal in number, but far outweighing them in any balance that might be struck.

The captain repeated the conditions that he had told Emilie earlier.

Monsieur Charpentier blinked for a moment. Yet when he spoke his voice was firm.

"As the head of this family and the owner of this plantation, I will agree to sign any stipulation that ensures my land to me and permits no damage nor removal of my property. In this I speak for all here."

"Very good," the captain said. "But although I understand your relationship to this young woman"—he nodded toward Emilie,—"I am not given to understand that you can speak for Les Chandelles, sir."

"My father-in-law has spoken for me, as he just indicated," Emilie said firmly. "And what obtains at Les Saules obtains at Les Chandelles as well. You will have my oath."

The captain seemed visibly to relax. "Very good," he said again, and again repeated the gesture with his cap that Emilie thought would drive her mad should she see him do it one more time. "General Butler will be advised of your acquiescence as quickly as possible," the captain went on. Half turning towards Emilie, he said, "I can assure you that our use of your property shall in no way cause it any harm; rather it will receive the fullest protection of the United States Army."

"What use?" Emilie demanded, suddenly shaken. "We have promised to sign the pledge that will keep our properties in our own hands. Of what use do you speak now?"

"Being that Les Chandelles is the largest plantation for an area of many miles, including several other parishes, and because of its especially fortuitous position along the river, it has been designated the headquarters for Colonel Jason Phillips, who is in command of this area."

Emilie could not believe her ears. "Do you mean to tell me that my house is to be quarters for a Yankee officer?" she demanded.

"Yes, ma'am," the Captain confirmed.

"How dare you! Why was I not told this at once before you told me about the oath or confiscation? Why wasn't I informed that the use of my property would have bearing on this pact? You are no gentleman!" She felt fury seize her and her body began to shake.

The only barely steadier arm of the old man reached out and held her by the waist.

Emilie bit her lip to keep a hot flood of tears from falling. She would rather fall herself, dead, in front of this blasted Yankee before letting him see her cry.

"Les Chandelles was ours to take, whether you were willing or not," he said quietly. "Since you have decided to sign the oath of loyalty it is not necessary to take any steps against you or your property. I'm sure that you can see that this is much the better way."

"And if I had not complied?" Emilie demanded.

"Then we would have simply taken if from you," he replied. "By armed means if necessary."

"Am I then to be kept from my home while your

coward of a commander takes it for his own purposes?" she asked.

"No indeed, ma'am," the captain answered in a softer voice. "As I have stated there will be no damage or even inconvenience to you. We want the business of the plantation to be carried on as usual. The presence of Colonel Phillips and his men will scarcely be noticeable to you."

"I rather doubt that!" Emilie shouted.

"It is unthinkable, sir, that my daughter-in-law share her roof with a Yankee officer," Madame Charpentier spoke up. "Especially while her husband, my son, is at this very moment fighting for the protection and preservation of that very land of which you speak."

At the mention of Guy, Emilie felt her knees go weak. She did not know how she would be able to stand a single moment longer.

"I am sorry if you find our presence so disagreeable, Madame," the captain was replying, "but the necessities of war displace the niceties of peace. I am sure that we shall no more infringe upon your famous hospitality than you will offer it to us." There was irony in his voice, but it was completely lost on his audience.

"Emilie to be in that house with Yankees!" Madame Charpentier could only mutter again indignantly.

There was nothing to be done.

Madame Charpentier wanted to accompany her daughter-in-law back to her home, but Emilie insisted that she stay at Les Saules, where her husband and her estate needed her. She tried to quell her in-laws' fears as best she could, but her own head was in such turmoil she scarcely knew what she was doing.

At last Madame Charpentier seemed resigned to letting Emilie return. "Look in Charles' study and see if you can't find his pistol," she whispered to Emilie as she embraced her goodbye for the dozenth time. "Sleep with it under your pillow, and if anyone dares to come near you—"

"I will sleep as I always have," Emilie laughed, relinquishing her mother-in-law's grip on her, "with Missy between me and the door. Although now perhaps I'll have one of the yard boys sleep outside in the corridor."

But Madame Charpentier demurred. "How long do you think it will be before the Yankees have incited them to kill us in our very beds?" she asked.

At last the captain insisted that they make their final farewells. He had secured the loyalty pledges, both of Les Saules and Les Chandelles, and he was anxious to return to the latter in order to conclude his business there on behalf of his Colonel.

As they rode back home Emilie was once more

filled with terror. She did not know when this unseen colonel proposed to take over her home, and she knew it was imperative that they get the young Confederate off the property as quickly as possible.

If only there was some way, she thought, to get him across the river. The other side of the Mississippi was still in Confederate hands, and if he could get into the western part of the state he would be able to rejoin the Confederate Army there.

But failing that, she must at least get him off the boundaries of Les Chandelles. Guy had told her many times, in their farewells, that her first duty was to protect herself and her property. Anything else had to follow.

And now she realized solemnly that that was all she had left of him: his warnings, his endearments, the two letters that had reached her since he had gone, and the two days and nights of lovemaking that he had warned might have to sustain her forever. Emilie choked back a sob. Was he gone? Dear God, could Guy really be gone? How was it possible to put still and make cold all that glorious manhood, all that bright shining beauty, all that strength and sustaining hope of life and love that he had been? She brushed the thought from her mind and brushed the tears that were starting to form from her eyes. Missy knew nothing of the young Confederate soldier, and the fewer people who knew that he was there, the safer she would be.

There were Tess, and the maid who had brought her the news, and then Robert. These three knew, and there was no telling how many others, but it would have to be tended to immediately. Emilie stayed silent, drawn inwardly by these thoughts all the way home.

After seeing her safely back to Les Chandelles, the Yankee soldiers wheeled their horses about and left.

Emilie breathed a sign of relief, but she knew that the feeling was only temporary. She did not know how long it would be before more blue-clad soldiers rode up the drive and deposited themselves at Les Chandelles permanently.

Throwing her shawl down on a chair as she passed quickly through the front salon, she sought the passageway to the kitchen.

Tess was standing in front of the stove. "Where is he, Tess?" Emilie demanded quickly. "I must see him at once."

Tess dropped her spoon and wiped her hands on her apron. She didn't say a word, but walked quickly out of the kitchen, pausing only long enough to hold the door open for her mistress. Emilie followed as Tess shooed the black babies playing in the yard out of her path. Emilie followed the tall figure to an area she had not set foot in since she was a child herself. These were the storerooms and smokehouses that clustered among the trees beyond the kitchen. Some were used for the preserving of meats, others for the storage of fruits and vegetables. There was even a small closet-size structure that served as an ice house where the frozen substance that cooled their summer beverages could sometimes be kept. Tess went to one of the buildings farthest back in the trees. She glanced about quickly to make sure that no one else was following them. She pushed the door open and stood waiting for the mistress to enter in front of her.

Emilie's nostrils were assailed by what she thought must surely be the rotting of many pounds of potatoes. Through the cracks in the walls there was enough light for her to make out the figure of the fugitive sprawled on the floor. He started to get up as Emilie approached him, but the young woman dropped swiftly to her knees.

"Tell me quickly," she pleaded. "My husband—is he still alive?"

The man closed his eyes. It was as though he were afraid to face her. Then slowly he shook his head. Emilie sat there petrified, afraid that if she released her anguish she would never be able to stop it. The tall figure of Tess stood equally still. Then the soldier broke the silence.

"His last words were of you, ma'am," he said quietly. "He begged me to make my way back here to tell you that."

"How—how did you manage to leave the army and come here?" Emilie asked.

"I ain't no deserter, ma'am," the soldier answered quickly. "But after the battle in which the colonel was killed, it just wasn't the same any more. Our whole company seemed to break and run. We knew the Yankees would be coming to fight us down here, and I reckon most men were trying to get back to protect their own homes and families."

"The war is far from lost, I'm sure of it," Emilie said staunchly, but the words didn't seem convincing even to her.

She stood up slowly. "Are you from nearby?" she asked.

"I'm from Louisiana, ma'am, but not near here," he answered. "I come from up around Shreveport, near the Arkansas border."

"That area is still in Confederate hands, thank God," Emilie said. "If we can get you across the river, you should have no trouble rejoining the army in the west."

"Thank you kindly, ma'am. If you can just see fit to provision me I can make my own way out of here. I wouldn't want to be causing any trouble for you. Colonel Charpentier, he said—"

"We'll give you everything that you need," Emilie cut him off. "Tess will bring it to you by nightfall. I assume it will be easier for you to travel during the night."

"Yes, ma'am," he said.

"We can also give you some blankets and anything else you might need," Emilie added.

"That would be good, ma'am. I'm sure obliged to you."

"Would it be easier if you had a mount?" Emilie asked.

"You mean like a horse, ma'am?" he asked.

"I don't know as if we can manage a horse, but perhaps a mule," Emilie replied.

"I'm afraid not, ma'am, but thank you just the same," he said. "I could never get an animal across the river if there are any Yankees around. I'd be questioned and found out for sure."

"Perhaps we can give you a suit of clothes, then," Emilie said. "You would not be very safe if the Yankees were to find you in your uniform."

"True enough," he agreed.

"Very well, then," Emilie said. "Everything will be made ready for you this evening. I wish you Godspeed and I thank you for the comfort you gave my husband in his final moments."

"He gave me this to give to you, ma'am," the soldier said, and he reached inside his shirt. Then, standing up, he handed Emilie a round metal object.

When she took it from him she realized it was Guy's gold pocket watch. She held it in her palm for a moment, staring at it. Then with a start she realized it was ticking. "I can hear it," she said almost to herself.

"I've been winding it every day to keep it in good order for you, ma'am," the soldier said. "I figured that was the best thing."

"It's almost as though—as though his heart were still beating," Emilie said. She held the gold watch against her cheek. Its ticking seemed to match her own pulse. "I must go now," she said hurriedly. "Thank you again." She ran out of the small room without waiting to see if Tess was following. She ran all the way back to the big house, up the stairs and into her room, flinging herself, the watch pressing her bosom, on her bed and crying with sobs such as had never before rent the air of Les Chandelles.

Missy stood silently watching her for a moment, then slipped out of the room. It looked as if the mistress would be hysterical and inconsolable for a long time. When she felt in need of her servant at last, she could come and seek for her. Missy hurried downstairs, as far away from the dreadful noise as she could get.

Emilie did not know how long she stayed like that. Her body was so drained of strength that she could barely raise herself up on her elbows to stare out the window, through which she could see that darkness had fallen. It was as though the brightness of day had passed before her grief and would never return again. The long dark night would be all she would know now.

Too tired even to look for Missy or to remove her clothes, she fell asleep at last, the precious gold memento thrust beneath the pillow that was soaked with her tears.

The sun did rise, however, and woke her from the fitful agony of dreams. Her mind had spent the night walking in bloody battlefields, searching for her beloved. Bright daylight gave no respite to her grief. The night was still the setting for Emilie's soul, and fresh day with its new problems held out no hope. It was as though sorrow had found her and would not easily relinquish her. Rather it would grasp her by both hands and render her helpless for as long as it could keep her in thrall.

In the morning she remembered the messenger who had brought her the terrible news, and she turned around and went back into the kitchen.

"Has he gone yet?" she whispered to Tess.

The startled cook was taken aback for a moment, and then realized whom her mistress meant. "Yes, ma'am," she mumbled.

"Good, that's good," Emilie replied, hoping to herself that he had gotten away safely. "You gave him everything that he needed?"

"Yes, ma'am," the cook replied.

It was only then that Emilie realized that she didn't even know the man's name. In all her grief and the confusion she had forgotten this simplest of courtesies. Nor, she reprimanded herself, had she even thought to press into his hand some money, which she was sure he was in sore need of. Emilie shook her head and walked slowly back to the front salon. What is happening to me? she wondered. Have I so taken leave of my senses that I can no longer conduct myself as I should? She thought then of her mother and the derangement that she had gone through during the last few years of her life. Dear God, Emilie thought, I pray no such thing is happening to me. I must survive the loss of my beloved if only to protect his memory. She walked outside and clasped her hands against the side of one of the great round columns. She sighed again for the still-ruined mansion whose repair the war prevented and wondered when, if ever, she and her house would be whole again.

Emilie was shaken from her reverie by the sight of two Union soldiers coming across the great lawn dragging a cart between them. These were not any of the three young officers who had accompanied her to Les

Saules, she quickly realized. They seemed a much more common sort, and she supposed them to be ordinary foot soldiers. She started to call out to them angrily at their daring to trespass on her property and in such a careless way as to damage the carefully nurtured green of the wide swath in front of the house.

But as they came closer, she staggered against the pillar, her arms reaching unconsciously for its support. Dangling from one side of the cart was what she knew to be a human limb. But surely no living person could have been so unceremoniously heaped into the small hand vehicle that carried what she now knew to be a corpse.

As they drew closer, passing in front of her, Emilie gasped. It seemed to her that the sound she unwittingly made had been so huge as to echo back and forth against the house and back onto that green expanse, but the soldiers paid her no mind, continuing to trudge along toward the roadway, the now recognizable body of Guy's orderly slumped dead in their cart.

He wore the nondescript clothing that she had ordered given to him, but its dun color had so soaked up its wearer's blood that the garments seemed vivid scarlet now. Emilie clutched her hands in disbelief, mindless in her agony of the precious object she had been holding, unconscious of it indeed until it fell from her hands and smashed on the wooden planks of the veranda.

She looked down in shock at the sound. It was only then as the morning light caught the glitter of the gold that she realized what she had done. Guy's watch lay smashed and broken on the floor at her feet, little fragments of shattered glass glinting up at her accusingly.

13

By the next morning she had come back to her usual senses. The pressing routine of the plantation demanded it, and Emilie threw herself headlong into work that she had been neglecting. The Yankees had determined that the great sugar plantations, which represented some of the largest fortunes in the United States, North or South, must be maintained and continue in operation. The boats that came to carry off the hogsheads again filled the river once Farragut's fleet had done its work. In a short time, the Yankee captain had intimated, traffic on the roads would be restored to normal as well. Business was going on almost as usual. Once again the great plantations toiled and baked under the relentless sun, bringing to harvest and then to market the crop on which their economy depended.

The sound of horses approaching made her wonder if the roads had indeed been reopened to regular traffic already. Moving swiftly to the front of the house, Emily quickly realized that these were the sounds of no ordinary number of visitors. She stood stock still for a moment wondering whether to go out and see who it was or wait for the arrivals to announce themselves. She remembered the sight of her elderly father-in-law standing at the head of the stairs in front of his house when she arrived with the three Yankee soldiers. She decided she must do the same. Besides, if these were the Yankees, and they probably were, she would just as soon they not be obliged to step foot inside her house.

Robert held the door back as Emilie went out. Officers and men were already dismounting in front of the house, but what was even more startling to her eyes was the long line of additional blue uniforms that seemed to fill the driveway nearly as far as the eye could see.

At the foot of the veranda a black stallion was being held while a large man dismounted. Emilie caught sight of a fierce-looking black mustache and heavily browed eyes of the same color beneath a wide-brimmed hat. From the way his horse was being held and the resplendence of yellow braid that broke the monotony of his dark-blue uniform, she guessed that this man was an officer of importance.

He signaled to another officer, whom Emilie instantly recognized as the man who had been in charge of the first visit of Yankees to Les Chandelles. Once more he gave that odd salute of his and handed her a sealed envelope.

Emilie took it without a word and tore it open. She scanned the single sheet inside quickly, and although some of it was couched in rather difficult language she understood the main import: It was an order, signed by the military governor in New Orleans, stating that the plantation was to become the field headquarters of Colonel Jason R. Phillips. The mansion and all its facilities were to be opened to him and suitable area found within the confines of the estate for housing the tents of the company he commanded.

Emilie handed the letter back.

Not a word had been spoken. The silence was broken only by the sounds made by the soldiers farther down the road, unloading their equipment and calling to one another.

She completely ignored the tall figure of the rather formidable officer. But at last he disengaged himself from his men and stepped forward, looking directly up at her.

"I will require the use of a bedchamber for myself and a suitable room on the main floor of the house for use as my office," he said. "My junior officers will be bivouacked with the men out here."

"Surely not on my lawn!" Emilie cried. "There is more than enough space in the meadow between here and the river for your army, sir. It is not necessary that the beauty of my home be totally destroyed, I trust." Her lip was quivering.

"Of course not, madam," the officer said. His looks softened somewhat as he spoke. "I have quite forgotten my manners, I'm afraid. Please allow me to introduce myself. I am Colonel Jason Phillips, commanding the 71st Regiment, General Benjamin Butler's Louisiana."

"I am Madame Emilie Charpentier," Emilie replied.

"I believe you have already met my second in command, Captain Rogers here," Colonel Phillips said, indicating the officer who had accompanied Emilie on her brief trip to Les Saules.

Again she nodded.

"Again I must apologize, Madame Charpentier," Colonel Phillips went on.

Emilie nearly winced at the way he pronounced the name, the soft and fragile French syllables very nearly broken by his hard flat Ohio accent.

"Is there anything that you require of me?" Colonel Phillips was asking her.

Emilie looked at him sharply. His dark eyes and full drooping mustache frightened her. He very nearly fit the description of those Mexican desperadoes that the elder Charpentier described when recounting his exploits in the war of '46.

"Yes, Colonel," Emilie said. "I should like a brace of pistols, ammunition for them, and one of your officers to instruct me in their use."

The Colonel threw his head back and laughed. "Are you planning to join our forces?" he asked.

"I am going to defend myself, if need be," Emilie replied coldly. "I shall keep the pistols at my bedside constantly."

"You really are not in need of protection against me, ma'am," Colonel Phillips said, his voice gentler. "Since you have signed the oath of loyalty, the safety of your person, as well as that of your estate, is entirely my responsibility, and I mean to execute that responsibility as befits an officer of this army."

"And I am the widow of an officer in the Confederate Army of America," Emilie found herself saying, "and I mean to place my honor and that of his sacred memory in my own hands."

"I'm sorry to hear of your bereavement," the Colonel said. "When did your husband fall?"

"At Chancellorsville," Emilie said.

The colonel's face suddenly darkened. In one move he bolted up the veranda stairs, taking Emilie by the arm, walking her inside the house, and motioning for Captain Rogers to follow.

Emilie was unnerved by the suddenness of it all. "What do you mean, sir?" she started to demand as she regained her breath.

The three of them were standing in the front salon. She tried to wrest her elbow from his grip, but his fingers only tightened.

He turned to his captain. "We've controlled this entire area since the beginning of April," Colonel Phillips said. "Chancellorsville was fought in the early part

of May. How can she have found out about her
husband?"

Emilie was suddenly grateful for his hold on her
arm. Without it, she was sure, she would have fallen
to the floor.

"Your concern with honor, ma'am, does not seem
to extend to spying or the harboring of spies," Colonel
Phillips said. "How did you get this news of your husband?"

"From a simple soldier in his command who made
his way back here after the battle," Emilie answered.
She saw no point in further arousing their suspicions
by an obvious lie on her part.

"And where is this soldier now?" Colonel Phillips
asked.

"Dead," Emilie replied steadily. "I saw your soldiers
with his body."

"Your oath of loyalty to the Federal Government
expressly forbids your aiding and abetting rebels and
spies," the colonel said. "I'm afraid that your honor
did not extend there either."

"The soldier came just prior to my signing of your
oath, Colonel," Emilie said simply. "I can assure you
on my honor it has not and will not be violated by me."

" 'Your honor!' " Colonel Phillips echoed. "What an
odd concept of it that is."

"Not to the people of this state, I assure you," Emilie
said. "And if you do not understand that, I'm afraid
that your rule over us will prove to be very difficult."

"I believe that I am the one who should be sleeping
with a brace of pistols at hand while I am under your
roof, madam," Colonel Phillips said. Emilie could not
tell whether or not he was serious. He abruptly released
her arm and strode back outside.

"I'm sorry, ma'am," Captain Rogers said. "I had
hoped that our staying here would cause very little

difficulty both for you and for us. I'm afraid that what you've done will make that less possible. We are going to have to watch your activities a great deal more closely. I beg you not to do anything so heedless again, for your own sake."

"Captain, a man came here through great hardship to bring my husband's dying words to me," Emilie said. "Do you really expect me to have acted in any other way? There are women in the North, I am sure, who are being brought the same terrible news of their loved ones. Do you suppose my feelings to be any less than theirs?"

"No, ma'am, of course not," came the reply. "Still, your situation, because of the nature of the war, is quite different."

"I know that," said Emilie, "certainly now, if I hadn't before. We are a conquered land and being treated as a conquered people."

"I assure you that you will be accorded every courtesy and consideration," Captain Rogers said quickly. "On that Colonel Phillips is a stickler."

"Colonel Phillips has seen fit to make himself my enemy," Emilie said, "whether he is acting on orders or by his own design. We can never be anything other than enemies."

"If that's so, ma'am, it's for different reasons than you think," Captain Rogers said. "In that you stand no different than anyone else. But let me assure you again you have absolutely nothing to fear from Colonel Phillips."

Emilie was struck by what he was saying, and the slow grin that was spreading over his face as he spoke. "Indeed, Captain," she said. "And why not?"

"Because," came the answer from behind an irrepressible grin, "Colonel Phillips hates all women."

Under the relentless sun of the hottest time of the
year, Les Chandelles throbbed and sweltered with the
burden of its dual activities. In the brakes the cane
crop was being laid by, utilizing by far the greatest
number of field hands. Other slaves were equally busy
cutting the enormous quantities of wood that would
be needed to keep the fires in the sugar house going
for the boiling down of the cut cane. The more skilled
among the hands worked as coopers, fashioning from
staves of wood the hogsheads and molasses barrels in
which the syrup would be shipped downriver to the
port. Henrique had reported to Emilie that the ditches
which provided drainage for the growing lands were
much in need of repair, and several gangs of slaves
with shovels had to be assigned to this task in order
that the fields be properly watered for the next year's
seed cane, which would be laid in early fall.

At the same time as the plantation went about its
unending business, Jason Phillips kept his soldiers
equally, if not as fatiguingly, busy. The blueshirts had
been encamped in the meadows between the house
grounds and the river only a day before the entire
company was mustered and the work assignments
read out to them. There would be men stationed at
the entrance to Les Chandelles' long drive, as well as
at various points along its boundaries. Other men
were set to building a tall observation tower from
which traffic up and down the great river could be
easily observed. This activity had Emilie most concerned. Henrique had explained to her the need for
the vast amounts of timber that were cut each year,
both for the fueling of the sugar-house fires and for
the manufacture of the all-important shipping barrels.
As Emilie watched the Yankees' tower rising, she
thought bitterly of how much needed timber they
were taking from her.

Equally troubling was the amount of food being consumed by the ravenous army. Although they were supposed to be fed on field rations, much of which was shipped upriver from New Orleans regularly, they much preferred to live off the land. The acreage set aside for the growing of vegetables for both the great house and the quarters was being severely depleted by the soldiers. Farmers themselves for the most part, they delighted in being able to obtain the fresh produce they were used to getting at home.

It was the first occasion Emilie had had that required her to complain directly to Colonel Phillips. She had let all sorts of minor inconveniences pass by, willing to forgo justice in order not to have to confront him. But now Henrique's reports were too worrisome. She had been informed that Les Chandelles was expected to market its usual crop this year, but nobody told her how she was supposed to do it if she couldn't provide enough food for her workers.

She had felt rather pleased with herself and her ability to avoid the colonel. He slept in a bedchamber at the farthest end of the hall from hers. An orderly slept in a blanket roll in front of his door. Emilie kept Missy in her own bedchamber, and besides those pistols he had finally agreed to, she posted one of the yardmen in the corridor in front of her own chamber. She took all of her meals in her room, thus avoiding him at table, while the colonel, along with Captain Rogers and one or two other officers from time to time, ate in the dining room. Likewise, she continued to use the small office for keeping the plantation books and conducting her business with Henrique and the household staff, while Jason Phillips had taken the library for his headquarters and even now sat in the large black leather chair that had belonged to Charles Bonfils.

Emilie had to grit her teeth before approaching the

door to that room and the colonel inside. But she knew that the foraging for vegetables had to stop, and there was only one way to do it.

She opened the door. Jason Phillips was seated behind Charles' desk; Captain Rogers and another young officer were on either side of him. The desk itself was strewn with maps and papers that the three of them had been examining. They looked up in surprise as Emilie walked in.

"Madam Spy!" Colonel Phillips shouted. "How dare you walk in here without receiving permission?"

"This is my house," answered Emilie coolly. "And I am not accustomed to ask permission to enter one of my rooms. There is a matter of great importance that I must discuss with you."

"I must remind you that this is not one of 'your' rooms," he replied. "This is my headquarters, whether you like it or not. We are at war and the conventional niceties of your former life are of absolutely no consideration now."

Emilie winced, remembering how similar his words were to Guy's when he told her of the great change that would come into their lives. "What I have to talk to you about is of utmost importance," Emilie repeated. "It is a matter we must deal with at once."

"Very well," the colonel said, folding the maps and motioning his junior officers into chairs.

Emilie sat down, not waiting to be told to do so.

"Well, what is it?" Colonel Phillips demanded.

"Your troops are stealing my vegetables," Emilie said. "At the rate that the fields are being raided there will be no way for me to feed my slaves."

The three officers exchanged glances.

"If, as you said, your main concern is the maintenance of this plantation and its capacity to continue to produce a sugar crop, you'll understand how important this is and see that it is stopped immediately."

"An army travels on its stomach," snickered the other young officer, whom Emilie did not know. "Wasn't it one of your Frenchies who said that?"

"I really don't know," said Emilie, "and I really don't care. This army of yours is not traveling, in any case; it has fastened itself on my plantation and is rapidly depleting it."

"How many hands do you employ here?" Colonel Phillips asked.

"About two hundred," Emilie answered. "The same number as you have soldiers. Surely the same fields cannot be expected suddenly to nourish double the number of mouths."

"So Madame Spy has already counted our troops," Colonel Phillips remarked drily.

"My slaves must eat if they are to work!" Emilie cried, ignoring his slur.

"May I remind you, madam, that the blacks are no longer your slaves," the colonel said. "The Emancipation Proclamation issued by the Federal Government in Washington declares all hands in the slaveholding states to be free. Your employees can go whenever they wish. Hundreds have already walked off other plantations. Might I remind you that it is only our presence here that keeps your hands from doing the same."

"These people are mine," Emilie shouted, "just as this house is, the fields are, all of the land is."

"That temper is," the colonel said. "I am sure no one would wish to lay claim to that. Not even an order from Lincoln himself could likely control it."

"Lincoln himself!" Emilie very nearly spat out the words. "What does he know of conditions here? Of what life is like for us and what our needs are? How dare he meddle with things he knows nothing about?"

"He knows that people are meant to be free and that one is not supposed to own another," Jason Phillips said quietly. "And that is something that you are going to have to learn to accustom yourself to."

"I've been up North and seen your great mansions," Emilie said. "And I've seen your Irish servants who are made to do no differently from our slaves and lead much the same kind of lives."

The men looked at each other. "We are farmers," the colonel answered her, "and simple townspeople for the most part. We know nothing of cities and servants and the great mansions you speak of."

"Then I am forced to say to you, Colonel," Emilie replied disdainfully, "that I am more familiar with Yankee ways than you are with our Southern ones."

"I doubt that very much," the captain said. "Irish servants or indeed servants of any kind are not part of our way of life. What you may have seen up North is no more representative of our section than one woman living alone in complete mastery over the lives of hundreds of other people is true of the South. You too are primarily a land of farmers and small-holdings, and it is to those truer representatives of this section that this land will someday be returned. You and those like you have ridden on the backs of others, black and white, quite long enough."

This rather long speech on the part of the colonel left Emilie quiet.

"However, I do not think this is a subject I need discuss with you," the colonel continued. "Of much more moment, I agree with you, is the condition of the vegetable fields and how we are to deal with it."

He turned to Captain Rogers and gave him an order which the captain quickly copied out, to the effect that the men were to be fed from the usual camp rations and that they were forbidden to forage. Additional sentries were to be posted around the fields and a lieutenant assigned the task of overseeing the work there, in place of the slave who had been doing it.

"Very good, sir," Captain Rogers said as he finished copying the orders. With a gesture Colonel Phillips dismissed both men. Emilie rose to go, but he motioned her to remain seated. When the other officers had left the study, he said, "Now that the matter of feeding the hands has been settled, I must turn my attention to that of the mistress."

Emilie made no comment.

"General Butler is making a tour of inspection in this area," Phillips went on. "He will be here on this coming Thursday. I want you to take dinner with us at table that night. The general will be pleased to see that everything is going on as usual at Les Chandelles."

"But it's not!" Emilie protested. "And I will not sit down to eat with Yankees!"

"Yes, you will," he said, "and in your loveliest dress. We will sit down promptly at seven, but I will expect you in the small drawing room at six, to preside over cordials."

Emilie started to protest again, but one look at Jason Phillips and she knew it would be of no avail. Then she remembered something. "I thought you hated women," she said. "Why is it suddenly so important that one be in your company?"

If the remark had any effect on him it did not show. "We're at war, madam," he said, as if he had to remind her of the fact. "And we must all do what is necessary and with whatever material is at hand. You will be in the small drawing room at six, this Thursday." He nodded his head and bent down to write something.

Emilie recognized the gesture—she had used it herself so often as a means of dismissing an overseer or slave from her company. She rose and left.

"Whatever shall I wear, Missy?" Emilie asked as she picked up one dress and then another only to throw them back on the bed and chairs, where half her wardrobe had by now been heaped. It was just short of two hours before she was commanded to appear. She had watched the arrival of General Butler and his escort earlier in the day and had made up her mind that she would not appear to bid him welcome. Her orders were to be present at six o'clock, and she made up her mind that she would do nothing but obey those orders to the letter.

She continued pacing and then, inwardly cursing all Northerners, she remembered something. "Missy, where is that black-and-white dress I had made in New York? That's fit enough to wear for Yankees, I suppose." Missy went to fetch the gown from the chest where it had lain ever since Mistress Emilie had ordered her to put it there on their return. Now she drew it out again and Emilie examined it minutely, smoothing the wrinkles out of the skirt.

"Fold it up and take it around to the laundry room at once," she ordered Missy. "Have Lucinda or someone else who's good with the press iron make it as presentable as possible. And mind she doesn't burn it. Then bring it back to me and you can dress my hair."

Emilie looked at her reflection in the mirror. That dress had incited one Yankee officer to near-rape. She smiled mischievously to think what effect it might have on General Benjamin Butler and the colonel, the woman-hating colonel, whose prisoner she considered herself.

When the dress had been restored to its original splendor and her hair had been properly put up by Missy, Emilie regarded herself in the tall glass again. If only Guy could have seen me like this, she thought, but she brushed that sad remembrance from her mind, forcing herself to concentrate instead on the game at hand.

Being isolated as she was she knew very little of General Butler, only that he had been given command of the state and had sequestered himself in New Orleans, supposedly for the duration of the war or until the Confederate Army managed to blow him out and send him back where he belonged. But of what type of man he was, she had absolutely no knowledge.

At precisely six Emilie, regally gowned and with her small, seldom-used ivory fan in her hand, sailed down the grand staircase of her house, determined to act the very essence of the Southern belle she knew she had never been. Sweeping into the small front salon, she smiled at the two men seated there, one familiar to her, the other not. Both rose hastily, and Emilie was slightly amused to see that in honor of the occasion Colonel Phillips had donned full dress uniform. She was able to take in his full height and rather impressive military bearing before she looked away from him and cast rather flirtatious eyes on the man who held half of Louisiana in his power.

"Madame Emilie Charpentier, General Butler," Colonel Phillips said simply, and with that Emilie sat down in a large tufted velvet chair facing both men, who had reseated themselves simultaneously.

"I am sorry we have not seen you down in New Orleans," General Butler said as Emilie signaled the slave to bring the silver service. "I am pleased to say that society is nowhere more congenial. Many people have remarked to me on the fact that life is as active and gay as it ever was before the war."

"I am afraid that I am much too involved with my duties here to be able to partake of New Orleans society," Emilie said. "Additionally, I am in mourning."

"Madame has informed me that Stonewall Jackson was not the only illustrious leader that the Confederacy lost at Chancellorsville," Colonel Phillips said. "Her late husband, Colonel Charpentier, also fell in that battle."

"I don't remember seeing his name in the dispatches," General Butler said, "but then a great deal of papers cross my desk. I am sure you will forgive me if I am not familiar with your late husband."

"Of course," Emilie murmured.

"Our gracious hostess is the recipient of more detailed news than we are, General," Colonel Phillips continued.

"How is that?" the General asked.

"Really, I think the colonel is exaggerating, sir," Emilie replied. "The only information that I have ever received during the course of this terrible war is the news of my husband's death."

She glared at Jason Phillips, who seemed to be somewhat enjoying her discomfort.

"Well, again, I'm sorry that you have chosen to keep yourself confined here, my dear," General Butler said. "I think that the liveliness of the city would prove more healing of the wounds you have suffered than the solitude in which you must find yourself most of the time."

"I thank the general very kindly, but I must stay where my responsibilities keep me," Emilie said.

"As you wish, of course," General Butler said gallantly. "Although unless I am much mistaken I would guess that our Colonel Phillips does not provide much companionship for you."

"Nor would I wish that he did, sir." Emilie's voice was indignant. She felt as though the general were making sport with her, egged on no doubt by the insinuations of the colonel. She would have liked to have lifted the silver teapot and poured the boiling water directly on the officers rather than in her delicate Sèvres cups they each held.

General Butler changed the conversation by directing several questions to Emilie that concerned the workings of the plantation. Much to her satisfaction she found that she was knowledgeable enough to answer him quite fully.

At the same time, she wished that her New York dress were cut not quite so low at the bosom. Several times during the conversation she noticed Colonel Phillips staring at her as though he could not quite take his eyes from the place where a row of stiff black lace barely sufficed to guard her modesty. Emilie was acutely aware of how little coverage it afforded when she had to lean over slightly to pour. If he hates women so, she thought, then he shouldn't be looking at me at all. But she realized that he had no more power to stop staring at the rise of her flesh than she did to tinge with color every time she found him doing it. It was with great relief that she heard the tall clock against the wall chime softly and she picked up a silver bell from the table to announce dinner.

She rose and the two men stood immediately. Emilie smiled, offering her hand to the general and making a wide path with her belling skirt as she walked with him, enjoying the fact that Colonel Phillips could do nothing more than follow in their wake.

Dinner was elaborate, to fit the high rank of the distinguished, if not quite wanted, guest. Tess had prepared *daube glacé,* a highly spiced beef dish with aspic. Complementing the meat was *maque choux,* a mélange of tomatoes and corn, and mirleton, a vegetable known only in that area. Before these platters were brought to the table, slaves passed around steaming dishes of court bouillon, made with the fresh red snapper that Tess favored. Emilie had protested when the cook had suggested beginning the meal with oysters. She felt it was enough that they were preparing so elaborate a dinner for the enemy without making it appear a festive celebration. Emilie had told her cook to add plenty of ground chicory root to the coffee that was brewed for dinner. She thought that the strong and unfamiliar flavor might hasten the general's early retirement from company.

She need not have concerned herself. Although conversation at the table was as pleasant as could be expected under the circumstances, General Butler showed no inclination to linger afterward, neither over the coffee nor over the excellent rum that was distilled from Les Chandelles' own sugar. He complimented Emilie lavishly on her beauty and her hospitality, and then asked to be excused and shown to his sleeping quarters, giving his early-morning departure as the reason for his retiring.

"I shall follow the general's example," Emilie said when she found herself alone in the large front salon with Colonel Phillips.

"Are you making a hasty departure in the morning as well?" he asked, but the mockery in his voice was contradicted by the expression in his eyes as he stared at her.

Emilie was flustered, finding herself once more the target of such unwanted and undeniable attention from him. She did not return his gaze but sat silently, eyes downward, busying herself with her fan. She knew that if one looked at Colonel Jason Phillips without hatred it would be impossible to deny that he was, in his dark way, an exceedingly handsome man. It was only the strong emotion she did feel against him and against the position she was in that kept Emilie from having to admit that fact even to herself.

He took a few steps closer, hovering over her. Emilie could nearly feel the shadow that his tall form cast.

"I wish to speak with you," he said suddenly and softly.

Emilie was silent.

He took this as a signal to continue. "It is not really necessary for us to confront each other as enemies while we are both under this roof." He paused. "It would be so much pleasanter and easier, I am sure, were we to resign ourselves to the situation and agree to make the best of it."

Emilie looked up abruptly. "I do not make friends with the murderers of my husband," she snapped. "Nor can I understand this need for pleasantry from me in one who hates all women!"

His eyes blazed as if on fire. Before Emilie knew what was happening he grasped her arms and pulled her to her feet, still glaring down at her with those fiery tortured eyes. "I do not hate all women!" he whispered hoarsely. The whisper might well have been a shout, so strong and forceful were his words.

Emilie stared at him as if not quite comprehending the strong emotion that had seized him.

He loosened his grip on her arms somewhat, and when he spoke his voice was more its normal tone.

"I do not hate all women," he repeated then. "And I have nothing but admiration for your constant expressions of loyalty toward your husband. Believe me, madam, I am sincere in this."

"I believe you," Emilie replied without quite knowing what she was saying. He released her, and for a moment she thought she was losing her balance, so tightly had he been supporting her. She felt quite alone for a moment, then reminded herself sharply that this was the enemy who had so gripped her, and she was thankful to be out of his grasp.

She realized with a start that this was the first time he had ever touched her. Again she admonished herself for even thinking such a thought. She was furious with herself and suddenly aware that the conflicting emotions she was feeling were no doubt showing themselves on her face.

"Please sit down," he said quietly, and Emilie found herself obeying without quite knowing why.

"I do not hate women," he repeated, "although God knows I have reason enough to. But when I tell you how much I admire you, please understand I do not use the words lightly. I know the difference between women, if any man does."

"What has this to do with me?" Emilie asked.

"Because I want you to understand." There was a pleading note in his voice, almost a cry of something within him demanding to be heard. "Will you listen?"

Emilie nodded. For some inexplicable reason, she did not trust the sound of her own voice.

"I was living in Ohio, on my father's farm, when I got married," Jason began, and even with these few simple words, Emilie thought she could discern an element of unburdening in him. Not only did his voice seem steadier, but the tenseness seemed to have gone from his body. "My father was a good man, hardworking in the extreme. He believed in the simple life, but he had a great deal of earthly wisdom. He tried to warn me, but I didn't listen. Only when it was late, much too late, did I appreciate what he had tried to save me from." He paused.

Emilie took advantage of his silence. "Are you sure you want to tell me all this?" she asked.

"Yes," he insisted. "I want you to know. I can't tell you how important it is to me."

"Very well, then," Emilie replied. She wondered if he wouldn't do better to go to Père Lachaise to have his soul shriven. But she didn't suggest it. She wanted to help him, yet she felt herself already apprehensive about his revelations without knowing why.

"I found myself very attracted to a young girl from across the county. She was so pretty, so fresh a sight to a boy who saw little around him but the endless fields and hard chores of a farm life." He paused. "Her name was Margaret, and she was from a farm family, too. I had no thought then of any other kind of life, no thought of the law or the army or any of the things that have happened to me. I thought to be a farmer like my father, and take a wife well used to the same ways."

"Were you very young then?" Emilie asked.

"We were schoolmates," Jason said. "During the winter months, between the fall harvest and spring planting, we children went to a small one-room schoolhouse in the valley to learn to read and cipher. But as soon as a boy was old enough, fifteen or sixteen, to do a full hand's work, schooling stopped. That was when I knew how much I missed not seeing her every day."

Emilie's mind was drifting with Jason's narration. She tried to imagine the life he was depicting, up there in the cold North, its snows and schoolchildren. It seemed a world away, another sphere.

"During the planting months we met only at church on Sundays. There was little time to talk, but when I spoke to her, she didn't discourage me. Poor fool that I was, this seemed to me enough to go calling on her."

"And your father?" Emilie asked. "You said he tried to warn you."

"Yes." Jason sighed. "Somehow he saw or sensed something about her that I was too young or too naive or too smitten to see. He warned me, but I didn't listen. I spoke to her father, he gave his consent, and my father did as he always said he would—bought a fine piece of acreage for me so I could start farming on my own."

He looked down at his hands, large, powerful, sinewy, not those of a professional or a city man. "I built the house myself, with the help of my brother and some friends. I wanted everything to be perfect for her. I lived all winter out there alone while I was building it. Most nights I wished I could have started with the roof and worked down." He smiled and rubbed his arm as if remembering and still feeling that long-ago cold. "We married in the spring when the house was finished. I worked like ten men that summer, clearing the rest of the ground, planting, raising livestock. I had never been so happy—too happy I suppose, to see that she wasn't. Oh, Margaret did everything a wife is supposed to, kept the house and all, but she was—restless, I guess is the word. She was always reading books, and getting after me to read them. In those days, reading was schoolboy's chores, something to do when there wasn't any farming to be done, and you had to. I couldn't understand what she found in those books of hers."

"Do you now?" Emilie asked gently.

"Yes," he replied grimly, "and I should have been glad when she found it in her reading. All those romances and novels, I just never understood then. Margaret didn't want farm life. She wanted romance and excitement and—and all those things that I thought I was giving her."

Emilie raised her arm as if in protest. She didn't want to hear.

Jason caught her signal and knitted his brow, trying to find other words. "She was a pretty girl, and she wanted more attention than I could give her, although I tried everything to please her. She was forever after me to take her places, into town and to the county seat, even to Cincinnati. Gallivanting, my father called it. And he was right, old Angus, he truly was."

"What's wrong with a woman's wanting to go shopping or visiting her neighbors? It doesn't seem so terrible to me," Emilie said.

"Miss Emilie, you've got a great estate, with servants at your beck and call, to do all of your bidding. A farm isn't like that. The land owns you as much as you own the land. You have to work at it all the time. Everyone."

"That's so," Emilie said slowly. "My father used to say almost those very words. That he was chained to the slaves as much as they to him. He only left Les Chandelles on the most important business, never for his own pleasure, my poor papa." Tears were forming in her eyes at the memories of Charles, but Jason drew her quickly back to the present.

"There! I knew you would understand," he exclaimed. "But Margaret never did. Or perhaps, perhaps, it was something else that pulled at her. I thought then that she needed something to occupy her mind more, besides the books. I wanted her to have a baby. But when she realized this, she drew away from me. She had never done that before, always wanted me . . . " He left the rest unsaid, concerned for Emilie's sensibilities. "The more she left me be, the more I threw myself into the chores of the farm. By the next spring, I had cleared more ground than I could cultivate by myself. I went into town and contracted with a hired man for the season."

"Did this please your wife?"

Jason smiled the strangest grin Emilie thought she had ever seen. "Yes, but not in a way I ever expected. After all, there was twice as much work for her, two men to cook and clean up after and wash for, but she didn't seem to mind. In fact, she was like she had been when we were first married. We—we even started loving again, and she was singing around the place like a sweet bird. I was working harder than ever, wanting more and more to make a go of it for her, so I could afford to give her the things I thought she wanted.

"The hired man was working too, but he wasn't putting as much into it as I thought he should. We started out together in the morning, after Margaret made the breakfast, but he was always back in before me. Ben slept in the barn, but he ate in the house right along with us. One evening I was coming in and I noticed that his field was already done for the day. It angered me that my hired man was setting himself at my table before me, but I made up my mind not to say anything. It was only a few days before his time was up; if I fussed at him now, there'd be even less done. He was a big, strong, young fellow, but I decided I wouldn't re-hire him the following season.

"I went into the house. Everything was quiet. There was nothing on the stove, nothing on the table, no sign of Margaret. I went into the bedroom. She wasn't there either. I noticed a drawer part open, and I went to close it. When I looked inside, it was empty. I drew aside the curtain she hung her clothes behind. There was nothing there either. I just sat down and waited.

"I must have fallen asleep at the table. When I woke up, it was dark and still no sign of her. I didn't want to look in the barn. I knew that would be empty, too.

"They took the little buggy we had, and one of the horses, and all of Margaret's things. By then, I accepted that she was gone for good. It took me so long to realize it that it didn't hurt so bad when I admitted it to myself. The hardest part was saddling up the next day and riding out to tell my father that he had been right all along.

"Old Angus wasn't nearly as hard on me as I thought he would be. He just listened, and nodded, and never really said anything much while I was talking. Then after I had told it all he was quiet for a minute and when he spoke it was to say that my young brother Lemuel would come back to my place with me and stay and work alongside me.

"I had two other brothers, younger than Lem, and Angus said he would make do with them. Lem was to stay as long as I needed him to. The only thing he said about Margaret was not to waste my time looking for her.

"Lem and I didn't talk much, but it helped a lot to have somebody around. I was feeling the pain then, and not being alone helped ease it.

"One day in late summer she came back. It was just near sundown when we were fixing our evening meal. She stood just outside the door for a moment, looking at me but not saying anything. There were purplish bruises all around her throat and arms. She was wearing a new dress, at least one that I had never seen before. But it was in tatters, pieces of the fabric hanging from the sleeve and skirt. Her hair was just all piled up on her head, but it wasn't neat and shining like it had always been when she braided it long.

"Then she asked me if she could come in. I motioned her that there was nothing in the way, and she walked in and sat down at the table. Lem put some stew in front of her. She ate as though it was the first time in days. I waited till she finished and then told her to go and rest. She nodded at me and went into the bedroom. Then Lem and I sat down and we ate ours.

"I only went into that bedroom once that night, to get some spare blankets out of the storage box under the bed. I made two sleeping rolls, one for me and one for Lem, and we laid them out in front of the fireplace.

"In the morning we got up and went out to the fields before she had risen, but when I came back to get some food for midday Margaret was up and about. She was cleaning up all the stuff that Lem and I had neglected and was scouring the whole house down.

"Then she looked up at me and said, 'I'm sorry, Jason, sorry for everything.' Somehow I just couldn't find the words to say to her.

" 'I don't blame you if you don't take me back,' she said. 'Heaven knows you've got reason enough. More reason than you think.'

"I looked at her. 'I'm going to have a baby,' she said. 'His baby.'

"I felt as though the floor was rising up to meet me. I didn't know whether I wanted to hit her and order her away or to take her into my arms and try to soothe away all the hurt and the pain that had happened to both of us.

"I didn't say anything one way or the other, just decided to let matters be. I was glad to have her back again, there was no way of denying it. And Margaret seemed glad enough to be back. She worked around the house and the grounds as she never had before. As if she weren't even carrying that extra weight. She seemed ready to resume our old life, and I decided the best thing for us all was for me to do the same. Outside of my mother and father and Lem, no one really knew what had happened. I would accept the baby as if it were my own."

Emilie looked at him. She would never have guessed that he was capable of such compassion or would have the strength to make such a hard decision. "What happened?" she asked breathlessly.

"Everything was going well. Even Lem was talking more and eating more than I had ever known him to do. He had always been sort of a solitary youngster, and now with Margaret tending to him he seemed to be coming into his manhood." Again he smiled that tortured grimace that had stunned Emilie before.

"I needed something from the house one afternoon and I left the cornfield to go and get it. It was an oppressively hot day and I realized it was near lunchtime. It would be better for me to eat in the house than have Margaret come out to the fields with the sun at its zenith.

"I walked back, and when I came into the house I could hear voices in the bedroom. The door was slightly open, and without walking in I could see everything.

"Margaret was lying across the bed, her skirts drawn up. That great swollen belly all exposed, and my brother—"

"Please, sir!" Emilie interrupted. She rose quickly from the sofa, not wanting to hear another word.

But Jason was just as quick. He grasped her wrist. "My brother, simple innocent boy, was astride her."

Emilie gasped, but he held her firmly.

"Now do you see, now do you understand?" he demanded.

"Yes, I understand," Emilie breathed. "But I implore you, sir, you must let me go."

Jason released his hold on her.

"Good night, Colonel Phillips," she said, and turned on her heel and walked toward the staircase, rubbing the place on her arm where his fingers had left their mark.

He watched the retreating figure until it all but disappeared in the gloomy reaches of the upper story. He sat down, bringing his unfinished glass of rum to his lips. He stared down moodily into the liquid for a moment before drinking it. I am losing control, he thought. But the thought of Emilie, so close and yet so aloof, stirred him in a way he had thought no longer possible. It had been difficult enough when he had seen her daily, but then her coldness and severe high-necked, long-sleeved dresses had constituted an unmistakable barrier around her. He had smiled ironically to himself each night as he had crossed first the figure of her slave sleeping outside her door and then the soldier similarly on guard outside his.

But the sight of her tonight was something he had been totally unprepared for. The womanliness that he had only surmised before and never let occupy his thoughts for too long had suddenly been made dazzlingly, undeniably evident. The rising swell of her bosom from the low-cut gown, the smooth white arms so teasingly accentuated by the tiny puff sleeves, had combined to arouse in him physical longing for the need he had long told himself was dead. Now it was totally alive again, throbbing relentlessly in him and stirring him to misthoughts and misdeeds such as he had just committed.

He would need all the soldierly discipline he had to keep from making a fool of himself or even worse in this suddenly dangerous situation.

This little slip of a slaveholder stood for everything he didn't believe in. It was impossible to let her provoke him into forgetting not only all his ideals but all the terrible things that emotion for a woman had caused him.

He started angrily, wondering who had told her that he hated women. It was not true, he told himself for yet another time, it was only what a woman had done to him that he hated.

But this Emilie was not anything like his wife Margaret had been. He had to credit her with that much. The Southerner was as sharply loyal and attentive to the honor of her dead husband as Margaret had been disloyal to him while he was so very much alive.

Pain seared his mind. Even the rum could not dull it. Jason closed his eyes and frowned. He had been able to keep from thinking about it for so long, burying himself in the war and his responsibilities. Now after all this time, he had been fool enough to permit himself to relive all this agony. It was the fault of that little baggage who had just flounced upstairs.

But she was not that at all, he had to remind himself in the next instant. She was brave and loyal and loving and everything, he was convinced, that a woman should be. Not at all like that other. Not anything like his wife. Margaret, the farm, the neat sturdy landscape of Ohio, all seemed equally dim in his memory now. In front of him was the far different green and look of the canefields, the sultry insinuating air of the bayous and all the troubling ambience of the south. In front of him lay Emilie, perhaps the most troubling thought of all.

14

Emilie remained in her room for several days, using Missy to summon the various members of the household staff to her chamber as she needed them, rather than going about the house where they were busied. She realized she could not isolate herself forever, going downstairs only in the evening for the daily meeting with Henrique. But she wanted to avoid Jason Phillips as much as was humanly possible. She could not expect the man to remain in his quarters when it was necessary for her to be meeting with her overseer, but Emilie would have liked to use even that as a means of showing him how thoroughly upset she was by his narrative.

She was startled then one afternoon when a slave tapped lightly on the door and delivered a request from the colonel that she present herself at the dinner table that evening.

"I will not!" Emilie stamped her foot as soon as the slave had scampered out of sight. But she knew that she really had little say in the matter of her own movements about the house; she was, to all intents and purposes, the colonel's very prisoner under her own roof. She could not very well refuse such requests indefinitely without risking even more of a confrontation than compliance would.

She went quickly to her desk, scribbled a note of polite refusal, and called for Missy to deliver it. This time she could plead a headache; but the thought of the next invitation filled her with anguish.

Although Les Chandelles was virtually untouched by the war, Emilie found the Yankee occupancy more and more distasteful. She understood quite well why they wanted the work of the great plantation to go on as usual, and she did not wish to thwart them in this, since it suited her own purposes as well. But their continued intrusion on her land was a constant sore spot. If the army provided her with an uncomfortable rub, then the colonel was, at the very least, a pebble in her shoe which kept her limping and unable to do anything properly. His very presence was cause enough for consternation on her part. And now it seemed he felt something had been established between them by his revelations, a bond of intimacy, perhaps. Emilie shuddered.

Not that she liked any of the Yankees, but at least she was able to tolerate Captain Rogers. He always addressed her with civil courtesy, which Emilie told herself she appreciated very much.

Of course, Colonel Phillips had always treated her just as circumspectly, except for that one conversation on the night of General Butler's visit. But somehow his courtesy did not sit well with her at all. It was as though everything he said or did were an irritant. From nothing more than the sound of his voice she could feel her hackles rising and her temper ready to flare. Emilie knew that this was as much her fault as his, but she hated his being there with a burning intensity that she wanted neither to temper nor to extinguish. He was the enemy, he was the conqueror. He stood unwanted on her land and slept all too easily under her roof. All the rage and frustration she felt at the loss of her husband and the conquering of her country was directed toward him.

Yet Emilie knew that she was being unreasonable

in the excess of her feelings toward him. It wasn't so much the man himself she hated, it was what he stood for. He had treated her better than she had the right to expect; his unsavory narrative, while displeasing to hear, had nonetheless evoked a degree of sympathy from her that Emilie disliked admitting to herself. And the colonel had been a gentlemen. He had been true to his word, damaging nothing in the house or grounds and permitting no one else to do so. When she had complained to him of the soldiers' invading the vegetable fields he had promptly put a stop to it. He had in no way interfered with the running of the house or the plantation, and Emilie knew he could have ridden roughshod over all of them, herself included. Still, it was easier to hate him and find fault with him than to admit his good points. But even if she were so disposed, still it would be wrong to take her meals with him. If word of such a state of affairs traveled to other plantations, as it must, Emilie was sure her reputation would be severely damaged, if not totally ruined. She had all but decided to continue to evade his company when an orderly brought an envelope to Missy to deliver to her mistress.

Emilie opened the letter with steady hands. The flowing handwriting on its container told her that this was no official missive.

Indeed it wasn't. It proved to be a letter from Francine Desbrosses. Emilie could not have been more surprised.

She read it eagerly, following Francine's expansive hand and chatty style. The letter related how she and her husband, Gaston, had been detained in New York by the sudden outbreak of the war and only now permitted to return, by boat, to their house in New Orleans. Emilie had been the object of her friends' worry and concern ever since she had fled from New York. Now

Francine had managed to convince the Yankee governor in New Orleans that no harm could possibly be done by her visiting her protégé upcountry.

In other words, she finished with a flourish, the couple would soon be on their way to visit Les Chandelles.

Emilie was delighted. The letter didn't say exactly when they would be arriving, so she could anticipate it every day. She was hurrying from the chapel one morning back into the house when she was suddenly confronted by Colonel Phillips.

"I trust you are pleased that your friends have been permitted to visit you," he said.

"How did you know—" Emilie started, then stopped herself. "I should have realized that even so simple a thing as a social call would require your agreement. In that event I suppose I must thank you for permitting it."

"You're very welcome," he answered. "And I am looking forward to meeting them. Since the governor has no objection to this visit, neither do I."

Emilie saw at once that the matter of future dinners had been resolved. With company to be entertained —company he himself had approved—there would be no recourse other than the four of them sitting down at table, at least each evening.

Emilie had no time to comment as their attention was immediately taken by the sight of a curricle rounding the bend and coming straight up the drive toward them. The elegance of the matched pair that drew the carriage told Emilie instantly that this must be her awaited friends.

"I will leave you here to greet your guests yourself," Colonel Phillips said as he walked up the stairs to the veranda.

"Thank you," Emilie replied, grateful in this instance for his courtesy. She was anxious as could be to see the Desbrosses, and greeting them in tandem with the Yankee officer would have been awkward.

Within moments she and Francine were in each other's arms embracing happily as Monsieur Desbrosses stood by.

Presently Francine disentangled herself from Emilie's embrace and held the younger woman at arm's length, studying her carefully. "You left us a young maiden and now I come back to find you a woman," she declared.

Emilie dropped her eyes. "You find me a widow," she said.

"My dear!" And once more Francine hugged her to her bosom. "You must tell me everything, but not all at once. We shall have plenty of time to talk later on."

Gaston Desbrosses stepped forward, and Emilie embraced him as well. Then all three went into the front salon, where Robert quickly set out large trays of refreshments for the travelers.

"General Butler visited here recently," Emilie said. "I am glad that he saw fit to permit you to come and stay with me."

"Ah, but the general is off on military affairs," Francine replied. "We have a new governor now. His name is Michael Hahn and he is a civilian."

"But aren't we still under military rule?" Emilie asked. "We certainly are at Les Chandelles."

"Yes, everything is directed by the army, and they are everywhere," Gaston answered his young hostess. "But the German is not a soldier, although the mayor that they've appointed for the city is a brigadier general named Shepley. Seems a decent enough chap."

"How New Orleans must have changed!" Emilie said.

"Yes, but not really," was Francine's reply. "The

city is busier and more bustling than ever, and naturally the bluecoats are everywhere. And then there are so many slaves at work—the city has never been so full of blacks."

"Ah, but they are no longer slaves, my dear," Gaston reminded her. "They are hands who have left their plantations and are being paid wages by the army to work on the levies and repair the streets."

Emilie frowned. So the colonel had not lied when he had told her of the emancipation and the numbers of slaves who had quit their masters and been received and welcomed by the Federals. At least she had been spared that. He had promised her that the work of the plantation would go on uninterrupted, and so it had. Except for a few field hands who had walked off, everything was the same.

"But my dear Emilie, what misfortunes you have suffered since you left us!" Francine said, taking her hostess' hand in her own. "We had no idea when you left so suddenly what had happened."

"Neither did I," Emilie said. "I wanted to come home as quickly as I could, never dreaming of what I would find when I got here."

The older woman murmured an expression of sympathy and sighed deeply. "The loss of your parents and the destruction of the house must have left you quite inconsolable, my poor pet, and so alone. But then what are these new griefs you mentioned?"

"I married Guy Charpentier of Les Saules," Emilie said.

"That would be the plantation just north of here," Francine murmured. "I remember his mother quite well."

"I barely remembered Guy," Emilie admitted. "He had been in Europe for more than seven years. He left the parish when I was just a little girl. His younger brother, Stephan, was a friend of my brother's." She faltered for a moment, her lips trembling, her eyes burning with the tears that threatened to burst forth at any moment.

"What is it, my darling?" Francine was quick to see the anguish that her young friend was suffering.

"We had—we had only three days together before Guy had to leave," Emilie said.

"Dear God!" Francine explained. "My poor child! And what has happened since?"

"Just before the Yankees came," Emilie continued, in a whisper, "an orderly of Guy's made his way here. He told me that Guy had begged him to come and find me and tell me what had happened. He gave—gave me my poor Guy's gold watch. That was all I—I had. But they caught the soldier and shot him and the watch broke and I have nothing." Her words and tears were all jumbled together. "Nothing." She buried her face in her hands and wept bitterly.

Francine took a few hasty steps to her side and hugged the weeping Emilie to her breast. She too was crying, unable to restrain herself. "An orphan and then a widow. Oh, my dear."

Emilie tried to choke back her sobs, but it was impossible. "First sweet young André, and then my brother. Now—now my parents are gone, too. And my poor husband. Oh, Francine, we were only married for three days. Three days!" She clutched at her friend's sleeve, burying her face in the silk-covered shoulder, and wept piteously.

"There, there." Francine patted her back, trying to comfort her. "Cry all you must, my dear. It's better for you to have it all out." She guided her to a small settee and sat down next to her.

Emilie for once was oblivious of her surroundings. Even the fact that Monsieur Desbrosses was present did not cross her mind. She cried until her small lace handkerchief was thoroughly soaked, and until her body felt so wrenched and tired she could bring out no more tears. It was only then that she remembered her visitor and tried to apologize to him for her lack of restraint.

"Never bother about it, my dear, never bother," he answered her gruffly, rather unnerved by the copious flow of female tears.

They all sat silently for a while as Emilie composed herself.

"I think we shall all retire to our rooms now," Francine said, taking charge. "Gaston and I are tired from our journey, and I daresay you could use some rest as well." They all rose and Francine took Emilie's arm as Monsieur Desbrosses followed them up the stairs.

"I will come and knock at your door in a few hours," Francine whispered to Emilie. "Then we can have our private chat. I am most anxious to know what has been happening here."

Emilie nodded.

Missy opened the door later that afternoon to admit Francine into Emilie's boudoir. "You look somewhat refreshed, darling," the older woman said, soothing the tumble of black curls back from Emilie's temples.

"I do feel so much better now that you're here," Emilie said. She forced a smile.

Francine sat down at the edge of the bed and once again took Emilie's hands in hers. "Now tell me everything," she said. "I heard so much since I came back to New Orleans about your mysterious Colonel Phillips."

"*My* Colonel Phillips?" Emilie was startled.

"You know what I mean," Francine pressed.

"After all, he has been living under your roof all this time and I'm dying to hear everything about him."

Emilie was mystified. "But why?" she asked. "I don't like him, but must put up with his being here. I can't imagine what you find so interesting about him."

"If only you knew the stories I've heard down in the city," Francine said. "Nothing more than whispers, my dear, but that's what makes it all so intriguing. Nobody seems to know anything more about him than the most mysterious rumors."

"It would seem to me," Emilie said primly, "that with a war going on and our own land conquered, people would have more important things to concern themselves with."

"Ah, but you know what New Orleans is like, Emilie," Francine chided her. "Society goes on as usual, with all its parties and dinners and balls, and nothing is more important there than a juicy bit of gossip."

"So General Butler had said." Emilie was rather surprised to hear the general's boast so quickly confirmed by her friend. "He said that the city was as lively as ever."

"More so, if anything," Francine said. "What with all of those dashing young officers and suddenly important men all about. I declare all of the hostesses of the city are actively vying with each other to catch the most eligible officers for their dinner parties."

"But these are our enemies!" Emilie said, shocked. "How can they think of entertaining Yankees?"

"My dear, these are the facts of life," Francine answered. "The ladies of New Orleans are nothing if not practical. There is no telling when the war will end or how. It seems most likely that we are done for and these Yankees will be our governors for heaven knows how long to come. It makes so much more sense to be friends with them than adversaries. Life is so much more pleasant this way."

"Never!" Emilie protested. "I consider Jason Phillips an intruder at Les Chandelles and myself his prisoner. There is no other way of looking at it, nor shall there be." Her eyes blazed.

"Gently, Emilie, gently," Francine admonished. "The war is not going our way. If we are to preserve anything of the life we cherish we shall have to learn to do so with Yankee compliance."

Emilie was deeply perturbed, but said nothing.

"Now come and tell me everything you know about Colonel Phillips," Francine insisted. "They say in the city that he had the most scandalous past, but no one knows quite what it was."

"I am afraid I can enlighten you very little, if at all." Emilie sighed. "I have as little contact with your mysterious colonel as possible, and the only thing I know is what one of his officers once said—that he hates women and considers us all his enemies." She did not like lying to her friend, but she could never reveal the confidence he had placed in her, nor would she have wanted to repeat its more sordid aspects.

Francine was taken aback. "What could have happened to him, I wonder," she said. "Well, I shall soon have the chance to find out for myself, and I promise you I will do a far more thorough job of exploring than you have, my dear young friend."

"I'm sure you will." Emilie smiled. "If for no other reason than that you have a great deal of interest in Colonel Phillips, while I have none whatsoever."

"We shall all dine together this evening, I'm sure," said Francine, "and I shall begin my study of him then. I warrant you that when I return to the city I shall have much to add to the store of information about him there."

"I hope that won't be too soon," Emilie said. "I would wish that you could stay here with me for as long as possible."

Francine patted her hand. "I intend to stay with you as long as propriety and your hospitality will allow," she said. "I do not like the idea of your being so isolated here. Now that I know all of the tragedy that has befallen you I am even more loath for you to be alone."

"Thank you," Emilie said. "I have been away from Les Chandelles only once in many months now, and that was to see my in-laws. I had a military escort then, but I understand that traveling now is a far simpler matter. Perhaps we can both go and visit Les Saules."

"I'm sure we can," Francine replied. "The Yankees restored railway service a long time back, I'm told, and the steamboats are on the river quite actively. Now they are permitting authorized civilians to travel on the roads as well. I doubt that we'll encounter much resistance from your colonel should we request permission to go only so far as the next plantation."

Francine rose, claiming it was time for her to begin her toilette for dinner. She kissed Emilie's cheek and assured her that more cheerful times were ahead for all of them.

When Emilie was dressed and ready for dinner, she found herself troubled by the most confusing emotions. She did not want to spend all her time crying for Guy, but she was not yet ready for the gaiety that Francine assumed was the best antidote to sorrow. It was going to be difficult to be polite and open with her New Orleans friends while they sat at table with the man who raised such a conflict of emotions in her.

Emilie stared at her reflection in the mirror. "This is not the most difficult thing that I have had to do in my life," she muttered to herself aloud. "And I will do what I have to do." She lifted her chin, shook her hair back slightly, and went down to the dining room.

The other three were already at table. The men rose as soon as she entered. Emilie saw that the place at the head of the table had been left vacant for her, and a slave pulled out a chair as she went to sit down. She thanked Francine inwardly for her tactfulness in seating Gaston at the foot, as though he were host and master. It was a suitable role for him, considering his age and the closeness of their connection, and far more agreeable to Emilie than having to sit facing the colonel playing that same part.

Robert silently oversaw the serving of the vension and wild turkey, the stuffed mushrooms and deep-orange Louisiana yams.

"How do you like our land, Colonel?" Francine asked after the main course had been served.

Emilie busied herself with her food as he answered.

"I love this land," the colonel replied, and Emilie looked up, sharply surprised. "Although I had never looked with favor on the peculiar institution of slavery, I have always considered the United States to be one nation. Therefore I consider myself neither a foreigner nor an invader."

"Yet when this wretched war is over you will go back to your own lands," Francine countered.

"I think not, madam," Colonel Phillips replied. "There is much I find to my liking here. There is a feeling about this place that pleases me very much. It is a softer air here and, I believe, a gentler kind of life you live that would suit me very well."

"But what about your family?" Francine pressed.

Emilie did not lift her eyes from her food, but she strained to hear every word he spoke and to understand his expression, and what they meant.

"There are no ties that bind me anywhere," Jason Phillips declared.

"But you have declared yourself on the side of the emancipators," Gaston Desbrosses interjected. "How can you reconcile your old ideas with these new feelings?"

Jason smiled. "The war is nearly over," he said. "It is only a question of time before all the states are united once again. There is no question but that the union will prevail, and with it slavery must fall."

Emilie shot him a look, but said nothing.

"The South is going to see an era of growth and prosperity such as even your most patriotic boosters have never envisioned," Jason went on. "Freeing the slaves is going to provide more freedom for everyone else as well."

"But how can that be?" Francine demanded.

"You have too much capital tied up in your so-called chattel," Jason explained. "Pay them decent living wages like laborers everywhere else, and you will soon find you have the necessary money for investment in the equipment and machinery that an industrial society requires. Once this has been realized in the South, this section will be the fastest-growing part of the nation."

"I saw something of the factories and mill towns of the north." Francine shuddered. "They were vile, dark places. I should not propose to see our beautiful countryside transformed like that."

"That need not be either, madam," Jason said. "Even if this state were to become more industrialized it would not mean the end of great plantations such as this. Sugar is still a most valuable crop, and that it requires vast acreage to be most profitably grown is well understood. But even Les Chandelles can easily afford to pay her laborers and realize even greater profits ultimately."

Gaston Desbrosses shook his head. "You make it sound most admirable, sir," he said. "But I do not see how it is possible."

"There is a system which we have been studying that is called sharecropping," Jason said. "The great estates can be left physically intact, but by actually redistributing the ownership to those who will be responsible for working it, both employer and employee will profit. The individual laborer will be given a small portion of land and will earn his own way by taking responsibility for the continued cultivation of his plot."

"But what of the master?" Gaston demanded. "What of those to whom the land properly belongs? And how will these poor darkies, even free, be able to pay for their piece of land?"

"Payment will be made back to the original owners out of part of each crop," Jason explained. "That way the former owners will be compensated for the lands they give up and will be assured of a continuing interest in the crops. The freed men will be able to start tilling the soil immediately with seed and equipment lent to them by the original owners."

"I don't see how it will work." Gaston was dubious.

"It will work." Jason smiled. "Wait and see."

Emilie spoke up for the first time. "You make it sound as though the war were already over, Colonel," she said. "And as though we are indeed your vanquished."

"The war is all but over, Miss Emilie," he said. "But it is not our wish to treat the South in a way that will punish her. The most important thing is that we heal our wounds and bind the nation together once again."

He had used her given name, albeit it with the formal and proper "Miss" attached. Emilie did not say anything, letting the matter pass. She had no wish to be disagreeable at table, and in spite of herself she found the colonel's conversation most compelling. She had had no idea of his sentiments. She had always surmised that he despised both the land and the people he had battled against. Now he was displaying a totally different attitude from the one she had expected. She could not comprehend this changed system that he was proposing, but she knew she could not be expected to. It was a matter for men like Gaston and her factor in the city, Anton Bledsoe, to advise her on. Not that it would be merely a question of advice, Emilie realized. If what Colonel Phillips was saying about the war was true, they would be in no position to determine for themselves what was to be done with the slaves. She remembered what he had told her about Lincoln's Emancipation Proclamation and his reminder that it was primarily his being there with his troops that had kept her slaves on at Les Chandelles. What he had said about hundreds and possibly thousands of others walking off the plantations and going to work as paid employees in the city had been confirmed by Francine.

Emilie permitted herself a quick glance at this stranger seated on her left. She had to admit that the survival of Les Chandelles, its continuance in its normal course, was largely due to his presence. She wanted suddenly very much to hear what else he had to say. She wished he would go on.

As if concurring with her unspoken wishes, Jason continued. "There is a beauty about this place that cannot be denied," he said. "I know of no Northern city to compare with New Orleans. I am of half a mind to return there and resume the practice of law when all this is over."

"Indeed. And what is the rest of your mind conspiring, Colonel?" Francine asked gaily.

"To attach myself once more to the land, madam," he replied. "I am used to the hard life of a farmer and sometimes find myself sorely missing that feeling that only contact with the soil can give a man. Cane, in fertile lands like these, is as much a guaranteed crop as anything in nature can be. Surely when the conflict is over the demand for Louisiana sugar will be even greater than it was before."

"You mean to make a profit out of your military service, sir," Francine chided him, but the playful tone in her voice took any offense from her words.

"What is life for, then, other than profit and pleasure?" he asked her.

"Oh la la!" Francine shrilled, delighted with his answer. "Do find your way back to New Orleans, by all means, Colonel," she exclaimed. "You sound like a native already." She looked at him keenly and added, "Unless you have found the possibilities for both lying farther upriver than our gay city."

Emilie was shocked. It was as if that provocative statement had been meant to include her. Surely her friend could not make light in such a way of Emilie's so recent grief. Emilie saw that Francine meant to pull her into the present, kicking and screaming if she must, but she found herself not ready to go. She could not release herself from the grip of Guy's memory, and no matter what hardship it placed upon her, she was determined to withstand all temptations to turn her back on everything that had meant so much to her.

"Perhaps the colonel will be kind enough to issue us a pass," Emilie spoke up. "I have a great desire to see my mother-in-law and I know that you would

dearly like to visit with Madame Charpentier as well."
She directed her statement to Francine.

"Of course, my darling, we must see that it is arranged at once," Francine agreed. "Colonel, surely you could not find it in your heart to deny so small a request to our poor dear young hostess."

"Indeed not, Madame Desbrosses," Jason replied. "The pass will be written for you promptly tomorrow, and I will send an escort of officers to accompany you."

After dinner they withdrew to the large front salon, where Francine, with some assistance from her husband, told of the carryings-on in New Orleans since their return. When Emilie asked for news of the friends she had made in New York, she noticed that Jason Phillips was almost stiff with attention.

But he seemed to relax somewhat, his bearing softening slightly, when Francine's anecdotes were primarily of her cousin, Mrs. Porter van Nuys, and the inconveniences that the war had placed upon that estimable woman. It was almost as though he had been waiting for the name of a New York beau to pass between them, but when none was forthcoming he sat back in the chair he had taken and contented himself with listening to the vivacious Francine's account of New York life during the war.

"Have you ever been to New York, Colonel?" the lady asked.

"I am afraid that that city would be as unlikely for me as my Ohio countryside would be for you, madam," he said, smiling. "I am not used to those marble palaces and crowded thoroughfares that you describe."

"But yet you seem quite at home with the idea of New Orleans," Francine said.

"But New Orleans is lovely, quite unlike New York

sounds," Jason said. Then he turned to Emilie. "Do you like New Orleans?" he asked.

"I have not spent a great deal of time in the city, I'm afraid," she answered. "My father did not like me to be away from Les Chandelles. Except for the trip to New York, I'm afraid I have spent most of my life right here."

"It does not seem to have restrained you in any way," he said. "Your education seems to me to be quite remarkable for a young woman of your position."

"Thank you," Emilie said. "I believe my father to have been very careful in seeing that I learned as much as I could of what I would require in my life. It is only unfortunate that it has not turned out as he would have wished."

"No one could possibly have foreseen what has happened to you, my dearest Emilie," Francine cried. "And yet you have withstood it all as few women could. I declare it breaks my heart even to have to consider your tragedies."

"I join in those sentiments completely, madam," Jason declared. "Our hostess has conducted herself in a way that would do credit to any member of her sex, even one far older and more schooled in the vicissitudes of life. I would commend you, Miss Emilie, in any company."

"Thank you, sir." Emilie felt the color rising slightly in her face. She knew that he was scrutinizing her, and whether that or his compliment was making her blush she did not know. All of a sudden the room felt quite warm, and the colonel seemed uncomfortably close to her. She looked to her friend, silently imploring Francine either to change the conversation away from herself or to suggest that they retire for the night.

But Francine, though she caught Emilie's glance, was having none of it. She seemed determined to make Emilie the center of attention and for her young protégé to bask in the company and compliments of the men. Emilie was almost angry with her until she remembered how quickly Francine had secured approval for their trip to Les Saules. Surely, she reasoned with herself, a visit with Madame Charpentier would set everything straight in her own mind, and make things appear as they should be. Madame Charpentier would bring her level to what her duties and responsibilities were.

Finally Francine said, after much extended conversation, "Let us leave the gentlemen to their brandy and cigars, my dear. We have to make an early start tomorrow and should get a good night's rest."

Emilie rose gratefully and with a nod to each of the men followed Francine to the broad staircase. She would have liked to have acted on her friend's suggestion, and was surprised when Francine followed her into her own room, throwing herself down into a large stuffed boudoir chair, as if making herself ready for a long visit.

"It is obvious that the colonel adores you," Francine said happily. "That nonsense about his hating women clearly stopped at the entrance to Les Chandelles."

"Really, Francine, I am shocked!" Emilie said. "How can you even be thinking of such things?"

"Emilie, you need a man," Francine said bluntly. "You barely tasted the joys of marriage before they were torn from you. Now you must admit to what others can see but you cannot. It is not only of your own needs that I speak, my dearest, but of this great plantation as well. Emilie, I can only think for you as your own father would have, and what dear Charles wanted for you is what I carry in my heart."

Emilie looked at her, suddenly feeling herself almost on the verge of tears again. "But Francine, what are you saying? How could my father ever have wanted such a liaison as you seem to be proposing to me now? He despised the Yankees and everything they stand for."

"Charles is no longer here, Emilie. You must remember that," Francine said. "And not only is your father gone, but the world as he knew it—our world—is gone too. This is what we must face. The Yankees are here to stay, Emilie. But whether they or we are to conquer ultimately is as much in our hands as it is in theirs."

Emilie looked at her quizzically. She could not imagine what her friend meant. It seemed to her obvious that the Yankees would impose their own will and set up a new order entirely of their own making. Colonel Phillips had said as much.

"Let me explain," Francine went on in a more gentle voice. "You have heard Jason Phillips talk about this land. He loves it no less than your own ancestors did. And I tell you, Emilie, it is in your power to turn that love in any direction you want to, including yourself. Don't look so horrified," she said, catching a glimpse of Emilie's expression. "It is all for your own good and for the good of the land as well. If you mean to preserve Les Chandelles, I tell you this Colonel Phillips is the best means for doing so."

"What is it you mean me to do?" Emilie cried.

"In the first place, dear, you must try to see him as he is," Francine said gently. "Not the devil incarnate, but a man who has suffered, perhaps as much as you yourself have."

"I never thought of him that way," Emilie admitted.

"To me he seemed too cold and too unfeeling to have much emotion of any kind."

"That's just what I mean, Emilie," Francine said. "In your unhappiness and your anger at the Yankees you have construed him as a monster. Perhaps you are being unfair both to him and to yourself."

Emilie sat staring into nothing. "Tomorrow we go to Les Saules," she said.

"Yes, we go to Les Saules," Francine echoed. "Will you tell his parents about Guy? What strength that is going to take!"

"I suppose I must," Emilie said. "They must know."

"Perhaps that will be the last great sadness of your life, Emilie," Francine said hopefully. "Perhaps with that mission behind you, the book can be closed on all the terrible things that have happened. A new volume full of love and life for you can begin."

"Perhaps." It was as much as she could dare to hope or say. Jason Phillips—everything about him, every thought or mention of him—threw her into confusion.

The next morning, the Desbrosses curricle was brought around to the front of the house. A lieutenant and two soldiers formed their escort. The morning was sunny, crisp, and beautiful, without the overpowering heat that so often enveloped the area. They were settled in the elegant vehicle and off at a smart trot when Francine turned to Emilie.

"I must say that I am more and more taken with your colonel," she confided. "I cannot help thinking of the way he spoke last night. I had expected him to be quite dry and military, little more than one of those crude Yankee farmers he claims to have been. But I declare, Emilie, there is poetry in that man's soul. I could hear it when he spoke about the South."

"I was quite surprised myself," Emilie had to admit.

"I had no idea he had formed such a fondness for our land, and he does seem to understand about sugar and the necessities surrounding the raising of it."

"Then you are more disposed toward his finding favor in your eyes." Francine smiled.

"No, I didn't say that," Emilie answered quickly. "I merely said that perhaps, like you, I had judged him too quickly in some regards. But I cannot think to open my heart to him, Francine. Not to him or any other man. Not yet."

Francine patted her knee. "No one is trying to rush you, *cherie*. We shall see."

Emilie found herself growing more apprehensive as they drew closer to Les Saules. As hard as it had been to be the recipient of such news about Guy, it would now be a thousand times more difficult to be the bearer. She tried to compose herself and think of what she would tell her mother-in-law. But no matter what words she thought of, they did not seem kind enough or sufficient enough for their dreadful import.

But when they arrived at the stately house and got out of the carriage, Guy's mother needed no more than one look at his widow in her mourning dress to know what had happened.

"My son, my son!" she gasped, staggering forward. Emilie ran to catch her. "It's over, isn't it?" she asked, looking up at Emilie.

"Yes," Emilie said. "He is gone, *chère mama,* he is gone." Her voice was muffled from behind the heavy black veiling she wore but the words were unmistakable. The women grasped each other, crying as they knelt on the ground of the home Guy had loved and come back to defend.

Madame Charpentier choked out a sob. "This earth he loved, these trees—" She lifted her hand helplessly as though to encompass everything that Guy had held so dear and was now lost to him as he was lost to it forever.

Emilie helped the old woman rise. Still holding her protectively, she drew her up and helped her climb the stairs to the front salon. Francine followed quietly behind.

Once inside, Madame unfolded a lacy lawn handkerchief and wept unchecked. She stopped every now and then to pat her wet cheeks. But the handkerchief was completely soaked and of no use. "He stood to inherit, you know that," she said to Emilie. "He would have joined Les Saules with Les Chandelles, and our families would have been united for all time. Now there is nothing—nothing. The name Bonfils is gone, and now Charpentier falls as well. Soon we will all be gone and everything we knew gone with us."

"But you have another son," Emilie reminded her gently. "There is still Stephan."

"Stephan?" Madame looked up. "Stephan is never coming home again either. I know it."

Emilie looked quickly again at Francine, who could only shake her head.

"But Stephan may come home," Emilie insisted. "There is still hope."

"No, my dear, there is no hope." Madame's voice sounded strong for the first time that morning. "Stephan will not return any more than his brother will."

The three women sat silent for a moment. Then Madame Charpentier spoke again. "When this bitter war is over I shall prevail upon my husband to leave Les Saules and retire to our small house in New Orleans. There we can pass the rest of our lives with fewer burdens and fewer memories than clutch at us here."

"But what will become of Les Saules?" Emilie asked. Other than Les Chandelles there was no place on earth dearer to her than this beautiful house and its gardens.

"What is to become of all of us?" Madame asked, and bitterness filled her voice. "It is over, my child. We are finished."

"Oh no, *chère mama*, it isn't. It can't be!" Emilie leaped from her chair and threw herself on the floor at her mother-in-law's feet, grasping the old woman by the knees and looking up at her imploringly.

Madame Charpentier smoothed the shiny black hair that nestled against her lap. "You are young, my child," she said, forcing a smile. "Perhaps you can carry on and see it through to a better day. But as for me, I am tired and have seen enough." As if to emphasize the words she closed her eyes and rested her head on the back of the chair.

Emilie sat for a few minutes, not wishing to move, not wanting to disturb the old woman. But at last she rose to her feet. "I think, Francine, it would be best if we started for home now."

Emilie leaned over to kiss her mother-in-law gently on the forehead, but the old woman did not respond. Emilie motioned to Francine and the two of them slipped quietly from the room, leaving Madame Charpentier undisturbed.

Outside, birds twittered in the treetops and the sunlight made dappled shadows through the leaves. It was as if the peaceful air of Les Saules had never been disturbed. Emilie inhaled deeply; thinking that each breath of it might be her last.

They were helped into the curricle and went back in infrequently broken silence to Les Chandelles.

Emilie retired to her room and directed that a dinner tray be sent up to her. For once Francine did not reproach her, but seemed to understand her need to be alone. Emilie thought that once within the privacy of her bedchamber, despair would surely overtake her again, but she was somewhat surprised to find she had no tears left. Perhaps that was the end of it, she thought. Perhaps my love and I have, between us, spilled blood and tears enough to suffice. Now I must find a more lasting way to keep his memory.

Francine was right. Emilie suddenly saw the wisdom of what her friend had been saying. People in their generations came and went, and none lived forever. But the land was always there, and the land could be protected, preserved, and maintained if only one was strong enough to do it.

She walked to the window and gazed out at the wide expanse of Les Chandelles, its lawns shimmering in their light greenness, its darker forest standing staunch and majestic where it separated the house grounds from the canefields. And the cane that she could see only in her mind's eye stretched, she knew, for miles and miles until its own rich green met the blue horizon.

She clutched at a brocade curtain and continued to gaze on all that was hers. "Les Chandelles *shall* stand, and Les Saules too. I swear it!" Emilie declared out loud, fierce and determined as the unchecked words of her vow. She stood silent then, not moving, as if standing guardian of her domain. She would do what had to be done and by any means. She had done man's work since her father died, had scrawled her signature on a piece of paper to keep it from being snatched away by the Yankees, had defied soldiers and overseers, practice and custom. But the world that had taken everything else from her—lover, parents, husband— would not take this. Les Chandelles would be hers until the day she lay buried under it. And that day, she determined, would come none too soon.

And even when it does, I won't let go, Emilie declared inside herself. There will be others to carry it on for me. I shall seed my body as I seed my land.

him each day. That was good; that was as it should be. So would she have treated him had she been wife to his child, all of them back among their Yoruba tribespeople. It was well that the girl thought of him thus; it would have been better had the grandson-husband been here as well.

Now other young men in the quarters would stop and speak to him of freedom, not in buried tones as Young Jess had, but openly. The great war that was being fought not far away would bring freedom to all of them, some of the young men told Old Jess. They had heard of other plantations where slaves by the dozens and then hundreds had walked off, and no one could stop them. Some of the young hands wanted to leave Les Chandelles as well. Although conditions in the fields were better now than they had ever been, the thought of freedom being so close consumed their minds. It was the presence of the soldiers that kept most of them from wandering off.

If freedom was indeed so close, then it would be coming to them. Meanwhile, until it was known for sure, a man was better off to stay where he knew there was food and shelter and someone to care for him.

He knew, in a way that none of the field hands born in slavery could, what freedom really meant. If there was no work outside the plantation and the slaves had no goods to barter with, as indeed they didn't, then freedom could be nothing more than a taste of ashes in the mouth and the cold wind for a cover in the night. It was better to stay and wait. Already, since Henrique had been made overseer, the lash and whip had been banished from the fields. The Yankee colonel had ordered that the work start an hour later in the morning and end an hour sooner at night. There was fresh cool water in the brakes for whoever needed it, and food was brought for midday meal instead of the hands having to wait for the hoecakes at the end of the day. Although Old Jess did not know how much truth there was to the rumors of freedom, the fact that things were already better in the fields seemed to prove that change, big change, would soon be upon them. As long as he had lived at Les Chandelles there had never been a shortening of the hours or a lessening of the punishment to mark one year from the next. Now so much had already happened it seemed to him that more change must indeed be on the way. He wished he had heard from Ephraim. The priest's slave had come to say good-bye when he left the parish for New Orleans at the first advance of the Yankees. Ephraim would tell him if it was good for the people to leave or stay. But Old Jess had never heard from him again.

Old Jess was tired, tireder than he had ever been in his life, and he knew full well what this meant. He didn't have much time left, and now with the days sifting through his fingers, he knew he had one last great duty to perform for his people. One field hand had been killed. He had to prevent the others from leaving before the time came when it would be right and safe to do so.

He told Missy, by word and signals, that he wanted to be helped to the front of the little house in time for all of the hands to see him when they came in from the cane that evening. She was surprised and mystified at his instructions, but she helped him out and plumped blankets and straw around him so that he could sit up.

The word went swiftly through the quarters that the old man was going to speak to them. As the weary hands trudged home from the fields, they assembled quietly in the dusty street. Some of them squatted on the earth, others sat in front of their own houses or leaned against them. The world that they had always known and hated was slowly changing all around them, and while the changes that had been made had been for the better, change in and of itself was a new and frightening thing for overworked and uneducated plantation slaves.

No one doubted the importance of an occasion that caused the old man, known to be weary and almost at the end of his days, to pull himself up and speak with them. An air of hushed expectancy settled over the quarters as more and more workers came to a halt at the end of the street where the old man's hut stood.

Old Jess smiled wanly at his people. He glanced about the crowd, judging closely when he thought that nearly all of the quarters' inhabitants were there.

He would need all of his strength for this.

But all of it and more he was prepared to give for them. He knew that his voice was weak and would not carry far, but that was no great matter. The ones who could hear would repeat to the ones who couldn't, and in the process Old Jess would have time to think and conserve that melting strength he had somehow gathered.

He looked about again. It was time.

"My people." Not another sound could be heard except for the distant barking of some hounds.

"My people, a new time is upon us. So far, it has brought some good. So far, it has brought some death."

There was a murmuring among the hands as they remembered the burial of only a few days earlier.

"I too have heard of many who have left their places and gone to freedom." He shook his head. "But nothing have I heard of those who have gone. We have no knowing of what they have found there. We have knowing only of our own dead brother, killed when he went to look for it."

There was a slight uneasy stirring among the crowd.

Old Jess knew that it had been a long hot day in the fields. Most of them had had but one meal, hours earlier, and perhaps most had not stopped for water in a long while. They would be anxious to get to their simple huts, their food, and their rest. He mustered up all his strength to speak with them as quickly as possible.

"I know freedom. I was born in freedom in the home country, not here in slavery. But I say now we stay here. We learn what freedom in this place means. The master we serve is a master we know. And the master we know is always a better master than the one we do not know.

"If freedom is here, it will be here for all people. Freedom will find us. Let us stay, my people. Here we can live. Out there"—one frail shoulder gestured toward the world beyond the woods—"we can die while we look. Out there, each one is alone and weak by himself. Here we stay together and we will be strong, the many as one. The soldiers have come to help us. We must not give them reason to kill. We must wait.

"Wait, my people, wait. I will wait with you, although my soul longs to taste what my youth knew so well. But I will not risk you. I will wait. You wait with me."

He raised his hand in a simple gesture that told them he had finished speaking. Those who had been sitting stood, and singly and in groups the people dispersed to their huts. It was not the time for talking over the old man's words. It was a time instead for each to be silent and listen inside his head to what he had heard. Later would be the time for words again.

Old Jess watched as they left, satisfied with what he had said and with the way they had attended him. The quarters would be quiet tonight. By tomorrow, men would stop at the hut to speak with him apart and say

mistress would react. She knew Emilie was supposed to hate all the Yankees, but she knew too how white people stuck together against black. She stared, not speaking.

"Missy, what's happened?" Emilie asked for the third time, trying to put a gentleness in her tone to quiet any fears.

The girl drew a deep breath and then spoke. "It was—it was one of the soldiers, ma'am," she said. "Came at me from the woods when I was coming back from the quarters."

"One of Colonel Phillips's men!" Emilie was shocked. "We must inform him of this at once!"

"Oh no, ma'am please," Missy begged. "If I tell on him, he'll hurt me for sure the next time. He told me so."

"Hush, Missy, there won't be a next time," Emilie said. "Whoever he was, he's going to get punished severely enough so that this doesn't happen again. I will not allow my people to be so abused."

Missy closed her eyes, saying nothing.

"Come into the kitchen now and let Sully look after you. I can see you've been hurt," Emilie said. Then she stopped for a moment. "Tell me quickly, Missy—did he do anything else to you?"

"No, ma'am," Missy whispered. "I got away in time."

"Thank God for that!" Emilie exclaimed. "Come, let us go into the kitchen to get you taken care of. Tess can give you something to drink to calm your nerves."

Solicitously, as though she were caring for a child, Emilie led Missy into the back of the house and saw that she was seated in a kitchen chair. She stood by, watching as the other slaves carried out her instructions and ministered to the frightened girl. As soon as everything had been done, Emilie announced, "Come along now, we're going to see Colonel Phillips and tell him this dreadful thing."

Missy got up and the two of them walked back through the passageway to the door of Colonel Phillips' study.

A soldier stood posted there immobile, as Emilie knocked on the door. At the sound of his voice bidding her enter she grasped the handle of the door and walked in, pushing Missy slightly in front of her.

Jason looked up in surprise at the two of them.

"Tell the colonel exactly what happened, Missy," Emilie coaxed.

Missy stood there speechless. She did not want to suffer the embrassment of having to disclose the sordid details to this strange man, but she could not disobey a direct order from Miss Emilie.

"Sit down, Missy," said Emilie quietly, "and explain, however you want to, what has happened."

Missy sat down. "One of the soldiers came out from the woods and pulled me in after him." Missy spoke in a low voice staring down at the floor. "My bowl broke and I tried to get away, but he—he pulled me down and then I pushed him off me and ran." She looked up at Emilie as if to get her approval.

Emilie nodded. She turned from Missy to stare at the colonel.

Jason got up from his desk. He walked around to Missy and took her hand. "I cannot tell you how sorry I am that this has happened," he said, "and I assure you that everything will be done both to punish your assailant and to ensure that it does not happen again." He looked up at Emilie, who was still standing. Again she nodded. He turned to Missy. "Could you identify the man if you saw him?"

Missy looked up at Emilie, bewildered.

The young mistress caught the meaning in the girl's

eyes at once. "Colonel," she said softly, "I'm sure that Missy would recognize the man, but surely after this ordeal we cannot expect her to have to face every man in your force in order to pick him out. Surely there is some way we can at least narrow the possibilities and save her this further embarrassment."

"I think we can," Jason said, relinquishing Missy's hand and returning to his desk. "I'll send for all of the duty rosters. We will be able to ascertain which men were either free at the time or close by the area where it happened. As soon as we can eliminate the majority of men to be questioned, I will advise you and we can take whatever steps are next necessary."

"Thank you very much, colonel," Emilie said. "Come, Missy," and she put her hand out for the girl to get up and follow her.

As the door closed behind them Jason could not help but curse. Everything had gone fairly smoothly in his occupation of Les Chandelles over the last several weeks; with the somewhat obvious help of Francine Desbrosses, he was sure he had done much to reduce the fair Emilie's hatred of him. Now, with a setback like this, she would again be thinking of all Northerners as conquerers, beasts and worse. He would lose all the ground he had gained unless he could somehow bring this sorry affair to a just and quick conclusion.

He called to the sentry in the hall and asked that Captain Rogers be sent to him at once. When his second-in-command arrived, Jason described the incident and put him in immediate charge of the detail to find Missy's assailant. He explained that he wanted a list of all the possible suspects before that evening and the men listed held for questioning by him that very night.

"To get this matter completely resolved before

dinner," he told Rogers, "would be my prime desire. But if it proves impossible, then by all means it must be resolved tonight. I will question the men myself if necessary."

"I understand perfectly, sir," Rogers replied, saluting. Then he stepped back smartly and left the office.

Dinner that night was not a lively affair. Emilie, as if to underscore her anxiety over what had happened to her maid, insisted that she had to confine herself with Missy in her bedchamber and that a tray be brought up. The nastiness of the attack sobered even the usually vivacious Francine. Jason was much relieved when the meal was over, and even more so when he stepped out into the passageway after Madame Desbrosses and found Captain Rogers waiting to report to him.

"We have the culprit, sir," Rogers announced. "I took the liberty of questioning the man myself while you were at dinner, and the rascal confessed almost immediately."

"Good work," said Jason tersely.

"He admits to having waylaid the girl, but claims that she got away before anything worse could be done to her," Rogers said in an undertone.

Jason nodded. "The girl said as much."

"What shall we do with him, sir?" Rogers asked.

"I want him locked up for the duration of our stay here," Jason answered. "I don't think they've got a stockade on this plantation. If I'm mistaken, use it. If not, dispatch a detail of an officer and two soldiers to bring him to the military prison in New Orleans."

"Very good, sir." Rogers saluted and left.

Jason followed Francine and Gaston Desbrosses into the front salon. "I would like to impart this news to Miss Emilie as soon as possible," he said. "I wonder if we might send one of the servants to fetch her?"

"Of course." Francine smiled as she always did when he insisted on using the word "servant" instead of "slave." It was as if the latter word could never cross his lips unless he were chastising his hostess for her ownership of them. He could talk about slavery in the abstract, but never did he refer to those who served about the house or stables as slaves.

Emilie made her appearance soon after.

"The man has confessed," Jason said at once.

"I am very grateful to you," Emilie breathed. "Does this mean that Missy will not have to go through the ordeal of facing him?"

"Exactly," Jason affirmed. "Since the man has confessed and his version exactly corroborates hers, there is no need to put her through any more suffering. I leave her to your own good hands and tell you again I will do everything in my power to see that nothing like this occurs again."

"Thank you, Colonel," Emilie said. "I fully realize the hardship that this occupation imposes on your men, and I think it is a good measure of their respect for you that such an unfortunate outrage has not occurred before. I am sure it is far from an uncommon occurrence in other places."

Jason smiled at her. It was quite the longest and most complimentary speech she had ever addressed to him. "Might I ask then that you join us for at least the small remainder of the evening?" He smiled. "I am sure your guests will agree with me that company here is not quite the same without your lovely presence."

Emilie opened her mouth to say something, but stopped. He had gone a little further than he should in his flattery of her, but she had no wish to stop him. Instead she returned the smile and settled herself into an armchair that faced the sofa he had risen from.

They talked of things that were linked to plantation matters. Again Emilie was amazed to see how
much he had learned of the running of the great estate
and the cultivation of the cane. She sat with them in
the salon for just past an hour and then quietly made
her adieux.

She was thoughtful as Missy helped her undress for
the night. She could not help but think about Jason
Phillips and how entirely different he was from what
she had first perceived him to be. But she was not
ready to concede, as quickly as he and the Desbrosses
were, that the war was almost over and that the south
had lost.

Like the cane, she would bide her time to see which
way the wind was blowing and accept the destiny that
came at the season's end. Until then she would make
no unnecessary enemies. If Jason Phillips was indeed
a factor in determining the destiny of Les Chandelles,
then she would give him the widest path possible in
which to walk away from her hatred.

The next day Emilie was handed a letter. It was
from Anton Bledsoe down in the city, announcing that
he had received permission to make the trip upriver
to see the crop being cut as he usually did. Emilie
welcomed the news. It was a long time now since the
Desbrosses had arrived with their wagonload of the
latest information. It would be good to hear what
new events had taken place in the world so far removed
from her.

The news that he brought was not very welcome, if
one was hoping to hear of victories dear to the Southern
heart. Bledsoe confirmed everything that Francine and
her husband had said. If it was true that life was going
on much the same as usual in New Orleans, Anton
Bledsoe was quick to state, it was because the jaded
inhabitants of the city had resigned themselves to the

fact. Ladies who in the first months of the occupation had spat on Yankee soldiers in the streets now invited the officers into their homes. Business was going on at a brisk rate. The Yankees did not want to fall masters to a land that was desolate and needy.

"The port is as busy as ever, if not more so," Anton Bledsoe said when they were all seated at dinner that night. "Our commercial importance has not and will not fall victim to this strife."

The next morning Emilie rode out with Bledsoe and Jason to the cane. The colonel helped her alight from the carriage and they listened as the factor looked over the crop from the commercial man's point of view.

He conferred briefly with Henrique, who told him the number of field hands employed and the quantity of cane each had cut. Bledsoe nodded gravely. The figures were good.

Then they walked over to where freshly overturned soil, looking black and raw, was spread out.

"My soldiers were somewhat idle for the last month or two," Jason explained. "We set them to cutting down some additional acreage of unneeded timber." He pointed to indicate the extended area. "Now this section too has been matalayed. Miss Emilie has all of this additional acreage now under cultivation for next year's crop."

Bledsoe smiled. "Your domain has been expanded rather than curtailed as had been my great fear, my dear," he said, taking Emilie's hand. "Not many of the great plantations have fared so well during the occupation as Les Chandelles."

"Yes, but for how long?" Emilie asked ruefully. "More acres than ever to be grown and harvested, and very soon, the colonel tells us, there will be no more slaves to do the work."

"I have explained to Miss Emilie the system called

sharecropping that has been devised for the benefit both of the owners and the former slaves," Jason said quickly. "We are convinced that it will lead to even greater productivity in the future, once the system has been implemented."

Bledsoe looked thoughtful. "I've heard about this idea," he said. "In theory it sounds quite feasible, but I don't think it will ever work the way you suppose it will."

The men argued the merits of the system for a while as both Emilie and Henrique stood silently listening. Finally Bledsoe turned to the black overseer and grasped him by the arm. "You have done excellently well here," he said. "I am sure that your efforts will not go unrewarded when the proper time comes."

"Thank you, sir," Henrique answered quietly.

As they drove back in the hackney, Emilie thought about Bledsoe's words. She knew there was justice in what he said, yet she could not help but wonder how indeed she was to reward her overseer. Freedom would be his, indeed all of theirs, without her so much as lifting a finger. From the way the men were speaking it seemed as if even that decision would be made by others and merely imposed on her. She would have little or no say in what was to happen.

She thought then about each of the men sitting with her. Bledsoe would continue to handle the business of the plantation in the city, as he always had. But Jason—what part was he to play? This was a question that loomed more and more frequently in Emilie's mind every time she tried to set it on the future.

She had to admit to herself that had Francine not outlined her position in so coldblooded a way, she might have found herself more naturally inclined to the Northerner. There was no question that he was making every effort to please her and bend her favorably toward him.

She gazed keenly from the hackney to the endless fields they were driving past. Cut down and shorn of its green glory, the cane stubble was no such majestic sight as it had been only a few weeks earlier. Yet the vast extent of her holdings was even further emphasized by the stricken stalks and overturned earth. The Bonfils, save her, were all dead, Guy was dead. And everyone told her that the dreams and the glory of the South were, if not dead, quickly dying. Only the land still lived, only Les Chandelles continued on as though nothing had happened. Not even the few hundred blue-clad soldiers sheltered on her land greatly changed it. And nothing shall, Emilie determined once again.

16

Christmas had passed and with it the boiling down of the last of the old crop. 1865 dawned bleakly and rather quietly on the great plantation. An ancient bottle had been exhumed from Charles' old wine cellar, and a few toasts to the new year and to peace had been drunk in the salon by Emilie, Jason Phillips, and the Desbrosses, whom Emilie had urged to stay until the war was over, if possible, and until everything was settled. Monsieur Desbrosses obtained permission passes from Jason occasionally to go down into the city to tend to his affairs, but he always returned after no more than two or three nights' absence.

Always he brought news with him, and always the news left Emilie desolate.

She tried not to show it in front of the others, especially Jason. It wasn't that long ago that he was still considering her perhaps a dangerous Confederate spy. Now she assumed instead a mask of acquiescence, which in fact quickly became no mask at all. She was resigned to the Union victory and to making the best of it. This was the way that New Orleans had survived, her friends assured her, and it was the best way to protect her property and herself.

The seed cane had been planted in deep furrows in both the old and the newly cleared fields. Now, with plow and hoe, almost all the field hands were occupied with the cultivation of the new crop which would be laid by in early summer.

The spring months were routine in the fields. Emilie felt as though routine had overtaken the big house as well. Everything seemed to be going on as usual. Even Gaston Desbrosses' latest news, about the army that Robert E. Lee was bringing from Richmond, seemed to have no reality. Although the Virginian had been named commander of all the armies of the south, Emilie was given to understand that it was more title than anything else. The armies that he commanded were remnants, the battleworn and ragged survivors of four years of ceaseless fighting. Now they would gather up their dying strength and undying courage to make a great trek to Lynchburg and its storehouse of supplies, which could perhaps replenish and maintain them for yet another season's battles.

But an unruly Union general named Grant had other ideas. Soon rumors were heard that Lee had never made it to Lynchburg after all. At a small town in Virginia called Appomattox, the Southerner had surrendered his sword to Grant.

The Yankee soldiers were jubilant. They shouted and sang in the meadows, spilling over onto the driveway until their cheering and frolicking reached near to the main house. Their cries were not those of conquerors, but of men who could at last go home.

They were dispersed by a single soldier, galloping up the drive on a large black horse. The men fell to the sides of the road as the rider strained forward. The case protruding from his saddlebags showed that he was carrying a message of importance to the colonel. But although his business was urgent and official, he could not help smiling and shouting to the men on foot.

"It's over! It's over!" he yelled down at them, not

breaking gallop or stopping but urging his horse on.

The men resumed their cheers. Jason received the message in the large study. He glanced briefly at the short message and then turned to his orderly.

"Summon Madame Charpentier here at once," he instructed. "With the utmost civility." The terseness of his own order forced him to add the latter phrase. He did not want the soldier addressing Emilie with the same curtness.

Within moments she was in the study. He gestured her to sit down.

Emilie looked at him expectantly.

Jason spoke in a low voice. "Lee has surrendered to General Grant," he said. "It will be only a short time until the rest of the Confederacy follows suit. It is all over."

Emilie closed her eyes. "Thank God," she murmured. It was a relief to know that war was no more, even though defeat was now their lot. At least it meant an end to the killings and bloodshed and uncertainty. Emilie was grateful for that much.

"What will happen now?" Emilie asked.

"I don't quite know," Jason admitted. "There will be many in the South who will not take this defeat easily. There will be, I suspect, a long need for Federal presence here, whether civilian or military."

Emilie sat silent.

"Legally all of your slaves are free," Jason went on. "It is imperative that you act at once to determine the future of your estate. If Les Chandelles is to continue, you should make every effort to advise the people of that fact and what arrangements you will make for their livelihood."

Emilie nodded. "You mean something like the sharecropping you have been talking about?"

"Exactly," Jason replied.

"I don't know where to begin," Emilie admitted. She felt more uncertain than she ever had in her life, even more than when she knew that Charles was dead and that the entire burden of the plantation had been thrust upon her. Then it was simply a matter of continuing on. The plantation, slavery, everything was intact. But now that whole world had crumbled and a new one was opening up in front of her. She was being told that she must take her first tentative steps into it, but there was not even the memory of what her father might have done to guide her.

Jason read the perplexity on her face. "Miss Emilie, if you'll forgive me," he said. "I have taken the liberty during the past several weeks of devising a plan which might be useful to you. This is entirely my own doing, I assure you. There is no official sanction to this at all, but I knew that with war's end you would be facing this dilemma."

"Thank you," Emilie said in a dry voice.

"I did not want you facing it alone," Jason said.

Emilie looked up at him sharply. What motive had he, she wondered, to be so good to her, and so considerate?

"I think you should study these ideas and change them as you will," Jason went on as if not seeing her look. "If I may make a further suggestion—"

"Of course," Emilie interrupted.

"I think you should consult with your overseer and get his ideas as well. He seems to be a very capable fellow and he has done an excellent job for you, as your factor pointed out recently."

Emilie nodded. "Do go on."

"If you think I can be of further assistance I will be glad to sit down with you and Henrique and discuss this matter," Jason said. "And before you make a final determination I will get permission for Mr. Bledsoe to return here as well. He can advise you from a purely financial point of view as to your best interests."

"That would be extremely kind," Emilie said.

"I am assuming with all this," Jason said, indicating the papers he held in his hand, "that you are going to continue to maintain production at Les Chandelles."

"I did not think there was ever any alternative," Emilie said. "I have never considered that there was anything else to do. I was uncertain, though, as to the means of doing it, now the war is over and the slaves are no longer ours."

"That is the beauty of the plan," Jason exulted. "The land that belongs to you can be rented, and cultivated as it always has been. A part of the profits will go to you in order to pay for the land and whatever else you may provide them to get started with. The people will no longer be slaves but each truly free, each with his own piece of land to live on and section of field to cultivate."

"It will look as though nothing has changed," Emilie said, trying in her mind's eye to envision this new order of things.

Jason smiled again. "You're quite right," he said. "It will look exactly the same, and from your point of view it will be."

"Then if Les Chandelles continues and everything goes on as it has been, who has won the war?" she asked.

This time Jason's smile was broad and genuine. "We all have," he said. "Your life will be very much the same, my dear. You will have all of your servants, if they choose to remain with you, but you will pay them wages for their work, as is only proper."

"Dear me," Emilie said. "Wherever shall I get the money?"

Jason laughed. "That fellow Bledsoe must keep you

quite in the dark," he said. "You could have been paying all the people on this plantation for as long as its been standing and your family would never have felt the pinch."

"I see," Emilie said, although truthfully she did not quite. "But what if they do not want to stay?" she wondered. "What if Sully wants to leave or Tess or Missy . . ." her voice trailed off.

"Then by all means they must be permitted to do so," Jason said firmly. "They are free now, as free as you and I. I trust for your sake, because you have been a kind mistress, that those among your people whom you truly want to stay will choose to. But neither you nor I nor the Federal Government is going to force them to stay if they don't want to."

"You mean all of your soldiers who have kept Les Chandelles from losing its hands during these years will no longer do so?"

"That's right," Jason said. "With the war over we are no longer going to uphold these old contingencies. You must make you own arrangements with your people. I can only help guide you. In truth I am not required to do even that."

"Then I am all the more grateful to you," Emilie said. "Not only for the wise way in which you have helped to conserve my property during the conflict but for your extreme kindness in helping me now. I declare myself to be everlastingly grateful to you, Colonel Phillips."

He walked quickly from behind the desk and sat down beside her. "If only you could be more than that," he said. "If only you could learn to think of me in quite another way, as I do you."

"Sir," Emilie began, but she did not know what to say next.

"I love you, Emilie," he said simply. "This is not a

colonel speaking, nor a Yankee, but simply a man. I love you as a man loves a woman. I cherish you for all the beautiful and kind things I have seen in you. I know how difficult it has been for you to have us quartered here, especially for me to have invaded your home as I have, and I beg your forgiveness. Now, I ask only that as the nation binds itself together and all the dreadfulness of the war is past us, you look upon me as a man, and as a man who loves you very much."

She looked at him. The deep dark eyes she had once thought so fierce were brimming with kindness and concern for her now. Under the dark heavy moustache were lips that could speak tenderness as well as wisdom. She saw them move slightly now, almost trembling from the ardor with which he had spoken to her. Emilie felt the urge to lift her finger to his mouth to stop not only its tremor but the flow of words that would, unchecked, surely find their way to her heart.

For Jason Phillips did not speak lightly when he spoke of love. She knew that much. It would be so easy to lean upon his strength, to rely on his wisdom, to unshoulder the burdens that had nearly broken her these four long years. Yet easy as that all would have been, she felt a need to fight it, a confusion of emotions that paralyzed her will and kept her from acting. Yet this paralysis seemed a very boon to Emilie: She did not know what to say or do.

"My husband—" she faltered.

"He has been dead for more than two years, Emilie," Jason reminded her. "Because I knew how deeply you felt your bereavement, I never pressed my feelings toward you, although your period of mourning has long been over. I have waited all this time to savor not the victory of my side over yours, but the victory of holding you at last in my arms."

Emilie looked at him, her eyes widened almost in fear.

"That time has come," he said simply. "The war and the grieving are over. Now we can start a new life."

She closed her eyes again as she felt his arms slip around her. She started to resist but could not.

"I love you," he was whispering against her hair.

She tried to pull slightly away from him. "I cannot answer you now. I cannot tell," Emilie said. "You must give me some time."

"Of course," he said. "Only tell me, that I may continue to speak to you of my love and my feelings toward you and all that you hold dear."

Emilie smiled. "What woman would not permit it?" she asked. "I feel almost a traitor to my sex that I must beg you now to stop and let me return to consideration of those matters which you yourself have said are most in need of my attention."

"Of course." Jason released her gently.

"I—I cannot think of anything until the matter of my estate and the people has been settled," she said. "It is impossible for me to set my mind on any other sentiment, no matter how sweet or how sweetly said." She smiled at him with these words.

"What do you want to do first?" Jason was all business again.

"I would like to speak with Robert, my butler," Emilie said. "He is the mainstay here and I think will be very influential with the others."

"Shall I send for him?"

"Yes, please."

Jason walked to the front of the room and opened the door. It was, for both of them, almost as if the scene on the couch had not taken place. Once again all was business and the situation of the estate the foremost matter at hand.

Robert was summoned.

Emilie's announcement was terse. "The war is over," she said. "Everyone is free—free to go or to stay."

Robert smiled slightly, then resumed his usual bland expression.

"I would like everyone to remain, of course," Emilie said. "Especially you, Robert. I am able to pay wages for your services, and I think that with the help of Colonel Phillips I will be able to offer you and each of the others a fair amount. Then we can resume our lives here much as we always have."

"There will be some differences, ma'am," Robert said quietly.

Emilie stared at him.

"We will wish to live in our own houses, not necessarily attached to this house or down in the quarters," Robert went on. "We will want to live our own lives, free to marry and raise families as we choose."

"Of course, Robert," Emile said. "But are you speaking for yourself now, or for all of the others as well?"

"Although I have not been asked to speak on anyone's behalf, ma'am, I believe what I say represents the feelings of most of the people."

"Are you in love, Robert?" Emilie asked. She was suddenly consumed with curiosity about this man who had never shown any facet of himself other than that of the perfect servant. "Tell me, tell me, who is she?" Robert's emotional affairs were suddenly of more interest than anything else that was happening around her.

For once the butler seemed somewhat flustered.

"I have a fancy towards one of the girls in the house, ma'am," he answered at last. "That is true."

"But Robert," Emilie asked, "why did you not speak to me of this sooner?"

"I did not know that I would receive permission, ma'am," he said. "It seemed wiser to wait."

"But of course I would have consented, Robert," Emilie exclaimed. "What did you have to wait for?"

"For the war to be over, ma'am," Robert said proudly. "And to be my own master and to need not ask anyone."

"Well said!" Jason exclaimed, slapping the butler on the back. "I daresay she's a lucky girl, whoever she is."

"But one who will still be serving a master, even if only in her own house," Emilie observed wryly.

"If wages and other conditions are sufficient for my wife and myself we will remain," Robert said.

"I assure you they will be, and I thank you," Emilie replied jubilantly. "Now I would like to speak to the other house servants. Should we assemble them all at once or according to rank?"

"If you please, ma'am, I believe you would be advised to speak with Sully and Tess before the others, and alone. They have long service in this house and would feel belittled if spoken to along with the others."

"You're exactly right, as usual, Robert," Emilie said, "and if you would be so good as to ask the two of them to step in here, we can settle the matter at once."

He bowed his head slightly and walked out.

Emilie turned to Jason. "There," she said smiling, "I don't believe it's going to be so difficult after all. Do you?"

"No, I think what you want will be easily accomplished." He smiled back. "I think that Henrique should be sent for now, as well. By the time he gets here you will have concluded with the others."

Emile nodded, and Jason dispatched an orderly to the fields.

The usually imperious Tess looked nervous and ill at ease to be called so far from her usual domain. Beside her tall figure, Sully looked even more rotund.

Emilie told them to sit down, and the two women exchanged nervous glances. But the mistress spoke quickly and easily, telling them of the situation, putting them at their ease, praising them lavishly and expressing her great desire for them to continue in her employ.

Emilie's mind was growing dizzy with the possibilities of all the good she could now be doing. These trusted, loyal, loving servants could have neat little houses of their own and their leisure hours to themselves while she continued to have all of the comfort and privilege of their services. Life could go on after all just as it had, just as Jason had said, only as he had also said, even better. The prospect was lovely. Emilie had never felt truly comfortable with the conditions of her slaves. She had accepted it as a matter of course in the natural order of things, but there were always little prickling disturbances at the corners of her conscience. She remembered the day that André had spoken of black people living in freedom elsewhere and how harshly her father had silenced him. She remembered too the jibes of the Northerners which she had been so quick to dismiss. And most of all was the perhaps never-to-be-answered question of why Guy had left Les Saules and exiled himself to Europe for so many years, coming back only when he felt it his incontrovertible duty to do so. She remembered how impossible it was for her to conjure up a picture of Guy in the fields supervising, ordering, or meting out punishment to the slaves. It had been so out of keeping with his character that she had never been able to imagine it. Now she was sure that slavery was at the bottom of his uprooting. He had taken himself as far as he could from the institution he felt powerless to deal with and must have known himself powerless to change.

Emilie searched the faces of the two women seated before her. "Please stay," she said simply. "This has always been your home. Now it will truly be so."

Gaunt Tess nodded. Sully cleared her throat. "Yes, ma'am," she said. "We be free now but we will stay on here."

Impulsively Emilie leaned over and kissed each on the cheek.

The women went back to their chores.

"It has been settled with the house staff that they will stay on and receive wages," Jason was explaining to Henrique. "Now I know that Miss Emilie will have a generous offer to make to you too."

"I want you so much to stay, Henrique," Emilie said. "Not only for all you have done for me, but for all that you meant to my father. Your life has been lived mostly in bondage, but now you are a free man, as God, I am sure, always meant you to be." Emilie was almost surprised at her words, but not quite. There was something in his bearing that had always impressed her, and now that he had proved himself so completely she stood even more convinced.

"I have never been one for staying in a place too long unless I was forced to," Henrique said. "I am not dissatisfied with my place here or the opportunity you offer me, but I would like some time to think about it."

Emilie looked at Jason uncertainly.

"Of course, you will want to think it over," Jason said, "but your decision is of great importance. Not only because of the position you hold here. Most of the field hands who have left the other plantations have been employed by the army in New Orleans to repair the streets and other civic facilities. The army has hired as many people as it could afford, but there are already great numbers of idle unemployed ex-slaves who are wandering about the city with no place to stay and very little to eat. There is no telling when jobs can be found for them or if they can be trained to do work other than what they are used to. It would be a pity if all the men of Les Chandelles were to fall into this sad state of affairs. Far better for them to become planters and farmers themselves in this place which they have always known and can continue to live on as free men. What you do, Henrique, will influence the others."

"I understand that, sir," Henrique said.

"You would have a house of your own," Emilie said. "You could even have the house that St. Georges and his wife lived in. That's a good house, Henrique, and should you want to start your own family, of course you are free to do so. Perhaps you have a woman already. I mean—I mean—" Emilie started to blush furiously. "Perhaps there is someone whom you would like to marry."

"If there were"—Henrique grinned in spite of himself—"I would have done it by now."

"Yes, I expect you would have," Emilie admitted. "But please, Henrique, when can you let us know?"

"By tomorrow," he answered. "I must go back to the fields now. It is important that the men be spoken to. They must understand what is in front of them."

"I agree with you entirely, Henrique," Jason said. "And if you like I'll go back with you. I have tentatively drawn up a plan for the division of Les Chandelles into areas for all of the hands. Miss Emilie has not approved it yet, but at least we can give your fellows some indication of what they might expect if they stay." He turned to Emilie. "Is that acceptable to you, ma'am?" he asked in a most businesslike way.

"I would appreciate it a great deal, Colonel, if you would do that," Emilie said.

The two men went out. Emilie sat alone in her father's old study. She looked about at the well-known furniture, the walls with their shelves of seldom used books, the heavy curtains at the window. Then her eye was caught by another shelf that seemed somewhat in disarray. Curious, she went over to look at it. It was full of the journals that Charles had subscribed to, *DeBows Review* and *The Southern Planter,* volumes and volumes of them, plus one or two other guides she did not remember. She realized that the journals had been much used and consulted, and as she tried to decipher something written in the margin of an article about the marketing of cane, she realized that the handwriting was not her father's.

She took the journal over to the desk and compared it to something that Jason had left lying there.

The writing was identical. So that was how he had come to know so much about plantations and cane! Emilie smiled. He must have spent night after night down here studying and learning everything that he could from her father's shelves!

She walked slowly back and returned the journal to its place. She started up to her own room, oddly pleased at her discovery.

Then she remembered Missy. She was going to have to tell Missy about the war's end and being free. Emily was startled. She realized that she had no idea of how her closest servant would react.

But Missy's demeanor was characteristic. She stood

silently listening to Emilie's recitation of the facts and possibilities, nodding her head from time to time.

Missy's mind was jumbled. Here was her mistress announcing freedom, the freedom that Young Jess had run off to find. Now he was gone, could be anyplace, could be free or unfree, could be dead or alive. Here she was, still at Les Chandelles, from which he had urged her to run, but she, she was free now after all. It seemed unreal.

"Do you want to stay, Missy?" Emilie was asking. "I would love you to, and would be glad to pay the same wages you might receive were you to go look for work at another estate or in the city."

"I don't want to leave, mistress," Missy answered. "There's no place for me to go." If Jess ever came back it would be to here, and here she would stay. And wait.

"That's wonderful, Missy," Emilie declared. "And I'm going to find out about getting you a house, a little house, of your own. It won't be necessary for you to sleep in here any more. We'll work out all the details as soon as I can."

"Thank you, ma'am," Missy murmured.

"And of course if you want to get married, that's entirely up to you," Emilie said. "Is there a young man?"

Missy shook her head. "No, ma'am, not now," was all she could permit herself to say.

But the words stung Emilie. She took Missy's hand. "Was there someone, then?" she asked her.

Missy's head only hung lower.

"You can tell me, Missy," Emilie insisted. "If there's anything at all that I can do to help, I promise you that I will."

The tears began to roll out of Missy's eyes. "You can't help. Nobody can," she sobbed.

Emilie was at a loss. "Who is it?" she asked. "Don't cry, Missy. Tell me."

"Young Jess, ma'am," Missy cried, unable to contain herself any longer. "The one who ran off to freedom. Young Jess."

"Old Jess' grandson?" She remembered him now. She hadn't thought of him for the longest time, but now she remembered him quite clearly. She knew she hadn't seen him in a very long time. "Where is he?"

"He ran off and never come back," Missy said. "Now freedom's here but not Young Jess."

"Perhaps he'll come back, Missy," Emilie soothed her. "He'll want to see his grandfather if he possibly can." She looked at her servant's face and added gently, "And he'll want to see you again too, Missy, if he knows how you feel about him. Does he?"

Missy nodded her head.

"Don't worry about it, Missy," Emilie said reassuringly. "We'll wait for him together."

"This has been one of the happiest days of my life," Emilie declared gaily at dinner that night. "I cannot remember the last time I felt so good."

Francine laughed. "The role of *la chatelaine* becomes you, my dear," she said. "You are quite happy at being *la bienfaitrice* as well as *la mediatice.*

"And what could be more appropriate," Gaston declared, "when that is exactly what we are feasting on tonight." Robert had brought in a long tray of the French bread stuffed with oysters that had somehow assumed the name *la mediatrice.*

"I don't believe I have ever eaten this before," Jason said, biting into the delicacy.

"It is one of the great favorites of our Creole cuisine, my dear," Francine said. "I'm sure you will learn to savor it."

"As I do this fine wine," her husband added, twirling his glass slightly. "And," turning with a slight bow to Emilie, "the marvelous picture I have had of your activities today, my dear. We have long been bombarded with the most vulgarly conceived illustrations of 'Lincoln Freeing the Slaves' and I assure you I much prefer the picture described for me of Emilie freeing the slaves. I find it far lovelier."

In spite of herself Emilie joined in the laughter of the others. It had been a good day, highly satisfying to her.

Then she grew a little more reflective. "I cannot thank you enough, Colonel Phillips, for the help you have been to me during all of this," she said. "I must frankly admit I would have been completely at sea without your planning and good advice." She turned toward Francine. "And you, my good friends who have elected to stay with me all this time. I do not know what I could have done without you."

"We had to be with you," Francine assured her. "It was uppermost in my mind the entire time we were in New York. I wanted nothing but to get back here to stay with you."

"Thank you," Emilie said, "and please, I hope you will continue to regard Les Chandelles as your home for as long as you can. I fear that I will need you more than ever now."

"We will stay either until our welcome wears thin," Gaston Desbrosses declared, "or until your dear departed father's cellar runs dry."

Even Emilie was able to join in their light laughter.

She was still happy and slightly heady from the wine when she retired to her chamber later that night. She was in her nightgown with the covers drawn up when Missy slipped toward the door.

"Where are you going, Missy?" Emilie asked in surprise.

"It's freedom now, ma'am, and I don't have to sleep in here any more," Missy reminded her.

"Oh, yes, you're right," Emilie rejoined quickly. "But wherever will you go?"

"I'll go and make me a bed in the old man's cabin," Missy said. "I've been taking care of him all this time and I can do it better being there. He's awfully weak, Miss Emilie."

Emilie bit her lip. "Does he know about freedom coming?" she asked. She thought Old Jess one of the dearest people she had ever known, and certainly if anyone deserved freedom he did.

"I'm going to tell him about it now, if he hasn't heard already," Missy said.

"I wish I could go with you," Emilie said impulsively, but she knew that it was not quite the proper time to make an appearance in the quarters. "You go along now," she told Missy, "and I—I will come down to see Old Jess the first thing in the morning and talk with him myself."

"Thank you, ma'am," Missy murmured and went out.

The street of the quarter was filled with noise and people. The celebrating had begun as soon as they had returned from the fields. A few of the Yankee soldiers had even come over from their tented meadow to listen to the music and join in the festivity.

Missy made her way past the jostling, dancing crowd. She almost lingered to listen to the fiddle and the mouth organ that the field women were lifting their skirts and dancing to, but she was more eager to see Old Jess. She knew that the sound of the music would carry into his cabin. She hugged the blanket roll with her few clothes inside closer to her and made her way to the last little house.

He was inside on his pallet. A candle had been lit and stood burning on the table, casting its shadows along the walls.

Old Jess raised himself up on his elbow when she came in. He watched silently but approvingly as she spread her blanket out in a corner and found a shelf to lay her few belongings on. Then she went over and knelt down beside him. Her eyes were shiny with the excitement she had not dared reveal in front of the mistress.

"Did you hear, Old Jess? Did you hear?" she asked him eagerly. "It's freedom! Freedom's come!"

"I know." The words came in a hoarse whisper but the old man was smiling too.

"Now he'll come home!" Missy went on. "Now that there's freedom here, Young Jess'll come back, won't he?"

"Sure he will," Old Jess said. "Sure he will."

"And I'm going to stay here and take care of you all the time," Missy said, " 'cept when I've got to be up at the big house. I'm working for wages now. I'm going to have some money when Jess gets back, and the mistress she said it's all right for me to stay here with you till Jess gets back."

"That's right, that's right," Old Jess said, but the exhilaration seemed to have worn him out. He sank back on the pallet and closed his eyes. "That's right," he murmured again.

"You sleep now and rest yourself, Old Jess," Missy commanded. She smiled suddenly, realizing it was the first time in her life she had told somebody else to do something.

"Can you hear the music?" she asked softly, hovering over him as she smoothed out his blanket.

Old Jess nodded.

"You sleep now," she told him again. "I'm going to go out for a while and see the singing and dancing. I'm going to see the freedom. Then we wait till Young Jess gets home."

17

"'Soldiers getting soldiers' pay,'" Ben spat out, "like hell. They think we're nothing and we're getting nothing."

Young Jess looked around at the refuse and sprawling desolation that had just recently been a bustling army camp. He could not meet the eyes of his friends. There was nothing that he could say to them that would make them feel any better or make any difference in the miserable situation they were all in. The army had come in and made them promises. Now the army had moved out and had taken those promises with them.

Most of the men he knew had no place to go back to. The old plantations they had slaved on had been burned down, ruined, or left to decay by the deserting owners. There were no jobs waiting for the Union's veterans, at least not the black veterans who had begged to be allowed to fight and after having proved themselves in battle had been left to fend for themselves in the bleak aftermath.

Young Jess wondered if he had a place to go back to. He hated to leave these men who had come to look upon him as their leader, but he knew that there was nothing he could do for them any more. They would have to stay as they were or strike out on their own, until the government made up its mind about what to do with them.

They had heard the slogan "Forty acres and a mule," but nothing more. It had remained a slogan and a dream for the freed men who now had to take up their lives again.

The white soldiers of the North were for the most part slowly returning to the cities and farms that they had known before the war, but for these black comrades in arms there was no such return.

Jess felt as uprooted as the others. Yet he knew that he had a choice where they had none. He could go back to Boston, the city he was just beginning to feel at home in when the war had taken him from it, or he could stay in the South and make his way back to Les Chandelles.

Les Chandelles! He hated the very sound of the word. But there, if anyplace, was where his grandfather was, and maybe where Missy was too. If the war hadn't reached there, then it was possible that the place stood intact. Certainly if any man had been strong enough and hard enough to protect his lands it would have been Charles Bonfils.

Jess could feel his blood almost boil at the thought of having to confront his hated old master again. But the heat was tempered with the idea of seeing Old Jess again, of being with Old Jess in freedom at last.

The ties of blood vanquished the heat of blood, and Jess made up his mind to go back. Besides, the master would be master no more.

He bade farewell to his friends, the men who had gone into battle with him and emerged victorious. He scribbled his name and the name of the plantation and the parish on a piece of paper for each of them, telling them that that was where he was headed and perhaps could be reached. The other soldiers looked at the torn fragments as if each were a talisman that somehow would keep Jess with them. He said goodbye to each in turn, Ben and Johnny and the others. Then he left them and went to the small staff house that was all that remained of the once enormous camp. The head of the regiment, Colonel Higginson, had already gone back to Boston in triumph. Jess didn't blame him, nor did he need him. There was nothing that Thomas Wentworth Higginson could do for him now. Perhaps someday in the future they would meet again, but right now Jess had his own life to go back to, and there the Bostonian could be of no use.

What Jess needed was someone who could get him a suit of civilian clothes. He was going to have to cross the entire South to get from the Carolina coast to the Louisiana parishes, and going in the uniform of the Union Army was not the safest way to travel across the bitter and defeated land.

He got his clothes and a pass, as well as his discharge papers. The pass and the papers would be necessary when he went from one command to another, but Jess knew that if he were stopped by any Rebel renegades on the back roads they could cost him his life.

In some places the railroads had been put back into commission by the Union forces and Jess was able to cover the miles rapidly. Then he would run out of track going in his direction and would have to take to the road for days at a time. He didn't go hungry. The army had set up feeding stations at all its outposts in order to take care of the thousands of ex-slaves who came pouring off the plantations looking for help. Jess was shocked not only by the desolation of the countryside, which he had expected, but by the defeat etched on faces both black and white. He wondered more than once whether he might not have been better off staying with the army. Then at least he would have had some covering over his body at night and a sense of still belonging to some place and some task.

But the army had not encouraged the black members it had belatedly admitted to linger long once the fighting was over. Some of the Yankee soldiers he came across did not belive that he had fought in their army. Once he was even accused of having killed some unknown white named Jess Martin and stealing his papers. It was only when he was able to give an account of himself, his regiment, and all the officers whose names he could remember under General Saxton's command that he was released and permitted to go on.

There was a flatbed ferry that went across the river that formed the border between Georgia and Alabama, but the other passengers were mostly returning Johnny Rebs and they did not let Jess get on. One of the few not wounded pushed Jess when he tried to board and Jess found himself on his backside on the wharf. He wondered who had really won the war and was angry enough to fight the surly veteran, but common sense told him he had no chance, not with so many of them. Nor would his Union papers be of help—just the opposite.

Jess trudged along till he found a Union post farther downriver and was able to get transportation there.

Then he was walking again on roads that were full of people going in both directions. He couldn't understand why so many people would be anxious to get someplace that as many other people were anxious to leave. But the roads stayed clogged with refugees both black and white, sometimes whole families pulling their belongings in creaking carts, mothers carrying babies in their arms while small children clung to their skirts. Here and there an elderly person would be borne on a litter or atop the heaped-up belongings of a wagon, but almost everybody walked.

Jess saw the ruination of the South. Even where great houses had not been burned and ravaged, fields stood stark and empty. Masters and slaves alike had deserted, leaving cotton to rot in the boll, cane and tobacco and swampy riceland to spoil unattended. He was glad when, pitching even farther southward, he got to the coast and was able to get himself on a small vessel that was sailing from Mobile Bay to New Orleans.

Although he had seen the Crescent City only one time and then stealthfully as he was being smuggled through it, Jess knew that once he reached there he would have little difficulty making his way upriver to the plantation.

All the desolation he had seen frightened him, and he found himself almost wishing that despite his hatred for it, he would find the old place intact. He knew too well what the destruction of the land would mean to ex-slaves, and he could not glory in the downfall of the owners. Plantations deserted meant land wasted and no need for the ex-hands who now needed work more than anything else. Jess knew that freedom to starve was no freedom at all. He had enough of that before the war, and now it stung him that he was seeing so much of it afterward. On the roads, at the army camps where they lined up for handouts, in the streets and stations of the whole defeated South he saw the bands of aimless men, the long-overworked for whom there suddenly was no work. They needed to be taught, to be trained, to be employed, to be given places to sleep and something to eat. There was so much to be done that his very bones ached with the thought of it. Where would they begin? Where would it all start?

He lay on the deck of the boat that night, his head on his kit bag, tossing and turning, haunted by the hungry faces and vacant eyes that he had been staring at ever since he had left the camp. What was to become of the people now? They had left their bondage, as was their God-given right, but what were they to do next? No one had told them. All of their lives, they had lived being told what to do, and now suddenly there was no one to tell them.

What was worse, there was nothing to do. A man whose only means of life had been his strength now had nothing to put that strength to and thus no way to make a life for himself.

Jess didn't know what had angered him more, the sight of his unfortunate fellow ex-slaves or the rough treatment he received at the hands of the vanquished Rebs. Who *had* won the war? He didn't know the answer.

New Orleans, when they disembarked, seemed as normal to him as a place could be. It had the same bustle of activity, of noise and people, as Boston had when he had first got off the train there before the war had broken out. If cities were ruined and people were starving elsewhere in the South, New Orleans seemed to know nothing about it. Jess was heartened by the city. He saw the neatly dressed black work gangs supervised by union officers everywhere on the streets. There didn't seem to be as much bitterness on the white faces he saw, although more than once he caught the hateful stares of both men and women as he hurried past.

He wondered why they seemed so angry at him. He hadn't noticed anyone casting disdainful looks at the street workers. Other people seemed barely to notice them at all as they bent over their picks and shovels.

Perhaps that was it, Jess thought to himself. They are

so used to seeing black people with bent backs they don't mind it. I guess I'm walking too upright for them. He wondered if there was something still left of the military training in his bearing. If he carried himself like a soldier, these people would know for sure, even without benefit of insignia, that he had fought on the Union side against them.

Jess grinned to himself. It might be pleasanter if he slouched his shoulders and shuffled a little, but he was damned if he was ever going to do that again in his life for anybody. Besides, shuffling wasted time, and now that he was back in Louisiana and near the river he was growing more anxious every moment to get on with his journey and find Old Jess.

Churning up the great river, with as much frequency as before the war, if not even more, were the giant steamboats like the one on which Jess had made the first leg of his journey up North so long ago. Now he was able to take passage on one that would leave him at the landing a few miles below Les Chandelles. From there he would walk the rest of the way to the plantation, unless he was lucky enough to meet someone with a wagon or carriage who would give him a lift.

Jess stood at the rail of the bow of the smoke-belching steamboat. From what he could tell, the land seemed no different from when he had left it. There was no evidence of burning or pillage. The familiar green of the cane soon rose to meet him, although it was early in the growing season and the stalks had barely begun the climb that would see them tower and wave six feet and more in the air. The leaves too were of a color that bespoke new growth, but even this seemed a good sign to Jess. The cane, when he hated it most, was full grown. The tending it needed at this season was with hoe and rake to attack the weeds that grew so quickly in those fertile, watered fields and would choke off the growth of the cane. Backbreaking and mind-numbing as it was, still it was easier than cutting the tall cane in the blistering heat of full summer. If he had to come back to cane at all, this was as good a time as any.

Louisiana, on the eastern side of the Mississippi, seemed to have escaped much of the destruction that the Union forces had caused in the other places Jess had passed through. Maybe then times wouldn't be so bad for the people here, he thought; if the plantations stood, then the work would have to be done. And with freedom here, that work was going to have to be paid for. Maybe he had made the best choice after all, coming home.

It was early morning when they arrived at the landing. Nobody paid any attention to him when he got off, and Jess started walking, following the road north that would take him straight to the driveway of Les Chandelles. He shifted his bag back onto his shoulder and started off. It was lucky that the sun wasn't too hot, he thought; he was able to keep up a brisk pace. He smiled, thinking that this was the first time he had ever walked this road with shoes on.

From time to time a wagon passed in either direction, but they were always white people, smallholding farmers, he thought, and he did not want to ask for a ride. He wished he had thought to bring some food or water with him, but in his eagerness to get off the steamboat he had completely forgotten. Now his throat was getting dry. Jess thought he would keep his eyes open for some small creek that he might be able to drink from. He was still too far from home to be familiar with the area, but he knew that if he kept a sharp lookout he was bound to meet some running stream. He hitched the weight of his bag onto his shoulder and kept walking. He was grateful for the giant trees that lined the road, their thick-leafed branches shading him from the increasingly intense sun.

Jess blinked and quickened his pace when he saw the silver movement of a small brook just ahead of him. The shoulder of the road sloped down to a small gully where the water ran. Jess stepped down and followed it, glad of the sight of the clean running water over the stones at the bottom of the brook.

He took off his bag and put it down on the earth beside him and then leaned over, gulping mouthfuls of the running water.

"Get up slowly and don't reach for anything," a man's voice sounded above him.

Jess moved only his eyes, keeping his head very still. He caught a glimpse of the barrel of a gun beside his ear. He rose slowly as the voice instructed, not turning around to face whoever it was until he was told to.

"Who are you?" the man demanded. "What are you doing around here?"

"I'm headed for Les Chandelles," Jess answered. "The old Bonfils place."

"Oh yeah?" the man said. "What business have you got there?"

"I used to live there. I'm going back to see my grandfather."

"Back from where?" his questioner wanted to know.

Jess thought for a moment. His eyes took in the grimy faded gray of the man's clothing and the look of his weapon. He had to be a Reb, Jess knew, and he wasn't likely to take kindly to Jess' story.

"I've been down to New Orleans," Jess said. "They made me go down there to work. Now they say I can go back home."

"They?" There was a shrewd look in the man's face. "Who's they? And didn't they teach you to say sir when you were talking to your betters?"

"Yes, sir," said Jess, looking down at the ground. "Sorry, sir." He hated himself for doing it, for slipping so easily back into the rough guttural syllables of a field hand and even worse, the cowering acquiescence to the cracker's demands.

"That's better," the man said. "Now hand me over that bag, and no tricks, you understand?"

Jess nodded. He picked up his kit bag and handed it over. The man grabbed it with his free arm, still keeping his rifle trained squarely on Jess.

Jess tried to look humbly fearful. He was glad that he had his papers inside his shirt right next to his skin. All the man would find in the kit was some old clothes. If he realized that they were Yankee, Jess would confess to stealing them.

But the man didn't seem to care what he had, or where he had gotten it, only if it was useful as loot. But nothing was. He threw the bag disdainfully back on the ground.

"There, you pick that up," he snapped, "and you just walk on in front of me. Let's see if you're really going to where you said you was."

Jess walked in front as the grizzled vet mounted his horse. He ordered Jess to keep walking while he kept his horse at a slow clip and cradled the rifle in his arm. Jess was grateful for at least having gotten some water. It wasn't nearly so hard to walk now. Still, the humiliation of arriving back home as someone's prisoner instead of as a free man rankled him. For so many long months and years now he had an image of what it would be like when he at last returned in freedom to greet his grandfather. Now this damn interfering Reb was going to ruin it all. He was going to deliver him to the plantation much the same way the farmer Higgins had done the first time Jess had tried to run away and Higgins had bound him and dragged him back to Charles Bonfils.

The dust of the road tasted like ashes in Jess' mouth now. This was not the way he wanted to come back.

There was no way to break and run for it. The horse and rifle determined that. There was nothing to do but hope that the man would grow tired of moving at the slow pace Jess' walking forced on him, give up the game, and leave him as abruptly as he had found him. But Jess had no such luck.

His captor seemed happy enough to idle away his day following Jess, taunting and baiting him with every insult his mind could come up with. He jeered at the idea of freedom for darkies, although Jess knew full well from the man's speech and manners that he himself had never owned slaves. He insulted the idea of Jess' manhood and the easy whoring ways of all black women. He taunted Jess with what would happen to that freedom now that white Southern men were coming out of the army and back to their own homes to defend their lands and their women. "You think you were bad off as a slave, that ain't nuthin' to what's going to happen to you now, black boy," he taunted him.

Jess felt his spine go rigid. It would take no more than a sudden unexpected move on his part to grab the halter of the horse and spin the animal around so fast that the rider would be knocked down. He played with the idea for several moments, his thoughts at least giving him the benefit of blocking out the dreary unending insults that the man seemingly never tired of cackling over.

But if he misjudged his quarry, if the man were a better horseman or better marksman than he suspected him of being, it could be all over just as quickly, and with Jess sprawled out on the road with a bullet in his back.

It was not worth the risk. Every step he took brought him closer to the plantation. Once there he would be safe even if his entrance was not that of the conquering hero he had envisioned.

That was only foolishness anyway, he told himself. He wanted to look like a hero in Missy's eyes. He wanted to return as a conqueror to the defeated Charles Bonfils. But these things were no more than vanity, Jess reprimanded himself. His true reason for coming back was to see his grandfather and to speak of freedom to him. It didn't matter who or what got him back there. The important thing would be that they would both be together again, alive and for the first time simultaneously free. The conditions that Old Jess had known as a boy and Young Jess had known only in the past few years of fighting would at last mesh for them, at the same time. That was what was important. Maybe this old cracker was a blessing in disguise, protecting him the rest of the way to Les Chandelles from far worse things that might befall him. There was killing and looting all over the South, most of it perpetrated by the embittered returning veterans of the defeated Confederate Army. Maybe this one foul-mouthed Reb was saving him from being jumped by a gang who might easily kill him for the sorry contents of his pack.

They trudged on, rounding a slight bend in the road. Jess thought he saw water again up ahead. He was about to turn and ask if they could stop when a familiar but long-unheard sound greeted his ears—the hoofbeats of several horses coming at full gallop. Jess stood still and waited.

No sight could have been more welcome to him

than the blueshirted cohort that quickly came into view.

"Whoa!" the leader called, holding out his hand at the sight of Jess and the mounted gunman.

Two of the soldiers got down from their horses. They held their rifles in their hands and advanced toward Jess and his captor.

"Dismount," the captain, still on horse, commanded the Rebel.

The man got down slowly, still clutching his rifle until one of the soldiers took it from him.

"What's going on here?" the captain asked.

The Rebel looked up. "I was just riding up this road when I found this darky," he said. "Looked to me like he might be a troublemaker, so I was just bringing him back to where he belonged."

"And where's that?" the captain asked.

"He says he's from Les Chandelles, and I was taking him back there," the man replied.

The Captain looked down at Jess. "Is that right?" he asked.

"The part about my going back to Les Chandelles is right, captain, sir," Jess said.

The captain grinned. "How do you know my rank, boy?" he asked.

Jess returned the grin. "Corporal Jess Martin, First South Carolina Volunteers, at your service, sir."

"Active?" the captain asked.

"No, sir, been mustered out and I've come back," Jess replied.

"Why do you want to be coming back to Les Chandelles?" the captain asked.

"My grandfather, sir," Jess said. "I want to see him and if he's in fit condition maybe bring him back North with me."

"Back North," the captain echoed. "Back North where?"

"I was in Boston, sir, when the fighting broke out," Jess said. "I was thinking we might want to go back there."

"Let me see your papers, son," the captain said. Jess reached into his shirt and handed them up.

"Everything seems to be in order here," the captain said after looking through them. "Except," he added, "for your friend here." He jerked his head toward the man who stood between the two soldiers.

"Reckon he hasn't heard who won the war?" Jess grinned and quickly added "sir."

"Here," he replied, handing the papers to Jess. "Get up behind one of my men and we'll get you back in more style than your friend was going to." Jess picked up his kit and looked among the soldiers, one of whom quickly made room for him behind his saddle. Jess jumped up and put his arms around the man's waist while the horse adjusted itself to the additional weight. "What shall we do with him, Captain?" one of the soldiers on foot asked.

"Take his gun and send him off in the other direction," the captain ordered. "We don't want any firearms in the hands of these Johnny Rebs. In fact, I've got half a mind to throw him into the lockup, but I think he's learned his lesson."

The troop wheeled their horses around and started back in the direction from which they had come. Jess held on for dear life, smiling at the luck that had changed again and that would see him return with a group of fellow soldiers. Now he was sorry that he had discarded his army blues after all. It would have been nice to have come back in full uniform.

The captain signaled for the soldier whose horse

Jess was sharing to ride up alongside so that he could talk to him.

"What were you doing in Boston?" he wanted to know.

Jess related the story of his running away and his adventures until he found himself attached to Colonel Higginson.

"You'll have a good pile of stories to tell your children and grandchildren." The captain smiled. "Do you have a gal waiting for you back here?"

It was Jess' turn to grin. "I hope so," he admitted. "She worked in the house for the young mistress. I hope she's still there."

"Do you mean the one called Missy?" the captain asked.

Jess brightened. "Yes, that's her," he answered in surprise. "But how did you know?"

"Our outfit is bivouacked at Les Chandelles," the captain disclosed. "We've been headquartered there for the past two years. Reckon your Missy will be glad enough to see you. I don't think she's taken up with anyone else. Seems like a quiet girl. I guess she's been waiting for you."

"I guess so." It was hard for Jess to contain his glee. Then his mind grew somber. "Do you know my grandfather?" he asked quickly forgetting in his haste and excitement to add the necessary sirs that had been drummed into him. "He's an old man, the one they call Old Jess."

"I've never seen him," the captain replied, "but I think he's still there. It seems to me that I've heard about some old slave that all the others kind of kowtow to."

"That would be him," Jess said.

"Well, you'll know in a minute or two," the captain

said. "Here's the fork to Les Chandelles just in front of us."

"Can you let me off at the quarters, captain, sir?" Young Jess asked. "I want to see my grandfather."

He slipped easily off the back of the horse and, slinging his bag over his shoulder, made his way along the wooded area. Through the trees he could see a large group of blacks walking toward him, their heads bent, and except for a few dark murmurs, completely silent. Jess was surprised to see men and woman walking slowly together, back toward the quarter, at this time of day. It was much too early for work in the fields to have stopped. He knew that conditions would be different now that the war was over and they were all free, but this did not look like the kind of difference he had expected.

He adjusted his pack on his back and moved quickly through the live oaks and around a giant cypress to catch up with the slowly moving file.

"What's going on here?" he asked the first man he came abreast of. He didn't know his name, but he looked familiar.

"Funeral," was the brief muttered reply.

Jess's spirits sank. Of all the days he would have wished to be unmarred by any sadness, this time of homecoming was it. For so many years he had dreamed of this triumphant return and fancied the unalloyed joy that his reappearance in the quarters would bring. Now his return would be simply an incident in a day that had already been specially marked for memory.

"Do you know me?" Jess asked. "Do you know where my grandfather is?" He knew that Old Jess would lead the people on an occasion like this. Yet as he peered among the people still filing through the trees he caught no sight of him.

The man he had spoken to looked at him impatiently. He was anxious to get back to the quarters.

"My grandfather," Jess repeated. "Do you know where he is?"

"Dead." The man said the word and moved away quickly.

Jess stood against the cypress and supported himself on the gnarled black trunk. Old Jess dead! His mind reeled as tears flooded unbidden into his eyes. If this silent cortège was the aftermath of his grandfather's funeral, then he must have died within the past few days. By only so much had Young Jess missed seeing him. By only countable hours had they been kept from looking at each other in the freedom one had been born to and the other sought all his life.

He blinked back his tears. His sorrowing would have to wait for another day. There was nothing he could do for Old Jess now except to live in the hope and the promise that the old man had always held out for him. Jess put his hand to the stone that hung inside his shirt and whispered hoarsely, "Goodbye, old man, old grandfather, goodbye."

He walked away swiftly, cutting his way through the forested area and up toward the lawn above which the big house stood.

He was surprised to see the state of ruin it was in, the proud columns of the veranda battered and smoke-darkened. He wondered if there had been a battle fought on the plantation, but his war-wise eyes saw no other signs of fighting. He strode across the wide greens purposefully, until at last he stood in front of the mansion that for so long had stood for everything he most hated and feared in the world. Jess stared up at the mansion.

He remembered how he had been trained for the work of a house slave. How he had to walk silently, never speaking unless spoken to, always answering in a whisper, "Yes, ma'am" or "No, ma'am." Always silent, almost mute, damn near invisible, if they could manage that.

Jess smiled grimly. Now it was only the place where he would find the other one he had come questing for. No need to be quiet now.

"Missy!" he yelled with all his force. He shouted the name again, not caring if the noise brought the rest of the pillars tumbling down. "Missy!"

Robert stepped out on the veranda to see who was shouting so, but Jess didn't even acknowledge that he saw him.

"Missy!" he yelled again with all the force in his body.

Now he could hear the sound of activity from within. He grinned, paused, waiting to see what would happen next. Surely all of creation must have heard him by this time!

She came hurtling through the door, skirts flying, apron billowing, rushing down the steps and toward him with a fury he had thought only cannonballs capable of. She flung herself into his arms thrusting herself against him, hugging him, grasping him till she near knocked the breath out of his body. He tried to squirm out of her frantic embrace, laughingly trying to hold her at arm's length so that he could look at her, but she would have none of it. She clung to him with all the strength of her being. He could feel her body shake and tremble and then felt his shirt wet with her tears.

"Missy." His voice was gentle now. The time for shouting was over. "I've come back, Missy. We're free."

"I know, I know," she sobbed. "I knew you'd come back. I knew it!"

Slowly from inside the house others began gathering on the veranda to watch them. Robert stood silently, not admonishing any of the housemaids who stood close by. Even Sully came out, a smile brightening her round face.

From the yard, from the stables, others dropped their work and left their chores and came and stood quietly watching the young couple locked in embrace.

Nobody spoke, nobody said a word. The only sound was Missy, sobbing and trying to choke back the sobs, trying to say Young Jess' name and with it all the other things she had longed to say to him all of her life. But the words would not come, nor were they necessary.

Tess appeared from the kitchen, her helpers behind her, all solemnly watching; even the yard babies who followed their mothers from the quarters to the house and squabbled and sucked cane and played outside the kitchen door all day were quiet as if they too understood.

Emilie watched from a window inside the second story. The scene below spread out in front of her like a tableau, the groups of people clustered here and there on the lawn and the drive. There were others, she was sure, on the veranda, where she could not see them. She watched as they did, in silence, as Missy swayed slightly, still holding fast to Young Jess, as though she would never let go of him. Some Yankee soldiers coming up the drive, no doubt with some message for their colonel inside, stopped and stood as still as the others. Emilie noticed them, and she smiled, glad that they too had sensed the moment and had not interrupted it.

A voice at her shoulder broke the silence. Emilie jumped.

"What is it, my darling?" Francine Desbrosses was demanding. "What in the world is going on?"

"It's Young Jess," Emilie said simply. "Young Jess has come home."

18

Jason had sent an orderly to ask Emilie to the study. She sat facing him, wondering what he had to tell her that could not wait until dinner.

"I wanted you to be the first to know this," he said, looking at her carefully and comprehending her anticipation. "I have just come from Les Saules. I have tendered an offer to your father-in-law for the purchase of that property."

"Was your offer accepted?" Emilie asked.

"Yes, it was," Jason answered. "I wish it had not been under such circumstances, but the loss of the younger son has now been confirmed."

"Stephan." Emilie's hand went to her mouth and she bit down hard on her knuckle.

"I'm sorry, terribly sorry, to have to tell you that as well," Jason said tenderly. "I am sure that you were fond of your late husband's brother."

"He was Chaz' closest friend. Now they are all gone. Its—it's just as madame had said it would be. The house of Bonfils and the house of Charpentier are gone, all gone."

"No, not gone, my dear, you're mistaken there." Jason came around the desk and sat down next to her, taking both her hands in his. "As long as there is an Emilie, both families shall live on through you."

"I? I am nothing," Emilie said bitterly. "Only a

woman, and when I am gone there won't be anything left at all."

"Not so, my dearest Emilie, I assure you," Jason said quickly. "I am buying Les Saules not for myself, but for you."

Emilie looked up at him.

"Les Saules and Les Chandelles share a common border," Jason said, "and I want them to share a common destiny as well. Now that it's free, this land can be richer and greater than ever, and you and I can be a part of it."

Emilie did not answer.

"Les Chandelles and Les Saules can be one," Jason insisted. "Just as you and I can be. As Emilie Phillips you can preserve and protect all that you knew of beauty here and at the same time help me to bring this land forward to where it should be."

"Emilie Bonfils Charpentier Phillips," she recited in a dry monotone voice. "What a great list of names that is for anyone to undertake."

"Anyone but you." Jason smiled gently. "There's only one small holding between here and Les Saules," he went on eagerly. "It's a farm belonging to a man named Higgins."

"He's a horrible person," said Emilie with a shudder.

"Yes, but I'm sure we can compensate him amply for giving the place up and going away," Jason said. "I've surveyed the bayou that lies between as well, and I'm having some men from the engineering corps come up to see if it will be worthwhile to drain it and reclaim that land for growing."

"You make it all sound so simple," Emilie said, "so simple and so easy."

"Not at all, my dear." Jason's voice was grave. "I expect that things will be anything but easy for a long time to come. There are too many problems and no

quick solutions. But together we could see it through,
Emilie. Together we could build a life here that will
be so worth the living."

Emilie smiled a little. "I suppose I need at least as
much time as Henrique did to make up my mind," she
said.

"Not quite." He smiled at her. "Henrique was freed
only once, whereas you have been asked for by me
almost continuously. But I won't pressure you. When
you say yes I want your mind to be free and clear. I
want you to come to me entirely of your own choice. I
really don't mean to press you like this. It's only . . ."
He paused for a moment. "It's only that I want you so,
I cannot help but ask each time I see you."

"Then you won't leave me the time or the space to
come to you on my own," Emilie chided him.

"Perhaps I will just step outside on the lawn one
day and shout for you as Young Jess did for Missy,"
he teased.

"And then I shall come flying out to you as she did."
Emilie laughed. "Is that what you want?"

"I must admit it was one of the more fervent wel-
comes I have seen," Jason said. "I would not mind your
flying at me like that at all. In fact, I would love it."

"Somehow I cannot imagine you standing before the
veranda shouting 'Emilie, Emilie,' quite like that,"
Emilie said. "Although I must admit, there was something very touching and romantic about it."

"Jess is a man of many parts," Jason said thoughtfully. "I had rather a long talk with him the other day
and I must say I find him thoroughly admirable."

"Do you think he'll stay on?" Emilie asked.

"I doubt it," Jason said. "There really isn't anything
here for someone like Jess. I expect that he will pack
up Missy and move North. Jess wants to go someplace

where he will be of use to his people. He's a natural leader and teacher if ever there was one."

"But there's so much that the people here can learn from him," Emilie argued. "He could set up a school-house right here at Les Chandelles and teach the children, and yes, the older people too, to read and write and cipher. Have you talked to him about any-thing like that?"

"No, I must confess I haven't," Jason said. "I was so caught up in hearing about his adventures and his ideas that I really didn't discuss any possibilities with him at all. It is just my thinking that he will be off before long."

"But perhaps if we spoke to him now," Emilie said. "If he is all that you say he is I'm sure he can see how useful he would be."

"Your idea of a school is excellent," Jason said. "And I will talk to him about it tomorrow. Perhaps he can see, as I do, a whole new life that is ready to begin here and now. Certainly Jess can be an impor-tant part of it."

"A school and a hospital and anything else we need." Emilie spoke softly, almost as if to herself. "I want Les Chandelles to be the best place in the world for everyone on it."

"And Les Saules, too," Jason reminded her. "Have you already forgotten that I've promised it to you?"

"As a wedding gift," Emilie said. "No, I haven't forgotten." She was silent for a moment. "What will they make of us, Jason? A Yankee officer who conquers the land and then stays to run it? The other planters in the parish will see me as a turncoat for marrying someone like you, and the slaves—" she corrected herself—"the ex-slaves will brand you a traitor to the cause for staying here and marrying me. A fine pair we'll be."

Jason laughed, but it was not the laugh of humor. "I know there will be problems, Emilie," he said quietly. "Perhaps graver, harsher problems even than those I contemplate. The land is going to be filled with great unrest. The returning army is going to be frustrated and embittered, what's left of it."

"Aye," said Emilie, "what's left of it."

"Our own army will grow restless and unhappy, champing at the bit, to be in their own homes," Jason said. "In many ways, an army of occupation is worse than an army doing battle. Not many are going to love us, Emilie, for what I propose we do. But I promise you that I will love you enough to make up for all the dissidents."

She took his hand and held it for a moment. "Dear Jason," she said. "Already you *are* more dear to me than you can know. I think that it is only in moments like these, when you tell me of the troubles that lie around us, that I quite understand how taken I am with you. When you spin sweet dreams for me, it seems unreal and I cannot react as you wish me to. But when you talk, as you do now, of the hardships that lie ahead, then I see only your strength and your goodness and your honesty. Then I think I could love you."

"Now," he corrected her. "Now I am talking of these things, Emilie. Do you love me now?"

"Yes." She barely breathed the syllable. "Yes, I do."

"Then, by God, that is all I ask for in this world!" he said.

"My life has been so full of hardship and tragedy. I almost bring guarantees of them as a dowry." Emilie laughed harshly. "Surely you do not need a wife who'll burden you with all of this."

"I need you, Emilie." He pressed his mouth to her hand. "I need you, and that is all that matters."

She did not pull her hand away. "I need you too, Jason," she said, "although it seems unfair of me to wish myself on any man."

"Emilie, you're almost morbid," he admonished her. "All of us have had tragedy and unhappiness in our lives. You must not speak as though at has been only your lot, or worse still, that it is all that lies in front of you and all you can bring to those who love you. That is not so."

"Perhaps it would not be for the best if we married too quickly," Emilie said thoughtfully. "Perhaps it would be better for you to take possession of Les Saules and establish yourself there before we take such an important step. Since Henrique has decided to remain, I'm sure I'll be able to manage somehow."

"If this is what you want I will respect it," Jason said, "but I really do not understand the need for waiting. Whatever we want to accomplish here can so much more quickly and easily be done if we are together."

"I'm afraid," Emilie admitted. "All of the problems we have been talking about are very real. I think we have got to wait until everything settles down and we know that we are safe to pursue our private lives as we would wish."

"I have an army here, Emilie," Jason reminded her. "No matter what trouble is brewing in the South, I of all men have the means to protect you."

"All the armies in the world are no protection against the malicious gossip and even ostracism that are sure to fall to us," Emilie said.

"If that is what is worrying you, my dear, then you are not the Emilie I thought you were," Jason said. "Some impostor, incredibly beautiful but an impostor nonetheless, is sitting here in your place."

"It's not that alone, Jason, that frightens me," Emilie

said. "Of course not. But that is just a small part to be added to the problems that you yourself just outlined so convincingly to me."

"Obstacles are put in front of us in order that we may overcome them," Jason said.

Emilie rose. "I must go to bed now," she said. "If my in-laws are stopping here tomorrow on their way to New Orleans I must be up early and ready to greet them. I hope I can convince them to stay here for at least a few days. The change will be so great for them, leaving the home they so loved."

"As you wish." He kissed her hand again and opened the door for her.

Emilie went upstairs. She undressed herself slowly, no longer minding that Missy was not there to help her, and fell on her bed into a troubled sleep.

It was not yet daylight when an unexpected clamor wakened her. Emilie drew on a robe quickly. She started for her bedroom door, but her attention was caught by an unusual glow on the horizon to the north. She hurried to the window, wondering what the great clouds of orange and black could be. She stared for a few moments and then hurried downstairs.

Her in-laws had arrived at an unheard-of hour. Emilie ran to greet Madame Charpentier and to try to comfort her. She had never seen her mother-in-law in such a state of disarray and helplessness. She tried to soothe the older woman, and as she bent over, helping her to a small sofa, Emilie was aware that Jason had come downstairs as well.

The old woman looked up at him. "I regret to inform you, my dear colonel, that you will not be able to occupy my beautiful house after all," she said.

"What has happened?" Emilie cried.

Madame Charpentier turned to her. "They burned

it down around our heads because we had sold out to a Yankee," she replied.

Emilie looked up at Jason, terror in her eyes. "How can this be?" She knew that he had no more answer for it than she did.

Madame Charpentier was crying. "My house, my beautiful house," she sobbed, "and my roses, my gardens gone, all gone."

Emilie hugged her close and tried to put the old woman's head against her shoulder for support. "Who could have done it?" she asked.

"It was a bunch of those renegades," Monsieur Charpentier answered unexpectedly.

Emilie turned around to face him. "You know for sure who they are?" she asked.

"The same bunch that plagued us before the war," he said bitterly. "The ruffians and the patrollers whose services we were so glad to make use of. Now they're risen up against us too."

"But why?" Emilie asked.

"They blame us for losing the war," the old man said.

"But that's impossible," Emilie said. "No one has given more than you have. Your sons . . ." She let the sentence go unfinished.

"They care nothing about that, my dear," the old gentleman replied. "They are angry and embittered and mean to strike out at whomever they can."

"They might have killed you," Emilie gasped.

"No, they gave us warning. I'll say that for them," Monsieur Charpentier said. "But they've burned Les Saules. 'Better destroyed than to the Yankees' they told us."

"It has started," Jason said quietly. "And it may prove to be worse than the war itself."

"What about your people?" Emilie asked.

The old couple exchanged quick glances. "They burned and shot up the quarters," Madame said, her voice slightly steadier. "They made us leave before we could find how many had been hurt—or worse."

"Did you recognize any of them?" Jason asked.

The two shook their heads. "They had sheets and masks over their heads," Monsieur Charpentier said. "Looked like ghosts trying to frighten us. They said the same would happen to anyone who sold out to the Yankees or helped them."

Madame Charpentier threw a sharp warning glance at her husband, but the old man sat with his eyes downcast and did not see her.

"They said since the darkies didn't belong to us any more we shouldn't care how many got killed," he went on. "They said that this was only the beginning till all the Yankees and the Yankee lovers were driven out."

"Armand—" Madame Charpentier said. It sounded to Emilie as though she were trying to warn her husband of something, but again the warning went unheeded by the old man.

"They said—they said," he whispered in the same strained voice, "they said Les Chandelles would be next."

For a moment his eyes widened as he looked at them beseechingly, in turn, one after the other. His head twitched back momentarily and then jerked forward. He collapsed in his chair and fell to the floor.

Jason sprang quickly to help him, but it was too late.

"It has started," he said again dully.

It was all he could do.

Emilie slipped to the floor and knelt beside him. She put her arm on his shoulder and murmured softly, "Now I know what I must do. They cannot stop us,

Jason, nothing can stop us. I mean to have you and I mean to have Les Chandelles."

She kissed him softly on the cheek and leaned on his arm. He steadied her and together they slowly rose, silently facing each other.

A sheet was quickly brought and drawn over the slumped body of the old man who had gone to join his fallen sons. Emilie led the numbed silent Madame Charpentier up the wide staircase and helped her get settled for the night. When she saw her at last asleep, she quietly withdrew to her own room.

She started to undress, but was suddenly overcome with the greatest longing. The room seemed cold and frightening. Emilie was still unused to being alone, without Missy, all through the night. But it wasn't just the presence of another human being she needed now. There was only one place to which she could turn, and find the fears and chills of the night dissipated.

Emilie shed her long dress quickly and undid the constricting undergarments that bound her. She slipped into a soft, thin nightdress and tied a wrap at her chin and waist. Then she opened her door and made her way silently down the darkened corridor to the chamber where Jason slept. She rapped at the door, grateful, when he opened it, that his light had been extinguished and he could not see her in her dishabille.

Yet she could not keep herself from rushing into his arms. She ached for the comfort that he and he alone could give her. Once she had wanted it from Guy, but Guy had thought there would be a lifetime of loving for them. Guy had been wrong, but that had been a war ago, and everything was different now.

"Different, different than it's ever been," she whispered to Jason, trying to explain the sudden flood of fear and emotion that had sent her seeking him in the middle of the night. "There is nothing but death all around here, Jason, and I want life!"

"Emilie, do you know what you're asking of me?" he demanded.

"Yes, I know." Her laugh was harsh. "I'm asking that you forget your honor as a gentleman and your duties as a soldier. I'm asking that you give me life, Jason, instead of death. I'm so tired of death and dying." She pressed her lips to his, surprising him with the urgency of her need. He tried gently to dissuade her, but she would have none of it. "I've lost too many I loved to the grave. I won't lose you too!"

Jason drew her closer, holding her tightly as if to dispel all her terrors.

But that was no longer enough for Emilie. "I'm not a child anymore," she said. "I love you and I know I want you."

"You won't be sorry?" Jason had to know.

"No." She shook her head. "No matter what happens, I won't be sorry. I will always have this night."

He led her to his bed. They lay down together, Emilie drawing strength from strength as she wrapped her arms around him and felt herself gently encased between his legs. She felt a sensation, little known and long forgotten, course through her body. Then she knew she had chosen wisely. The fears and frights began to ebb with all the other memories and thoughts that tore at her. Everything was melting in the tremulous motions of Jason's lovemaking; everything outside that bed, beyond that room, slowly began losing shape, cognizance, and even existence in Emilie's mind. Soon nothing was except what was passing between them as the slow liquidity of the warmth that was gathering inside her shut everything else away.

She didn't need to see, to think, to know; all she needed was the length of him against her, the brush of his lips on her everywhere at once, his stilling of her limbs as they began to tremble without her doing. Then he was over her, then in her; Emilie felt her body as it floated up of its own will to meet his.

All of her being was gathered and concentrated where she felt him thrusting at her. Delighting, she leaped up again and again to meet him, to give him, to seal the joining between them that precluded all else.

"Jason!" she gasped, "love, my love!" unable to contain herself any longer. Then she felt the subsiding thrusts she somehow knew would follow, and she clung to him more fiercely that before, to keep him from leaving her embrace. At last she lay back, relinquishing him, and Jason leaned toward her, brushing back the tumbled black hair that framed her shining face.

"Was that what you wanted?" Jason asked tenderly. "Do you know now all that we can be to each other?"

"Yes, love, I know." Emilie smiled in the darkness, her fingertips stroking lightly the face, once thought so fierce, that she had grown to hold so dear. "No one can stop us now, nor can anyone ever come between us."

Jason kissed the fingers at his face. "I've made you mistress in deed as well as name," he said. "Now I must make you my wife and my own forever."

"Now," she repeated, then added, "and all the hurt that ever has been done to you, now I shall make right again for you."

He took her into his arms with a force that she thought would crush her very bones. "Emilie, my Emilie," he began, but before he could say more, she put her mouth against his with a fury that matched his body's claim on hers, and in their embrace, crushed out the words that she would gladly wait until the next morning to hear.

About the Author

Rochelle Larkin, who has written more than two dozen books, lives with her children in New York City. She is the author of *Harvest of Desire*, also available in a Signet edition. Currently she is working on the next book in this series.

More Big Bestsellers from SIGNET

SIGNET Bestsellers You'll Enjoy